Praise for Synithia Williams's Jackson Falls series

"Williams' skill as a writer [...]
ability to overcome their d[...]
[...] pick

A *Publishers Weekly* Buzz Books 2020 Romance Selection!

An Amazon Best Romance Book of the Month!

A *Woman's World* Romance Book Club Selection!

"Fans of second chances, reconnecting friends, friends-to-lovers, and political romance stories will enjoy this book." —*Harlequin Junkie*

Forbidden Promises

"The perfect escape. *Forbidden Promises* is a deeply felt, engrossing, soapy romance that manages to both luxuriate in its angst, while also interrogating something far more wide-reaching and universal than the admittedly sexy taboo appeal of its central conceit."
—*Entertainment Weekly*

"Emotions, relationships and business are tangled in this soap opera-esque tale, and readers will find themselves unable to look away from Williams' well-drawn and larger-than-life characters. It's impossible not to enjoy this entertaining glimpse into a world of wealth, political ambition and familial loyalties." —*BookPage*

"A romance for readers looking for equal parts passion and family drama." —*Kirkus Reviews*

"Fans of Elle Wright and Jamie Pope will be seduced by this charming and passionate family saga." —*Booklist*

"Politics, passion, and family drama combine to make a deliciously soapy second-chance, brother's-best-friend romance. Readers of Alisha Rai's Forbidden Hearts series or Reese Ryan's *Engaging the Enemy* will be tantalized and surprised by the many twists and turns."
—*Library Journal*

SYNITHIA WILLIAMS

Foolish HEARTS

HQN

ISBN-13: 978-1-335-91806-2

Foolish Hearts

Copyright © 2021 by Synithia R. Williams

This edition published by arrangement with Harlequin Books S.A.

For questions and comments about the quality of this book,
please contact us at CustomerService@Harlequin.com.

HQN
22 Adelaide St. West, 40th Floor
Toronto, Ontario M5H 4E3, Canada
www.Harlequin.com

Printed in U.S.A.

To everyone looking forward to a brighter tomorrow.

Acknowledgments

Writing a book is hard. Writing a book during a pandemic is excruciating! Thank you to KD and Dren for our Monday-night sprints. That dedicated time was just the boost I needed to kick-start my writing mojo for the week. I don't know if I would have been able to push as hard as I did without you two motivating me (and convincing me to buy way too much stuff online between sprints). I have to thank Ashley, Jada and Cheris. I started this book around the time we dealt with COVID-19 at home. Thank you, ladies, from the bottom of my heart, for everything you did to make that time easier. I love and appreciate you! Also thanks to all of my family and friends who texted, called and checked in to make sure we were okay. Thanks to Michele and Errin at HQN Books and my awesome agent, Tricia, for your support during those difficult days in 2020 along with your love for this series. Finally, to my readers. OMG, I love you all so much! Thank you for every email and social media tag telling me how much you enjoy the Robidoux shenanigans. They were a bright spot during a difficult year.

CHAPTER ONE

Ashiya scanned the numbers on her computer screen and grinned. Another profitable day for her consignment store, Piece Together. Another day that she'd kept the store she'd opened on a whim from being considered a contender for best dramatic performance by a Robidoux family member. Another day she'd taken that whim and turned it from "*that little store*," as her mom referred to it, into *the* place to shop in Jackson Falls for quality, preowned designer clothes, with a healthy helping of fashion tips and perfect accessories on the side.

She shimmied her hips in the chair as she hit Enter to save the day's profit numbers in her bookkeeping software. Six years ago, when she'd decided to open her store, she hadn't believed she'd be here for this long. Honestly, she hadn't believed she would be able to make it work. She might have grown up in the mix of the Robidoux family with all their drama, fighting for control, and business acumen, but she'd never wanted any of that. She wanted to live life on her own terms with little interference from her family.

Piece Together was something she'd known her mother, cousins, and uncle wouldn't care about. They'd let her "*play around*," and she'd get peace and quiet. Who knew she could actually run a business successfully?

A knock on the office door snapped her from her internal celebration. She glanced up from her computer to the door of her office in the back of the store. Lindsey, the store's assistant manager, stood there. She'd been one of the first people Ashiya hired to help run Piece Together when she'd opened. Lindsey, with her no-nonsense personality, straightforward style, and keen eye for fashion, had stayed by Ashiya's side through those early, lean years when Ashiya hadn't been sure the store would survive. Short, with a cute face, and an upturned nose that reminded Ashiya of a pixie, Lindsey could easily pass for one of the college kids in town despite being thirty-one.

"Hey, I've finished straightening up the front of the store. How much longer will you be here?" Lindsey pulled back her normally brunette hair, which was now colored a soft pink, into a ponytail at the base of her neck.

They always tried to walk out together. Downtown Jackson Falls wasn't a dangerous town, but that didn't mean they liked to tempt fate. Their parking lot was behind the building, poorly lit and after eight p.m. served as the overflow parking for a few bars in the area. They preferred to be safe rather than sorry.

"I just finished up." Ashiya hit the Save button one more time just to be sure she cemented the success of the day. "I've got to get out of here anyway."

"Hot date?" Lindsey asked with a wiggle of her eyebrows.

Ashiya barely stopped herself from rolling her eyes. She couldn't remember the last time she'd had a hot date. Not since she finally came to her senses and told her on-again, off-again boyfriend since college to get the hell out of her life. Every time she thought about the time and effort she'd wasted on that relationship, the good things she'd let pass her by, she wanted to slap herself. She would pay whoever invented a time machine all six years' worth of Piece Together's profits for the chance to go back and tell twenty-two-year-old Ashiya to stay away from that manipulative asshole and to remember that good sex did not equal love.

She pushed aside thoughts of her wasted years and sighed. "No hot date. My cousin Elaina's celebrating her engagement." Ashiya powered down her computer and stood.

Lindsey crossed her arms and tilted her head to the side. "So she's really getting married, huh?"

Ashiya barely contained her chuckle at Lindsey's dubious tone. "She is, and I actually believe she's happy."

Lindsey raised her brows again. "Good for her."

"I know, right?" Ashiya said. "I'm happy for her. I hope this marriage works out better than her first one."

Lindsey crossed her heart, pressed her hands together as if in prayer and lifted them to the sky. She wasn't overly religious, but Ashiya appreciated every bit of good vibes for a better relationship for her cousin. "I hope so, too. She can be…intense, but everyone deserves to be happy."

Ashiya walked across the small office, which was actually a former storage room that she'd converted into an office for her store, to the coat rack, where she'd hung her purse. A small black Louis Vuitton bag she'd found at a thrift store in Charleston the year before and today had paired with a simple white T-shirt and gauzy leopard print A-line skirt. She lived for finding deals like that.

"Now that she's engaged and happy," Ashiya said, putting the strap for the purse over one shoulder, "she's also making an effort to hang out with the family more. Tonight is ladies' night to toast to her good fortune."

"Sounds like fun," Lindsey said with what came across like forced enthusiasm.

Ashiya grinned. "It will be. I haven't gotten a chance to hang with my cousins in a while. I'm looking forward to it."

"I'm waiting for the day your family convinces you to quit running the store and start working at that huge corporation they own."

"I wouldn't abandon you like that." Ashiya flipped the lights off in her office.

"I wouldn't consider it abandonment. Just remember if you ever decide to go and start making big deals instead of scouring thrift stores for premium goods, I'll understand and take over the store for you."

Ashiya wrapped an arm around Lindsey's shoulders as they walked toward the front of the store. "Not gonna happen, but if I ever change my mind, I know I'll be leaving this place in good hands."

They did one more check of the front before locking up the store. This wasn't the first time Lindsey teased her about potentially leaving Piece Together to work for Robidoux Holdings. Lindsey believed Ashiya would take the skills she'd utilized to turn Piece Together and use them for bigger payout working for her family's larger holding corporation. Ashiya appreciated her friend's support, but she wasn't about to deceive herself into thinking she was smart enough to run anything bigger than this store.

She and Lindsey said their goodbyes as they left the store and got into their cars. As always, Ashiya waited until Lindsey had driven off before exiting the parking lot. She made a left and eased into the late afternoon traffic toward the Jackson Falls Country Club for ladies' night.

Honestly, she wasn't sure how much fun this would be. She didn't dislike Elaina, who was remarkably more pleasant now that she'd taken over control of Robidoux

Holdings and found happiness with herself and in her love life, but that didn't mean Ashiya immediately thought of Elaina when she wanted to go out and have fun. Thankfully, India, Elaina's younger sister, was going to be there as well. Ashiya refused to turn down any opportunity to hang out with her favorite cousin. Byron's new wife, Zoe, would also be there. Ashiya liked Zoe well enough and believed she was the reason Elaina had agreed to the night out in the first place.

Ashiya was happy for all her cousins. They'd found love and were living their best lives. She, on the other hand, was single again for the first time since the age of twenty-two. She didn't know what to do about her relationship status. Well, she knew what and who she wanted, but she'd burned that bridge, and there was no turning back.

She blasted the latest Megan Thee Stallion song on the radio to get her mind right for a night of fun, but her ringing phone interrupted the beat. A number she didn't recognize popped up on the car's console. She considered ignoring it, but she'd learned her lesson the hard way about ignoring phone calls. Even from unknown numbers.

Ashiya pressed the button on her steering wheel to accept the call. "Hello?"

"Hello, I'm trying to reach Ashiya Waters?" a woman's cool, professional voice asked.

Ashiya rolled her eyes. Telemarketer. Hadn't she put her number on that list that told them to leave her the hell alone or something? "Sorry, I'm not interested."

"Ms. Waters, this is Brianna Winters. I was your grandmother Gloria Waters's personal assistant," the woman said in a rush before Ashiya could end the call.

Ashiya frowned at the screen. Her Grandmother Gloria? Why would her grandmother's assistant call her? Ashiya hadn't had anything to do with her father's side of the family since they'd disowned him for marrying her mother. Resentment about her mother pursing her father to gain access to her grandmother's then-growing beauty company went long and deep. Ashiya vividly remembered being eight or nine and overhearing her Grandmother Gloria telling Ashiya's mother that she wasn't going to get a red cent of anything that would have gone to her son.

Ashiya kind of understood her grandmother cutting ties after learning the truth behind the reasons her mom pursued her dad. That didn't stop Ashiya from being hurt when her father's family didn't want anything to do with her. She loved her father and knew the estrangement hurt him, too, but she also loved her momma. Ashiya couldn't imagine ever wanting to be close to someone who hated her mom. As she'd grown, and the animosity festering from her parent's bad marriage and unresolved issues infected Ashiya's life in ways that still hindered her.

"Okay," she said slowly. "Why are you calling me?"

"Because you grandmother died two days ago." Brianna spoke in a direct manner with only the barest hint of sympathy.

Ashiya sucked in a breath. She squeezed the steering wheel. Every single memory she had of her grandmother involved her telling her dad he never should have married that raggedy whore in the first place whenever they visited. Eventually the visits stopped. That didn't mean Ashiya had wished her dead.

"I'm sorry to hear that," she said truthfully.

"I'm calling you because the reading of the will is this Friday." When Brianna spoke this time, her voice was warmer. "You'll need to be there?"

"Why would I need to be there? I'm pretty sure I'm not listed."

Brianna cleared her throat. "Actually, you are."

The thought of being in her grandmother's will was so absurd, Ashiya laughed. Probably not appropriate after receiving news of a deceased relative, but she didn't believe anything her grandmother left for her required her to attend the reading of the will. "Okay, so she left me a clock, or my dad's high school clothes. Can't you just mail them to me? I don't have to show up for that."

There was a pause before Brianna spoke again. "You're getting a lot more than a clock. Ms. Waters, your grandmother left you her entire estate. You are now the majority shareholder of the Legacy Group. If you'd like to avoid having your cousins contest the will, I'd suggest you be here."

ASHIYA SAT IN her car in the Jackson Falls Country Club parking lot. She'd driven there on autopilot while listening to her late grandmother's personal assistant talk about everything she was expected to inherit. Not only the shares in the company, but a home in Hilton Head, South Carolina, multiple properties throughout the Southeast, all her grandmother's money and worldly goods, and a vintage Jaguar vehicle.

The information whirled around in her head like clothes during the spin cycle of a washing machine. She didn't believe a word of it. She'd said as much while on the phone with Brianna. How could her grandmother's assistant know what Ashiya was getting if the will hadn't been read yet?

"I was with your grandmother when she made the changes with her lawyer, and I served as the notary. Believe me. You're getting it all."

Inheriting her grandmother's money made absolutely no sense. She hadn't seen her grandmother in years. Decades. Her grandmother hated when her dad married her mom and wanted to keep her mother from having access to even a penny of the money the company made. Ashiya always assumed her grandmother didn't want Ashiya to gain access to the company either since Gloria Waters never made any attempt to reach out to her or form any type of relationship with her. Now she was supposed to believe the company, money and property were all hers?

She had to get to the bottom of this. She couldn't go inside and celebrate with her cousins. She wouldn't be able to focus on anything. Yet, she didn't want to outright snub Elaina.

Ashiya got out of the car and dialed India's number. Her cousin answered quickly. "Hey, are you here?"

"Umm…yeah, but I can't stay. Can you meet me at the front door? And don't tell Elaina."

"Sure, let me step away so I can hear you better," India said, not asking for more information. "I'll be right back," she said not quite in the phone. Ashiya assumed she spoke to Elaina and Zoe.

Ashiya arrived at the front of the clubhouse and slid through the door. India came around the corner at the same time. Her cousin slid her phone into the pocket of her pink sundress. Her curly hair was twisted into a cute puff at the top of her head, and worry clouded her brown eyes.

India immediately came over and placed a hand on Ashiya's arm. India was two years younger than Ashiya, but they were more like sisters than cousins. "What's going on?"

Ashiya let out a humorless laugh. Where would she even

start? There were so many unanswered questions she was afraid to even try to begin to unravel.

"Something came up," she said. "I really need to go talk to Mom and figure out what's going on?"

India frowned. "Is everything okay? Did my dad do something?"

Ashiya shook her head. "No. For once this doesn't have anything to do with your dad."

Ashiya paced in front of the door. She wished her problem were tied to her Uncle Grant. She'd know what to do if that were the case. Thankfully, because Ashiya was busy with her "little store" Grant Robidoux didn't pay her any attention. She'd rather deal with her overbearing uncle meddling than inherit a fortune and the responsibility that came with it.

India reached out and took Ashiya's elbow in her hand, stopping her from pacing. A small line appeared between her brows. "Hey, what's going on?"

Ashiya took a deep breath and met her cousin's worried expression. "My grandmother died."

India blinked. Her head drew back, and she frowned. "Your grandmother?" India's eyes narrowed as if the idea of Ashiya having a grandmother was unheard of before her head cocked to the side. "You mean your dad's mom?"

India's surprise at the announcement was further proof that what Brianna said on the phone made no sense. Ashiya had no ties or contact with her grandmother. There was no way the woman would leave Ashiya with all of this responsibility.

Ashiya sighed and shrugged. "The one and only."

The confusion left India's eyes, and sympathy filled them instead. "Oh, no, Ashiya, I'm sorry." India pulled Ashiya in for a hug.

Ashiya stepped back after a second in India's embrace. She didn't deserve it. Sure, she was saddened to hear the news, but she wasn't devastated. She hadn't known the woman. And there came the guilt. A big, heavy weight in her chest. She didn't deserve sympathy, and she definitely didn't deserve money.

"Thank you, but I'm fine. Really, I am. I barely knew her, and according to my mom she is—was—evil."

India shook her head. "No one is completely evil. You told me yourself there was bad blood between her and your mom since your parents got married. There are always two sides. I'm sorry you didn't get the chance to hear her side."

Ashiya pressed a hand to her forehead. "You're right, I guess. But I got a call from her personal assistant. She wants me to come to Hilton Head for the reading of the will. She thinks my grandmother left everything to me."

India's eyes widened. "For real?"

"That's what she says, but I don't believe it. My grand-mother hated Momma, and she didn't like me. Why would she leave everything to me?"

"Maybe she didn't hate you and your mom as much as you think," India said in her very logical, let's-view-all-sides way.

"No, the hatred was real." She remembered the visits to her grandmother when she was young. The cold shoulder. The shouting behind closed doors. The names she'd called Ashiya's mom. Names like gold digger, whore, two-faced witch. Names Ashiya hadn't understood the meaning of back then but knew they couldn't be good.

She shook her head to rid her brain of the memories. "I can't believe it. I can't do it."

"Do what? Go to the funeral? I don't think it'll hurt just to pay your respects."

If only that's what she meant. She tugged on her ear and glanced around. No one was in the front of the clubhouse with them. "Take the company, the money, the estate," she said in a thin voice. "I don't know how to run anything."

India had leaned in to hear what Ashiya had to say. After Ashiya spoke, India grunted and leaned back. She gave Ashiya an are-you-kidding-me side-eye. "Ashiya, you run a business now."

"A small clothing store here in Jackson Falls. And not even new clothes. They're consignments. I can't run a corporation."

The thought of being in charge of million-dollar decisions, having to report to a board of directors, fighting for respect from people who'd spent their entire careers in the corporate world made her stomach twist in a dozen glass-encrusted knots. No, she couldn't do it. Wouldn't do it. They'd eat her alive in less than thirty seconds.

India rolled her eyes. "Girl, get out of your damn head. Before you start having a panic attack and telling yourself all the things you can't do, how about you first find out what exactly you've inherited and what, if anything, you have to do about that?"

Ashiya took a deep breath. Her stomach still twisted. Her palms sweat, but India's words took the edge off her anxiety. Until she knew for sure what was going on, there was no need to freak out. The freak-out could wait until she was sure Brianna was right.

Please, God, let Brianna be wrong. She sent up the quick prayer.

She met India's you've-got-this gaze. "You're right. I just never thought I'd be in this position. You know I never wanted to be a part of that world."

Understanding crossed India's features. India's desire

to stay out of the running for top billing in the Robidoux family was one of the reasons she and Ashiya had been so close. Ever since they were kids and India gave Ashiya her favorite teddy bear instead of laughing when she'd learned that at eleven, Ashiya was still afraid of the dark she'd mentally adopted India as her little sister.

"Not wanting to be a part of it and being able to survive it are two different things," India said in a supportive voice. "Regardless of what happens, I believe you can handle it."

Ashiya wished she had a tenth of her cousin's optimism. "Time will tell. Look, I need to talk to Momma about all this. See what she thinks and then make plans to go to Hilton Head. I guess I just needed to talk to someone first and get my initial freak-out out of the way. You know Momma. She'll tell me to calm down, act like a Robidoux, and take everything my grandmother left and more."

At times Ashiya thought her momma forgot that Ashiya was half Waters. That even though her dad had generated his own wealth, he'd given up the wealth from his family when he'd married her. Elizabeth Robidoux Waters had not known her husband knew he wouldn't inherit a thing if he married her. She also hadn't forgiven him once she learned the truth. He'd only wanted to be happy, and despite her parents' strained marriage, her dad had found his own way without the help of his mom or his wife's rich family. He was why Ashiya had tried to avoid being as cutthroat as some of her Robidoux cousins.

India nodded and patted Ashiya on the shoulder. "I'll tell Elaina that something came up. She'll be fine."

Ashiya reached into her purse and pulled out a card. "Give this to her, okay? I know she didn't want gifts, but I still thought I'd get her something. Tell her to enjoy it."

Ashiya had gotten Elaina a yearlong subscription to a

tea-of-the-month club. Since her cousin was cutting back on alcohol, she'd focused on using tea to calm her nerves. Ashiya hoped the gift would be welcome from the prickly Elaina.

"I will. You go. Talk to your mom and call me before you head out of town. If you need me to go with you—"

"No, I'll be fine. I may need drinks when I return."

"I've got you." This time when India opened her arms for a hug, Ashiya took it. She'd need all the emotional support she could muster if the inheritance was really hers.

They pulled apart, and Ashiya watched as India went back toward the dining area. With a determined sigh, she went to the door leading out of the clubhouse. She wasn't looking forward to this conversation with her mom, but she couldn't possibly go to the funeral and learn the contents of the will without saying something to her.

She pushed open the door at the same time someone pulled from the other side. She lost her balance and stumbled forward on her high heels. She barely stopped herself from falling. A warm hand reached out and steadied her by the elbow.

"Excuse me," she said.

"Sorry," a familiar male voice said at the same time.

Ashiya froze. The blood rushed from her face, and her lungs decided breathing wasn't necessary at that moment. Her eyes jerked up. Surprise, embarrassment, and regret sent her body into a confusing tailspin. The familiar face seemed just as surprised to see her. Her heart squeezed while the lingering touch of his hand on her elbow turned her limbs into jelly.

Russell. The guy she should have chosen. Fine as hell Russell. He would be the person she saw when she was already discombobulated.

Fine as hell was a weak string of words to describe Russell Gilchrist. Tall, broad of shoulders, thick of thighs, and sweet of heart, Russell was the perfect embodiment of good guy with just a hint of bad boy beneath to make a woman fantasize about seeing him lose control. The lights from outside the clubhouse added a silvery glow to his sandy-brown skin and brought out the gold in his hazel eyes. He'd offered her everything she said she'd wanted in a relationship, and in turn she'd broken his heart when her jerk of an ex came back and said all the right words with wrong intentions.

After recognition entered his gaze, he quickly snatched his hand back. "You good?" His voice didn't seem as concerned now that he recognized her. Instead it was cold, clipped, as if he couldn't wait to get away from her.

"I'm fine. I was in a rush and didn't—"

"Then I'll let you get going." He stepped to the side so she could walk away.

Ashiya sucked in a breath. Three years had passed, yet she still couldn't get used to seeing the cold look in his eye. Three years of seeing him occasionally around town or at parties and trying to accept the way he barely held her gaze or spoke to her in a tone warmer than an Antarctic. She'd seen his other side. She'd seen the adoration shining in his eyes. Heard the way he whispered her name when he was deep inside of her. Knew he could be the most caring person she'd ever met. Knowing that only made this side of him hard as hell to accept.

"Russell, I…"

"I'll see you around." He walked pass her and entered the clubhouse without another glance her way.

Heat spread through her cheeks. She looked to the sky and groaned. No matter what she said or did, she couldn't break through the silent treatment. Not that she could blame him. She'd toyed with him. Used him to make her ex jealous, and by the time she realized she was falling for Russell, it was too late.

She wanted to rush back into the clubhouse and demand that he talk to her. That he let her explain. That he give her, *them*, another chance. Instead, she sighed and walked to her car. Getting Russell back was still on her bucket list, but she couldn't focus on that particular goal at the moment. Right now, she had to figure out how to get rid of a million-dollar inheritance.

CHAPTER TWO

THE ENERGY THAT jolted through Russell's bloodstream whenever he came close to Ashiya Waters wouldn't go away, even though his brain knew she was bad news. He tried to ignore the sound of his *pulse* pounding in his ears, the short breaths, and the shock of awareness in his every nerve ending as he spoke to the hostess at the Jackson Falls Country Club and followed her to the table where his cousin Isaac waited.

Tried and failed.

He pulled out the chair across from Isaac, sat and glanced around. "Where's the waiter? I need a drink."

Isaac stopped giving a woman sitting alone his customary come-here-girl look coupled with a lip lick that would put players all over the world to shame, and looked at Russell. Typical Isaac. As soon as puberty hit, his cousin had realized the effect his light brown skin, dark eyes, thick lashes, and full lips had on girls and had taken advantage.

Isaac's lips lifted in a smirk as he raised his drink, more than likely a Crown and Coke, and gave Russell a curious look. "What the hell happened to you?"

Of course, Isaac wouldn't show any sympathy in the face of Russell's obvious irritation. Not because his cousin didn't care. If Isaac believed Russell was really in some type of trouble or had a problem, he'd be the first person to ask who they were fighting. Isaac had teased Russell since they were kids but also took him under his wing as a pseudo brother when Russell's older brother, Rodrick, disappeared ten years ago.

Russell shook his head. "Nothing."

"Oh no. You've got that look." Isaac's dark eyes narrowed, and he leaned over the table to peer at Russell.

"What look?" He glanced around for the waiter again.

"The I-want-to-get-the-hell-out-of-here look. Sorry, bruh, but you can't leave yet. I just joined this country club, and I need to be seen here for these people to respect me."

"I'm not leaving," Russell said, trying take the bite out of his voice. It wasn't Isaac's fault he was thrown off center. Only one person could toss his emotions around like that with just a look or touch.

Damn, why did she still have to smell so good?

Russell shook his head to get the thought out of his mind.

"Good," Isaac said with a firm nod. "My real estate business is finally taking off, but I'm tired of selling hundred-thousand-dollar homes. I'm ready to sell million dollar homes. I need to find the bigger, more lucrative clients, and I can make the connections here."

"I know that. That's why I agreed to come here and help you out. Though I don't have as many connections as you think."

Isaac sucked his teeth. "Bullshit. Not only is your aunt marring into one of the richest families in town, but you work for the company. People love your goofy ass. I need some of that to rub off on me."

Russell laughed despite his cousin's words. Isaac didn't mince words with anyone. Especially with him. His cousin's brash manner served to at least take the edge off of his encounter with Ashiya and brought his mind to the reason he'd come here in the first place.

"I'm not in as good with the Robidoux family as you think. Now that Elaina has taken over the company, I've got to work twice as hard to get on her good side."

Russell had put the work in to get on Elaina's father, Grant's, good side. Grant talked a lot of shit and liked to throw his weight around, but Russell quickly noticed that if he listened to the advice Grant gave, then he was willing to take you under his wing and guide you. Once Grant's son, Byron and his best-friend, Tyrone left the company, Grant needed a mentee, and Russell had never been one to turn down an opportunity. Not since realizing that the people who could get things done and receive justice were the ones with money and power. He'd vowed long ago not to feel helpless because of his social status. He'd been willing to use Grant to get higher. He just hadn't anticipated Grant losing his position to his daughter.

"I heard she can be mean as hell," Isaac said.

"She can be, but she's smart as hell, too. She doesn't take crap from anyone."

"Well, you know how to be charming. Just use that on her." Isaac said as if charming Elaina Robidoux was a simple matter. His cousin obviously didn't know the woman.

Russell shook his head. "Charming doesn't work on Elaina. Honesty delivered with a ton of respect works best."

"You know you can get your aunt Patricia to help."

Russell scowled at the suggestion. "Nah. The kids don't like her. Using Aunt Pat will only make things worse. I've got to do this without reminding them that my aunt is marrying their dad. Plus the thing with India…"

Isaac laughed and took another sip of his drink. "Oh yeah, you did try to hook up with her."

Russell avoided Isaac's gaze and looked for the waiter.

He caught the eye of a young man heading their way. "That was all Grant's idea."

"Still, you tried to hook up with her."

The waiter interrupted them. Russell was thankful for the interruption. He didn't want to relive his weak-ass attempt to get close to the Robidoux family while also getting back at Ashiya. He ordered his drink, and they both ordered food. After the waiter walked away, he looked back at Isaac and hoped his cousin was ready to change the subject.

"So, about you and India." Isaac said with a smirk.

So much for Isaac changing the subject. Russell sipped his drink, savoring the bite of the gin and tonic, before he sighed and answered. If he avoided the topic, it would only make Isaac press harder. "India was cool. I liked her, but there wasn't anything there."

"Tell the truth. You went along with it because Ashiya played you, right?"

Russell's hand balled into a fist on the table. "She didn't..." He couldn't even finish. She'd played him like a fiddle. He hadn't seen it coming, even after he'd thought he'd learned his lesson once about bad-for-you women in college. He'd done the fall-in-love-and-have-your-heart-broken thing once before. When he'd met Ashiya, he'd thought they were both too old to play games or tell lies. That had been his first mistake.

"She played you." Isaac continued to smirk.

Russell shifted and sat up straighter. "Well, she's not playing me again," he said with determination.

He remembered the look in her eyes right before he'd walked away from her earlier. The look that said she wanted to talk. She regretted what happened. She wanted them to try again.

How in the hell could he try again? How could he trust her again? She'd sworn she was over her ex when he'd started dating her a few years back, and then what happened? She'd dropped him as soon as that asshole came calling. Strung him along while she talked to the ex to figure things out. She swore she hadn't cheated on him, but he'd never forget her ex's parting words after Ashiya broke things off with him and admitted she had *too much history* with Stephen to give up now.

"Nobody gives it to her like me. You tried, man, but she always comes back for this."

He'd felt like a fool. Falling for Ashiya despite all the warning signs that he shouldn't.

"You know," Isaac said in the slick way he had, usually before he tried to convince Russell to do something stupid. Usually with mixed results.

"Know what?"

Isaac lifted a shoulder. "You could use her to help you. And by helping you, that helps me."

Russell leaned back and sipped his drink. "Don't start."

Isaac shifted forward. "Nah, hear me out. Ashiya is close with India and Elaina. If you start hooking up with her again—"

"No. Not just no, but hell no. I am not getting tangled up with Ashiya again just to get on Elaina's good side. I've got enough entanglements with that family as it is. If I'm going to get anywhere with Elaina, then I have to prove it at work."

"Bruh, don't you know half of success isn't what you know but who you know? You want that new CEO position, right?"

Russell nodded. He wanted the position. Not just for the job, but for the money and power that came with it.

His family had been helpless after his brother's disappearance. No one had cared about a Black kid from a lower-middle-class family disappearing on spring break. Fifteen years later, even though Russell had garnered money and connections, they weren't enough to get answers about his brother's case. People like the Robidoux family had the wealth, pull and network to get the answers to whatever questions they had. Russell wanted that kind of pull.

"Then use your connections. Ashiya finally dumped her ex, and you said she's making puppy dog eyes at you again."

"I didn't say that. I said she acted jealous when I dated India and wanted to talk."

"She wants you. Use that to your advantage. She used you, so I have no sympathy for her." Isaac finished, as if that was more than enough reason.

She still smelled fucking delicious. Like cinnamon and honey. Just that small touch reminded him how soft her skin was. Then there was the way she looked at him. As if she really were sorry, she really wanted a second chance, she really cared about him. The idea of being with her again was tempting even without the potential benefit of getting closer to her family.

But he also remembered how she'd hurt him. The lies she'd told. The promises that she was over her ex and ready to be with him. He'd be a fool to sign up for that again.

Russell took a long swallow of his drink and shook his head. "I'm better than that. I can get the CEO position without Ashiya's help or influence. I was dumb enough to get caught up with her once. I'm not about to sign up to be caught up with her again."

ASHIYA USED HER key to enter her parents' custom-built home in the neighborhood adjacent to the Jackson Falls

Country Club. Seeing India before coming to face her mom had been the right thing to do. She still didn't think she could handle being left with the majority of shares in a large corporation, but India's insistence that she could handle anything thrown her way had soothed her frayed nerves. India wouldn't say any of that if she didn't truly believe the words. Her cousin always saw potential in Ashiya that she rarely saw in herself. Her mom would push her to take the inheritance to further the Robidoux family goals even if she doubted Ashiya's capabilities. Sometimes Ashiya still felt like that scared eleven-year-old waiting for someone to come find her.

Ashiya crossed the threshold into a too-quiet interior. "Mom?" she called. She dropped her keys in her purse and walked down the hall toward the downstairs living area. The thick carpet runner over the hardwood floors muffled the sound of her heels.

Her mom should be home by now. Elizabeth worked for the Robidoux Foundation overseeing the company's philanthropic endeavors. Though the position kept her busy, her mom hadn't mentioned having anything scheduled for this evening when they'd spoken the night before.

She passed the living room on her way to the stairs and froze. Blinking twice to make sure her eyes weren't deceiving her; she took two steps backward to get a better look in the room. "Dad?"

Her father slowly turned away from the fireplace to her. The corners of his mouth lifted. "Hey sweetheart."

Ashiya's cheeks hurt from the smile that lifted her lips. She hurried across the room and gave him a hug. "What are you doing here? Mom didn't say you were coming to town."

Her dad hadn't been in Jackson Falls for almost a year.

Her parents hadn't filed for divorce, or officially separated, but in the twenty years since the blowup with her father's family, the two rarely stayed in the same place together for more than a few weeks at a time. Her father had left her mom the house since, in his words, she'd wanted it so damn much, and traveled. His job in banking kept him busy enough that her parents could claim the frequent separations were due to her dad's job. Ashiya was pretty sure everyone in the family knew the frequent travel had more to do with the strained relationship than any banking emergency.

"I surprised her today," he said when he pulled back. Her dad had the same honey-brown skin and hazel eyes she did. He was only a few inches taller than her own five-foot-six and he'd gained weight since she'd last seen him.

Ashiya was about to ask why he was there when realization struck. She frowned and grabbed his hand. "I'm so sorry about grandma."

Pain flickered across his face before he nodded and patted her hand. "I'm sorry about that, too."

Regret filled his voice. The blowup that imploded her parent's marriage was also the last time Ashiya remembered seeing her dad and her grandmother together. Even though they'd fought, Ashiya knew her father had cared. She couldn't imagine the pain he must feel knowing any chance of a reconciliation was over.

"When was the last time you…" She didn't want to ask the rest of the question, because she didn't want to make him feel worse.

"A year ago," he answered, surprising her.

Ashiya's eyes widened. "Did you two make up?"

He shook his head. "My mom was very stubborn. Even

until the end. We made peace with each other, but I wouldn't say we made up."

Ashiya let out a breath. The tightness around her heart eased a little knowing that her father at least had found peace. Still, that wouldn't dampen the sorrow of losing a parent. "I'm sorry, Dad."

He tried to smile, probably to reassure her, but his lips formed more of a crooked line instead. "It's not your fault. I was just as stubborn as she was. Despite knowing I'd made a mistake, I couldn't admit that to her."

Ashiya forced herself not to flinch. The mistake her dad spoke of was marrying her mom. If it weren't for her, would he have admitted his mistake? She was their only child, his only tie to Elizabeth. One night when her parents had fought, her mom asked why he stayed. His answer: he wouldn't leave Ashiya without a father.

He'd lived with them until she'd gone to college, then traveled for "work" frequently afterwards. She'd never ask because she knew he'd never confess it, but she was the reason he'd never admitted to his mother he'd married the wrong person, the reason he hadn't gotten the inheritance promised to him, the reason he'd been stuck in a loveless marriage for years.

"How did you find out about your grandmother?" he said before she could ask more about his estranged relationship with his mother.

He walked over to the sofa and sat. Ashiya followed him. "I got a call from Grandma's personal assistant. I didn't know she was still working."

Her dad leaned back in the couch. This time his smile actually curved the corners of his lips. "She wasn't working at the company anymore. She had a personal assistant to keep up with her correspondence, help her manage the estate, and basically be a companion."

"Oh," Ashiya tried to imagine having a person whose sole job was to handle personal things for her, but she couldn't. She valued her independence too much to leave personal details of her life to someone else. How did her dad know so much about his mom's life? She guessed his making peace with his mother probably meant he'd had more contact with her in her final years than he'd let on to Ashiya or her mother.

"So, what did Brianna have to say?" he asked.

His use of Brianna's name confirmed her suspicions. Could he have known the call from Brianna, the promise of an inheritance denied to him, would come her way?

"She said I need to come to Hilton Head for the reading of the will." She watched her father closely as she spoke for any signs of surprise or shock. There were none. "I told her I didn't need to do that. I haven't seen Grandma since I was a kid. I'll go to the funeral, but there wasn't any reason for me to attend the reading of the will."

"Except there is a reason," The words were a statement and not a question.

"She left me everything?"

Her dad took a long slow breath, smiled and nodded. "Good. At least she did one thing right."

"You knew about this?"

"I asked her to do it. It was the only thing I asked her to do. My family made it very clear they wanted nothing to do with me, and I'm happy with the life I have now. But that company was built by my grandmother, was passed down to my mother, and should have been passed to me. Since it's not, I'm happy it's coming to you."

The sureness in his voice, the confidence that all was

right in the world, knocked her speechless. Of all the people in her life, her dad was the one she would have considered least likely to get involved in her life. He'd always supported her in her quest to not be a part of the power plays in the Robidoux family. Was that only because he'd always planned a bigger play? To give her everything her mother always wanted?

Ashiya stood up from the chair. "But I don't want it." Nor did she want to be a part in another attack in the war between her parents.

A shocked scoff came from the door. "How could you not want this?" Elizabeth Robidoux Waters's smooth, cultured voice didn't hide her disbelief. Or maybe that was disappointment.

Ashiya spun around toward the door. Her mom stood there, eyeing Ashiya with, yes, that was disappointment, from the threshold. Elizabeth was taller than Ashiya and in heels could tower over her husband by a few inches. Her skin was the color of dark honey and she wore her thick salt-and-pepper hair in a tapered style. Since there was no event tonight, her mom was in her usual loungewear of silk pajamas, tonight the color of deep purple.

"Why would I want it?" Ashiya said, ignoring her mom's eye roll. "I've tried to stay out of all of the Robidoux family fighting for money and power. What in the world makes you think I want to fight Dad's family for the same thing? Besides, I didn't do anything to deserve it."

Her mom crossed the room with a smooth, almost regal air. She sat primly on the edge of the chair across from Ashiya and her father. "You're his daughter. That's why you deserve it," Elizabeth spoke as if that were enough to erase the years of neglect and animosity between Ashiya and her dad's family.

"If I wasn't good enough to acknowledge as her grand-daughter, then I don't deserve it. It's a headache that I didn't ask for. I'm going to figure out how to get out of this."

Elizabeth raised one manicured finger. "No, you're going to take this, and you're going to use this to the family's advantage." She didn't raise her voice as she spoke, but her tone hardened with the reprimand.

Her dad grunted and stood. "Still trying to get your hands on my family's company, Elizabeth."

Her mother's chin rose. "What would you tell her? You wanted her to get the company. Now she has it. Of course she should use it to her advantage."

George pointed to Ashiya. "Her advantage. Not yours or Grant's. This is for Ashiya to break free and live her own life without interference from you or anyone else."

Elizabeth shot to her feet and glared at her husband. "This is for Ashiya to finally get what is rightfully hers and take her place as the head of that family as she should."

George shook his head and scoffed. "You're always concerned about getting more wealth, more power. Do you ever think you've gotten enough?"

"No," Elizabeth said without a hint of a regret. "I don't have enough and never will. I haven't forgotten where my family came from. Descendants of slaves and share-croppers to what we have today. I will not apologize for accepting every red cent anyone in my family can earn."

Her dad scoffed and shook his head. "You try to make it sound noble. Hard to do when I know you don't have a heart."

Pain flashed across her mom's face. She'd never admit it, not after all these years, but her mom loved her father. Ashiya believed that every time she'd overheard her mother crying whenever her dad left, or saw how Elizabeth stalked him on social media when she thought no one was looking, or stared at George longingly whenever he was in town. The rift between them was so big after all these years. Her dad's love dried up after the heartbreak her mother had caused. Ashiya let go of childish hopes they'd reconcile, but she still hadn't figured out how to stop playing peacemaker between them.

Ashiya stepped between them and held up her hands. "Both of you stop. Please." They turned towards her. "I don't care what you think is rightfully mine." She looked at her dad. "Or your need to get a hold of what you've always wanted," she said to her mother. "This is exactly why I should turn it down. The will hasn't even been read yet, and you're both already making plans for me. In case you haven't forgotten, I have a life. A pretty good life and a successful one. I'm going to the funeral, and I'll go to the will reading, but after that I'm calling my lawyer and finding out how to sell everything she gave me."

She turned and walked out before they could stop her. Footsteps followed. She spun, expecting it to be her mom, but was surprised to see her dad. He held his hands in front of him in a hold up gesture.

"I'm serious, Dad. I don't want this."

"I get it. You've watched the fight for power and money tear the family apart. I don't blame you, but don't make plans to toss out your legacy before understanding what you've got."

"I can give it to you." It was really his legacy. He was the one who was denied everything. She should give it all to him.

He shook his head. "From the moment you were born, my one regret was giving up what my grandmother built and not being able to pass it to you. The Robidoux family has a legacy, but so does my family. You're part of that. Understand it. Maybe you'll have better luck with my family than I did. Learn about them before you turn your back on them the same way I did."

CHAPTER THREE

RUSSELL OPENED THE door to Just Drips, the coffee shop not far from the Robidoux Holdings office, and breathed in the rich scent of coffee. His latte-a-day habit was one he knew he should break. Especially since he had a fancy machine at home that mixed up everything from a basic cup of coffee to the most intricate expresso. He didn't like using his machine. It was the last gift Ashiya had given him right before their relationship imploded. He didn't have the heart to throw it away, nor could he bring himself to use it. Therefore, Just Drips got his money.

He'd ordered ahead using the store's app, and his large vanilla latte with an extra shot of expresso should be waiting for him at the counter. He made his way through the thick wooden tables and past the long line of patrons toward the pickup location.

"Good morning, Beta," he called out when he reached the counter.

Beta, his favorite barista, lifted a hand and waved. "Morning, Russell. I just finished your drink."

"My girl," he said, grinning.

She chuckled and put a lid on the top of his drink. She picked up another cup read the label. Glancing up, she called out, "Ashiya!"

Russell's body stiffened. No. Seriously? He'd just run

into her the other night. Fate couldn't be messed up enough to have him bump into her again.

"Right here," Ashiya's sweet voice called from behind him.

Her voice was one of the things that had gotten him from the start. Soft, and teasing. Like the caress of cotton or silk across his skin whenever she laughed or spoke his name.

He sensed her coming up next to him before seeing her in his periphery. The sweet and spicy scent of her perfume barely drifted to him. Not enough to overpower, but tempting enough to make him want to lean in closer.

"Excuse me," she said softly.

Russell realized he was blocking her access to the pickup counter. He quickly shifted to the side. "Sure."

Beta's friendly smile turned into a look of concern when Ashiya stepped forward. "Here you go, Ashiya. I'm so sorry for your loss."

As much as he knew he should avoid looking at her—looking at her only made the stupid part of his brain long for her—he still glanced in her direction. The clench of his gut at the sight of her in a blue-and-white sundress that clung to her full breasts and flared out around her waist was exactly why he shouldn't have looked. A white jacket draped her shoulders, and her wavy hair was pushed back by a pair of white-and-gold shades that gave off a sixties vibe.

Ashiya stiffened and hesitated before answering Beta. "Um…thank you," she said quickly, as if she wasn't sure how to respond.

Beta held out the drink. "I put an extra squirt of chocolate and whipped cream on this for you. Please know that you're in my prayers."

Ashiya nodded awkwardly as she took the drink. "I appreciate that."

Beta's words of comfort were so unexpected that despite his efforts to pretend as if Ashiya Waters didn't exist, he faced her fully. Her eyes darted in his direction, then glanced away. A flush appeared beneath her smooth brown skin. Dark circles shadowed her eyes, and though she smiled at Beta, her lips were stiff.

"You be safe on the drive, okay?" Beta said.

Ashiya took a long deep breath. A move he remembered meant she was measuring her words before speaking. "I will." She lifted the cup. "Thanks again."

Ashiya darted one more quick look his way before turning and heading toward the door. Russell frowned after her. Sorry for her loss? What had happened? Surely nothing with her mom or dad. He would have heard about that.

"Here you go, Russell," Beta said, holding out the cup with his drink.

He jerked his head back around. "Thank you." He took the cup from her.

"See you tomorrow? Same thing?"

It was on the tip of his tongue to ask what was up with her interaction with Ashiya. He hated that he even cared to know. He'd staunchly avoiding trying to overhear or participate in any gossip related to Ashiya. That was typically easy to do because, unlike her cousins, she tended to stay out of the spotlight. Most people in Jackson Falls loved her, her store, and her bubbly personality. They didn't realize there was a cold heart beneath all of her outward sunshine. Something he wished he'd learned long before he'd trusted her with his own heart.

Instead he nodded at Beta. "See you tomorrow." He turned and walked toward the front.

He didn't need to be concerned about what was going on with Ashiya. They'd broken up, and he was moving along. While he had to see her occasionally due to working for her cousin Elaina, he wasn't involved in her life anymore. Whatever was going on with her wasn't his business.

Outside, the warm spring morning air was already thick with humidity and the promise of a hot day ahead. He headed toward his car parked not too far on the street from the coffee shop. Camille Ferguson and Ashiya stood in front of his car. His footsteps slowed. Camille's family owned a brewery in town, and she loved to brag about it. She wasn't a friend of Ashiya's, either, which made the pained expression on Ashiya's face even more honest. Just like that, the urge to help Ashiya one last time bubbled up.

"I was so sorry to hear about what happened," Camille was saying as Russell approached, her hand pressed to Ashiya's shoulder. "If you need anything, just let me know. Of course, I'm going to tell your mom the same thing. You know I would do anything to help you all out."

Ashiya smiled tightly and stepped back, causing Camille's hand on her shoulder to drop. "Thanks, Camille, but I'm fine. I promise."

"But it must have been a shock. How did you find out?"

Ashiya's lips pressed into a thin line. A glint came to her eye that meant Camille was about to get cursed out. Russell hurried over. "Ashiya, do you have a second?"

She turned to him, relief clear in her eyes. "Yes." She looked back at Camille. "Will you excuse us?" Despite the question, her voice warned Camille walking away was the only option.

Camille lifted her chin. "Of course. Remember what I said." She smiled at Russell before sauntering away.

Russell walked over to Ashiya. Now that he'd rescued

her from what appeared to be an awkward situation, he didn't know what to do. It was the first time they'd been alone together in months. They stared uncomfortably at each other for several long seconds.

Ashiya pointed over her shoulder. "I should go."

"Are you okay?" he asked at the same time.

She blinked, and her lips parted. She didn't have on lipstick, but the gloss she wore made her full lips look tastier than the latte in his hand that he'd craved all morning.

"Depends," she said.

Don't ask. Don't ask. It's not your business. "On what?"

The second the words came out, he bit the inside of his cheek. Damn his brain and his tangled emotions for not staying on the same page this morning.

Ashiya shifted her weight to one foot and eyed him warily. "Are you asking because you care, or because you're just as nosy as everyone else in this town?" Resentment filled her voice.

His defenses immediately rose. He did care, but he couldn't tell her that. He'd spent the years since their breakup denying any hint of a thought about wanting her back. The problem was, some of his tangled emotions wanted to believe her pleas for forgiveness were sincere. He wanted to forgive her, and that pushed bitter frustration through his veins. He wasn't supposed to care about her.

"I was trying to be nice." His voice was harsher than he'd intended.

She took a deep breath and pressed a hand to her forehead. "Look, I appreciate it. I'm fine." She glanced at her cell phone. "I've got a long drive. Thanks for saving me from Camille." She turned and walked away before he could say anything else.

Russell swallowed the need to call out and ask her to

come back. Find out what was wrong. Fix whatever caused that look in her eye.

She broke your *heart. Remember?*

He did remember. He'd been played by love once in college and then later as an adult. He wasn't about to sign up to be fooled a third time. He knew very well that Ashiya would make a fool out of him.

RUSSELL ENTERED THE conference room on the top floor of Robidoux Holdings with the rest of the research and development team. He'd been shifted over as the head of the division after Alex Tyson quit to take a job teaching at the local college. Since then, he and his team had successfully completed testing several new products that were now ready to introduce to the public. The quick comeback hadn't been easy after the company shock of Elaina being fired, Alex stepping in temporarily before leaving, and Elaina ultimately buying a major stake in the company and ousting her father.

Russell was proud of what they'd accomplished. Proud enough to believe he was the best fit as chief operating officer to partner with Elaina, who was president of the company. Too bad he wasn't as confident in his ability to get the position. Elaina was a hard person to read.

She entered the conference room shortly after the rest of his group. Her beige suit jacket was open, revealing a silky top and the matching pair of tailored beige trousers. Her black strappy heels clicked with her confident strides as she crossed the room. She smiled and nodded coolly at everyone before taking a seat at the head of the table. After settling into her chair and straightening her jacket, she looked at Russell.

"How are we coming with the new bioplastic?" she asked in a no-nonsense voice.

Russell nodded and spoke confidently. "We're ready to start internal testing. We think it'll be a good alternative for Kamanda Motors."

She raised a brow and eyed him skeptically. "Are you sure?"

"I'm positive." He picked up the dark blue folder in front of him. "If you take a look at page six of our report, you'll see that the flexibility and strength make it a perfect alternative to chemical plastics for Kamanda's new line of hybrid vehicles."

"Prove it," she said, her voice a challenge.

Russell only smiled in the face of her skepticism. For the next hour, his team went over the details of the new bioplastic they planned to manufacture using the hemp Robidoux Holdings processed through Elaina's recently acquired company. Elaina drilled them on strength, reliability, and life cycle costs, and they answered every one of her questions. By the time the presentation ended, she'd given them the go-ahead to start manufacturing on a small scale for internal trials.

"Good job, Russell," Elaina said once they were finished. She scanned the rest of the people in the room. "All of you. I look forward to the results of the trails."

His team smiled and nodded. Elaina stood, and so did the rest of the group. Without another word, she walked toward the door. Not surprising. Elaina had warmed somewhat in the past few months, but she was still a straightforward businesswoman. Russell preferred her get-to-the-point style and directness more than he did Grant's manipulation and innuendo.

"Elaina, can you spare a second?" he asked before she could leave.

She glanced at her watch. "I've got a lunch meeting. Can you walk with me?"

"Sure." Russell followed Elaina out of the office.

"What do you want?" she asked in her typically blunt fashion.

He knew her well enough to understand that beating around the bush would only irritate her. "Have you made a decision about who you'll choose for your CEO?"

She stopped at the elevator and faced him. Her chin lifted as she watched him with mild interest. "Are you asking because you think I should consider you?"

"I know you should consider me."

The corner of her mouth lifted. "Why is that?" She crossed her arms over her chest. Her voice was mildly bored, but the interest hadn't left her eyes.

"Because of what I've done with research and development in the time I've been here. Many of the products that were held up before I took the position have either finished testing or gone on to market."

The elevator doors opened. "Many of the products were held up because I refused to let Alex be successful."

True, and he was surprised she would even admit that. He, along with many people in the office, hadn't believed it when Elaina and Alex ended up together. He'd thought they were more likely to kill each other than sleep together. Then again, Ashiya was proof he wasn't the best at reading a room and understanding relationships.

Elaina walked onto the elevator, and he followed.

"Despite that, you can't deny the quick, and successful, turnaround after things with you and Alex smoothed out."

"No, I can't deny that," she said with a hint of praise.

"I am impressed by what you've done. I will admit that your group was able to bounce back despite everything that happened."

"Which makes me one of the best people for you to consider."

Elaina's direct stare met his. "You are one of the best, but you're also my father's man. My dad may have accepted might taking over without much of a fight, but I know that won't last forever. One day he may try to come back. How can I trust you?"

He'd expected the question to come sooner or later. In the past, he had to be Grant's guy because he'd wanted the respect, power and privilege that came with climbing the ladder of the Robidoux corporation. Without climbing that ladder, he'd be no closer to finding answers about his brother's disappearance. But being Grant's guy didn't mean he'd make a decision that would compromise his own integrity or that of the company. He wanted Grant's privilege, but not to be like Grant.

Russell pressed a hand to his chest. "I'm not your dad's man. He hired me, and I do respect and admire him, but at the end of the day, I work for you, and I'm loyal to you."

Elaina's gaze sharpened. He had the weird feeling that she'd been waiting for him to offer her his loyalty. "Then you'll have to prove it. I've worked hard to get control of this company. Whoever I hire to be the CEO will have to be someone I can trust not to go behind my back and tell my father every move I make. I'm still not convinced you're the right person to do that."

"What will it take to convince you?"

As long as whatever she asked wasn't immoral or illegal, he was willing to do whatever it took to prove his loyalty. Elaina, though she could be cold, wasn't callous.

She'd push him, but she wouldn't push him into something that would compromise the company.

The elevator doors opened. Elaina stepped off, and he followed her. She stopped and faced him. "Are you still seeing Ashiya?"

He flinched, and his steps faltered. That was the last thing he'd expected her to say. "I wasn't seeing Ashiya." The old habit of denying their relationship made him respond automatically. He spoke in a rush. The words sounded like a lie even to his ears.

As far as he knew, Ashiya's family wasn't aware they dated. They'd kept it quiet because Ashiya didn't want her family "meddling." Later he'd learned it was because she didn't want too many people to know about her fooling around with him while she was on "break" from her ex, Stephen. Discovering that had done more than bruise his ego, it pulverized his heart and shattered his confidence.

Elaina's lips lifted in a patronizing smile. "Don't be ridiculous. You may have kept it from my daddy, but I was well aware of what was going on. You two breaking things off and her getting back with Stephen is the only reason I didn't say anything when Daddy tried to hook you up with India. Now that Ashiya has finally come to her senses and dropped Stephen, I wasn't sure if you were back in the picture."

"I'm not. Whatever was between Ashiya and me is over."

Elaina made a noise and smirked. "Hmm…that's too bad." She turned on her heel.

He started to let her go, but her mention of Ashiya brought back his curiosity from that morning. The way people kept stopping Ashiya and offering their condolences. Elaina was at work, and no one had said anything about her family being in trouble. As much as he hated asking, he couldn't stop himself.

"Elaina."

She glanced over her shoulder and lifted a brow. She was growing impatient. He quickly asked the question.

"Is Ashiya okay? This morning, people seemed to be worried about her."

"Oh, that. Her grandmother died," Elaina said, some sadness coloring her voice. "She's on her way there now."

Russell watched, stunned, as Elaina walked away. Ashiya's grandmother died. She'd never spoken of a grandmother before. More proof of how superficial their relationship had been. He understood how painful it was to lose a relative. The gaping holes in his heart after his brother's disappearance hurt every day. If Ashiya felt a tenth of that then he empathized with her. As he turned back to the elevator, he sent up a quick prayer for her strength. Ashiya might have broken his heart, but he could never feel good about the thought of her in pain.

CHAPTER FOUR

ASHIYA ARRIVED AT her grandmother's home, a huge, two-story house on a secluded lot overlooking the bay, late that afternoon. She was greeted at the door by Brianna, her grandmother's personal assistant. Based on her stiff tone, and her father saying she was more of a companion than an assistant, Ashiya expected Brianna to be older. Instead, a woman who looked close to Ashiya's thirty-two years, with sienna skin and curly hair cut into a short, tapered style, gave her the tour of the eleven-thousand-square-foot home.

"Would you like something to drink?" Brianna asked once they were settled in the downstairs library.

Brianna wore a black sleeveless silk shirt and black slacks. The funeral was the next day, but Ashiya wondered if Brianna wore black out of mourning for her late grandmother. Every time she'd mentioned one of her grandmother's favorite spots in the house, she'd spoken with fondness and sadness. She might have been an employee, but she seemed to have cared about Ashiya's grandmother.

Ashiya shook her head. "No, I'm fine. I am curious to know why you asked me to stay here instead of getting a hotel."

Brianna smiled at Ashiya as if she were a silly child. "Because once the family reads the will, this house is yours. I thought you'd want to get familiar with it."

Ashiya shook her head. She jumped up from the couch

she'd settled on as if it burned her. "No, I'm not here to count my inheritance. I don't have to stay here."

"It's what she would have wanted." Brianna's voice was tinged with sadness.

Ashiya rolled her eyes and barely stopped herself from snorting. "I doubt that."

She'd thought about what her dad said earlier in the week. This inheritance, if it really was all coming to her, wasn't about what her grandmother wanted for her. The gesture was intended to make her father feel better, and her father would feel better knowing Ashiya was getting the very thing her mother always wanted.

Brianna was unfazed by Ashiya's skepticism and spoke with conviction. "I'm telling the truth. Your grandmother was a… stubborn woman, but she did have regrets. Unfortunately, she realized that too late."

She slowly eased back down onto the couch. "Which is even more reason I don't need this house or anything else. Just because she had a last-minute realization that her relationship with my dad was screwed up doesn't mean I should get anything."

"It's about more than her relationship with your dad. Your grandmother admired you and what you accomplished. She believed you would do better with all of this—" Brianna waved around the house "—than your dad would."

Ashiya crossed her arms. "How could she admire me when she didn't even know me?"

"She knew about you. That's all that matters." Brianna glanced at her cell phone. "I've gotten the house cleaned and the sheets in the master bedroom changed. Your grandmother spent her last days here, surrounded by her sisters."

"Wait, she died in this house?" Ashiya glanced around as if waiting for her grandmother's ghost to pop out.

"She passed away at the hospital. She had to be rushed there, but she was here before..." Brianna's voice trembled. She cleared her throat and glanced back at her phone. "Anyway, the house is cleaned and ready for you. The funeral is tomorrow at two in the afternoon. You'll meet with her sisters before the funeral. I thought you'd rather wait until you've had a night's sleep before dealing with them, and then the lawyer will read the will at five in the afternoon once the funeral is complete."

Ashiya blinked and tightened her arms. "That fast?"

"That fast." Brianna said with a self-satisfied smile.

Brianna already had things organized and ready for her. "Did I inherit you, too?" Ashiya said with scoff.

"No, but your grandmother did leave a stipend for me to assist you with the transition into the company."

Ashiya held up a hand. "Hold up. I was only playing. I don't need a personal assistant."

Brianna's bless-your-heart look almost made Ashiya feel like a five-year-old. It might have if Ashiya's mother hadn't perfected the look decades ago.

"Maybe not," Brianna said. "But I was at your grandmother's side for the past five years, and I know as much about her hopes and plans for the company as she did. I'm just as invested in the success of the Legacy Group as she was, so I look forward to helping you. But that's not the reason the funeral and will reading are happing so fast. Your cousin Levi insisted."

"Levi?" Ashiya asked.

For the first time, the confidence in Brianna's features wavered into something more pensive. "Yes. He's currently running the company. He expected to inherit, since he's the only one of the cousins who's actively involved in the business."

Ashiya sucked her teeth. She'd spent years avoiding infighting on the Robidoux side, only to be tossed in the middle of another fight with her dad's side of the family. How could she be this unlucky?

"Seriously, he's already trying to get his hands on my grandmother's money?"

Brianna's eyes widened. "No, it's not like that. It's just, he's worked for the company for most of his life. He wants to make sure things at the company continue to run smoothly after the death of your grandmother."

"I guess I'm going to mess that up."

"It will be hard for him," Brianna said, almost as if she felt sorry for him.

Maybe she did. Ashiya was the person who'd never been around. Now she was supposedly inheriting everything. Brianna might care about the company and obviously cared about her grandmother enough to respect her wishes, but that didn't mean she wanted Ashiya to take over instead of someone who'd been around all along.

"Well, this Levi can have the company. No matter what the will says, I don't want it. I'm turning everything over."

"Seriously? But…your inheritance is worth millions."

"My sanity is worth more."

The sound of the door slamming made both of them jump. They stared in silence for several seconds before they spun toward the library door.

She glanced over at Brianna. "Are you expecting anyone?"

"I was hoping he would wait," Brianna said at the same time.

"He who?"

"Levi," Brianna said. "He found out you're coming, and he wasn't happy about it."

Heavy footsteps preceded a figure filling the door of the library. He was tall, almost as tall as Russell, she thought, then hated that she'd thought of him again. Her cousin Levi had skin the color of pecans, with eyes as dark and hard as onyx, and a determined set to his jaw. Ashiya immediately guessed he wasn't going to welcome her to the family with open arms.

"You're Ashiya." He stated in a cold, arrogant voice that matched everything about his appearance, from the condescending look in his eye to the tailored blue-and-white-striped dress shirt and navy pants.

Having grown up in the mix of the Robidoux clan, Ashiya wasn't afraid of a challenge. She didn't want the inheritance or to be a part of another family game of tug-of-war, but that didn't mean she was going to be bullied.

She stood, straightened her shoulders and met his stare. "I am."

The corner of his lips lifted in a sneer. "Already here to try and snatch your fortune."

"I'm here because my grandmother wanted me here," she said matching his sharp tone.

He scoffed. "Your grandmother? What right do you have to call her that?"

She may not have any rights. She hadn't seen her grandmother since she was a kid, and that hadn't been a warm and fuzzy meeting. Despite any of that, she didn't like the accusation in his eyes or his voice. No matter what Levi thought, Gloria Waters had been Ashiya's grandmother, and she'd wanted Ashiya to have her fortune. Ashiya might not want it, but what right did he have to undermine her grandmother's wishes?

Ashiya placed her hands on her hips and glared at her cousin. "Again, she wanted me to be here. That's my right."

"If you think you're going to come down here and take everything away from me, you're mistaken."

"I'm not here to snatch anything from you."

He pointed. "Then turn over the inheritance. You don't deserve it."

The matter-of-fact way he said that further raised her defenses. "She gave it to me."

"Aunt Gloria was sentimental in her old age. She may have gotten softhearted, but that doesn't mean you deserve it."

"You don't know anything about me or my relationship with her."

"I know your mother married your father for money. When the money didn't follow, their relationship was strained. I know you're the lame duck of the Robidoux Family. The owner of a little thrift shop that's barely making a profit. You're out of your league, and you know it. If you're smart, you'll sign the paperwork over to me the second after the will is read."

His words hit their mark. Hit the mark and drew blood. Still, Ashiya refused to bleed out on the floor in front of him. "And what if I don't? I have other cousins I can sign things over to."

"If you don't, I will ruin you and your family." He looked her up and down as if she were nothing. "And it won't be hard."

He spun on his heel and stormed out. Ashiya stared at the empty doorway with her mouth wide open. She pointed at the door, then turned to Brianna, who still stared in the direction he'd taken.

"Did he really just threaten to ruin me?"

Brianna let out a long, sad sigh. When she looked at Ashiya, her eyes were filled with empathy. "Welcome to the family."

THE INSISTENT BUZZING of her cell phone's alarm forced Ashiya's eyes open the next morning despite the sleeping pills she'd taken the night before luring her back to sleep. She didn't sleep well when she wasn't at home in her own bed, which was why she'd taken the pills. Back when she'd dated Russell, they'd typically meet up at his place or in hotels. She'd never had a problem sleeping when he was next to her. He'd reach over and rub her back whenever she tossed and turned. His warm hand always soothed her anxiety, and she'd drift back to sleep, feeling safe and secure next to him.

That was her first thought as she reached for her phone and swiped off the alarm. She lay in the king-sized bed and stared up at the ceiling. Very much groggy and still in the remnants of sleep, she didn't stop her mind from wondering what Russell would have done if he'd been there with her. He would have held her the night before. He would have rubbed her back while she talked about all of the mixed-up emotions rumbling through her. Why would her grandmother put her in this situation? Why did she think Ashiya could handle running a major corporation, or would even want to? How was she going to get out of this?

She had no answers. She let out a long breath and pushed back the covers. She had the funeral to prepare for. No more thoughts about Russell and what things would be like if he were there. She had enough on her plate to worry about besides how she'd messed up that relationship.

There was a firm knock on the bedroom door before it opened. Ashiya jumped up in bed with a gasp. She jerked the covers to her chest, even though she'd slept in a nightgown and wouldn't flash whoever decided to come in. Brianna stopped right on the other side of the threshold.

Ashiya let out a long breath. Her heart struggled to go back to a normal pace. "Brianna, what are you doing?"

"I'm here to make sure you're up and tell you about your schedule for the day," Brianna said as if Ashiya should have anticipated her barging into the bedroom first thing in the morning to update her on the schedule.

"You couldn't wait until I was up and came down-stairs?"

Brianna stopped in the middle of opening the curtains and turned back to Ashiya. For the first time since Ashiya had met her, she appeared unsure. "Oh, sorry. I'm so used to coming into your grandmother's room in the morning to go over her plans for the day. Now that you're here and—"

"And I'm not taking her place." Ashiya held up her hand. "Let's get that straight."

Brianna turned away from the curtains and clutched the tablet in her hands to her chest. Her lips lifted in a pacifying smile. "If you say so."

"I do say so." Ashiya shot back. She pushed back the covers and got out of the bed. "Since you're here, you might as well tell me what the schedule is for today. I mean, there's the funeral, then the reading of the will. That's it."

"Those are the main things, but first you have to meet The Dragons."

Ashiya froze. "The what?"

Brianna's lips twitched. "Your grandmother's sisters. They're the matriarchs of the family. Though they'd do anything for any of their kids and grandkids, they can also be a bit…challenging to work with. That's why they are affectionately known as The Dragons. They pretend to be fierce, but they're really cute."

"There's nothing cute about dragons," Ashiya said,

going to the closet where she'd put her overnight bag and toiletries.

"Their growls are worse than their burns."

Ashiya groaned. "I don't like growls or burns."

Brianna chuckled as Ashiya pulled the pink toiletry bag out of her luggage. Brianna updated Ashiya on the schedule and plans for the day while giving her a rundown on the different family members Ashiya would be meeting. Not only were there "The Dragons," but also their various offspring. Cousins who were successful in their own right.

A small kernel of excitement bubbled in her chest at the thought of meeting the rest of her family. Her introduction to Levi hadn't gone well, but he wasn't the only new family she had. She enjoyed hanging out with her cousins, aunts and uncles on the Robidoux side. The idea of having more cousins to get to know was the one good thing about this entire debacle.

"Don't get too excited," Brianna said later as they made their way to the church where her aunt's funeral would be held. "Your cousins aren't close at all. They get along during family events, but they don't hang out with each other."

"Why?"

Cousins not hanging out was foreign to Ashiya. Though the Robidoux family fought for dominance, at the end of the day they always had each other's back. No matter what happened, she couldn't imagine not being able to go to India, or even Elaina, for help if she really needed it.

"It goes back to The Dragons," Brianna said as she smoothly turned the black Lincoln Town Car onto another street. "They all married well, but while your Aunts Maggie and Gertrude both worked to help your grandmother build the Legacy Group, your Aunt Helena didn't. There wasn't really any animosity between the sisters, but when their kids didn't want to work for the Legacy Group, there were some hurt feelings. Not to mention the rivalry between the husbands all vying for their positions of dominance in a matriarchal family. Some of the hard feelings spilled over to their children and the grandchildren, aka your generation. Your grandmother and her sisters pretended to be okay with the way things are, but I know they all want the family to come back together again."

Ashiya absorbed all the information. She could easily see how the same thing could have happened on the Robidoux side. Her mom and Grant were committed to Robidoux Tobacco and the legacy they could build from that, which could have easily created a rift between their other siblings and family members. Except Grant and Elizabeth insisted on keeping the family close and bringing everyone together every few years for a family reunion, because family connections were important to them both. Sounded like that hadn't happened on this side of her family.

"Is that part of the reason why she left me everything?" Ashiya asked. "To bring me back to the fold?"

"Yes, but it's a small part. Your grandmother knew about you, your shop, the way you've been able to stay out of most of your family's drama. She admired your spunk."

Ashiya smiled. "My spunk. I fear she grossly overestimated me."

Brianna glanced at her out of the corner of her eye. "I'm not so sure about that. I've seen some of your spunk as well."

They arrived at the church before Ashiya could inquire more about her family. Brianna led Ashiya to a private room in the back of the church. Three women sat on separate couches in what the gold plate on the door labeled the pastor's office. All of them appeared to be in their late seventies to early eighties. One had short, tapered natural hair that was white as a cotton ball. She eyed Ashiya up and down while taking a drag on a cigarette. The second's hair was jet black and styled in perfect curls. She gave Ashiya a welcoming smile while her hands flew as she crocheted purple yarn into what looked like a blanket. The third's hair was a soft honey blond, also short and cutely curled. She reached into the black bag next to her, pulled out a peppermint and held it up for Ashiya.

Ashiya took the candy because she didn't have a good reason not to. "Thank you."

The one with the cigarette spoke first. "So, you're Gloria's granddaughter."

Ashiya nodded. "I am. And I guess you're my grandmother's sister?"

"I'm Helena Drakeford, your oldest aunt. That's your Aunt Maggie Salvant." She pointed to the one crocheting. "And that's your Aunt Gertrude Gaillard," she said about the one who'd given Ashiya the candy.

"Nice to meet all of you," Ashiya said.

"You've met us before," Maggie said in a sweet voice.

"I did?" Ashiya tried to remember. She'd only gone around her father's family a few times before they'd disowned him.

"Yes," Maggie continued. "Right before your mom turned your dad out and forbade him from coming around family." Maggie's voice kept the same syrupy sweetness. Her hands never lost a beat while she crocheted.

Ashiya coughed and cleared her throat. "Well, sorry, but I don't remember."

"You were young," Gertrude said, taking another piece of candy out of her purse and opening the wrapper. "I didn't think you'd remember."

"I'm glad to meet you all now, but I wish it were under better circumstances."

Helena took another long drag out of her cigarette. She eyed Ashiya through the smoke. "Your grandmother wanted you here, so that's all that matters. I suppose Brianna already told you what we know."

Ashiya glanced at Brianna standing next to her, but her face didn't give away anything. "What's that?"

Helena's head tilted to the side. "That you're about to inherit everything. I don't think she should have given it all to you."

"Of course, my Levi should have gotten it since he works for the company," Gertrude supplied before putting the candy in her mouth.

Aha, so that was Levi's grandmother. "Levi. I met him yesterday. Nice guy," Ashiya said.

Maggie shook her head and stopped crocheting long enough to give her sister a dubious stare. "Levi is an asshole and a bully and you know it, Gert."

Gertrude lifted a shoulder. "Don't hate on my baby because he's confident."

"Confident my ass," Helena said, taking another long drag from her cigarette. She focused on Ashiya again. "Pay your respects to your grandmother and relax while you can. Once they read the will, you're going to have a fight on your hands."

Ashiya shook her head. "But that's the thing. I don't want—"

The door to the office opened, and a short Black man wearing a preacher's robe came in. "Ladies, we'll be starting soon. The rest of the family is arriving."

Ashiya didn't get to finish her statement as they were ushered from the office to the larger fellowship hall to gather with the rest of the family. There she was introduced to everyone by Brianna. All of them eyed her as if she were a new toy they couldn't wait to play with. If she hadn't grown up around the Robidoux clan, she might have been intimidated.

Instead, she hid her nervousness behind a confident expression and kept her face solemn as everyone gave her condolences on the loss of her grandmother. Even though they all knew Ashiya hadn't been close to her grandmother. Her dad had decided not to join the family. When Ashiya spoke with him the day before, he'd decided to drive up and planned to sit in the back of the church.

"I don't want to deal with the drama after all this time. I'll go to the church early and the graveyard late. I'll pay my respects to my mother without the rest of them watching me."

Just as Brianna predicted, her cousins were there, but there wasn't any real comradery between them. There was Levi, arrogant and glaring at her as if she were there to steal the bibles from the church. She started to say something snarky about him to Brianna but stopped herself when she noticed the way Brianna's eyes turned mushy whenever she looked Levi's way. Ashiya really hoped Brianna realized she could do ten times better than Levi. She also met her cousin Preston, Maggie's son and a writer currently living in Greenville. She heard about Antone, Helena's grandson, who was a professional wrestler too busy to return for a funeral. His sister, Shanta, was there. She was a school administrator and eyed Ashiya as if she were a kid sent to the principal's office. After that she lost count of all the various aunts, uncles and cousins she was introduced to.

The funeral was long. For someone who hadn't gone to church in years, Ashiya fought not to fidget. She listened as the preacher gave words of comfort and the choir sang every song in the hymnal, and she barely stopped herself from groaning when the praise dancers came out. She threw glances at *The Dragons* sitting in the front pew and sobered as she watched them wiping tears from their eyes. She might not have known her grandmother, but the women had lost a sister. Ashiya settled into the seat and got through the rest of the funeral.

The anticipation of her family grew at the graveside. The shifting, whispers and restless movements increased with each scripture reading and selection from the deacon board. As if she knew everyone couldn't wait longer, Helena directed everyone back to the fellowship hall after the graveside service to "get things over with."

Ashiya sat at the back, her fingers crossed under the table as she prayed Brianna, The Dragons, and her father were wrong. She didn't want the company. She wanted to appear poised and calm, to hide her dread about the contents of the will. Instead, her palms sweated and she fidgeted with the gold cross she'd worn with her black dress. Her stomach was so twisted in knots that she could barely swallow a sip of water. Silently, she prayed for this all to be a dream, for Brianna to have been mistaken, but as the lawyer pulled out the paperwork and read, Ashiya's worst fears were confirmed.

"I, Gloria Dewalt Waters, do hereby leave my entire estate to my only granddaughter, Ashiya Robidoux Waters."

A collective gasp went through the family. Dozens of eyes flew to the back of the room to Ashiya. Helena's rough laughter came through the growing whispers.

Levi jumped up. "I contest this."

"Boy, sit down," Helena said. "You can't contest it."

"Aunt Gloria wasn't in her right mind," he said.

"That's like saying me, your mom and your Aunt Maggie aren't in our right minds. She knew exactly what she was doing."

Levi pointed at Ashiya. "She can't have the company. She doesn't know how to run a corporation. She's just a thrift store owner. Are we really going to let her take things over and ruin it?"

Ashiya's spine stiffened. Heat spread through her cheeks, and anger flooded her system. She didn't want the company, wasn't sure she could run it, and didn't deserve any of this. But she sure as hell wasn't going to sit there and let an asshole like her cousin Levi tell her that she couldn't. Ashiya slowly stood, straightened her shoulders, and stared him dead in the eye. "I can and I will run this company. If you don't like it, then get the hell out of my company."

CHAPTER FIVE

RUSSELL WAS USED to spending time at various Robidoux family parties. From political campaign events to galas designed to show off the family's influence, he attended, networked, and charmed his way into the affluent lifestyle he wanted. He'd enjoyed some parties and hated others, but none made him as curious as the one he was attending that day.

He arrived at Elaina and Alex's engagement party forty minutes after it was scheduled to start. He was late partly because he hadn't wanted to be one of the first people to arrive and partly because the rain had made traffic terrible. The party was at Alex's parents' farm on the outskirts of Jackson Falls. Dozens of cars lined the long driveway leading to the house. Rain belted down in thick sheets as Russell parked at the end of the line. He grabbed his umbrella and the gift he'd purchased before getting out of the car and rushing to the house.

A tall, smiling woman who had the same tawny-brown skin and assessing black eyes as Alex answered the door. She wore dark jeans and a black T-shirt with Groom's Awesome Mother emblazoned in gold glitter letters across the front. "Welcome. Come in out of the rain." She waved him into the house.

Russell left the umbrella on the porch, wiped his feet on the mat and entered. The sound of conversation and laughter overtop old-school music came from the rest of the house. "Hi. I'm Russell Gilchrist. I work with Elaina and used to work with Alex."

"Well, Russell, I'm Alex's mother. I'm glad you made it. Gifts go in the dining room. Food is spread out in the kitchen. We're packed inside because of the rain, but we're still having a good time. Elaina and Alex are in the family room right now."

Alex followed her into the house. After putting his gift with the others in the dining room, he made his way through the crowd to find Elaina. The house was large, but it was jammed with partygoers. He recognized many from the country club, or work, and of course Elaina's family was there. Everyone except for her father.

Elaina and Alex were on the couch in the family room. Two women who also resembled Alex's mother flanked them. They wore black T-shirts with the same gold lettering except theirs read Groom's Awesome Sister on the front. Alex and Elaina were in white T-shirts. Elaina's read I Said Yes in pink glitter, and Alex's read She Said Yes. Russell's lips quirked at the sight of Elaina and Alex together with the matching shirts. He wondered which of Alex's family members had come up with the idea. He couldn't imagine someone from the Robidoux clan doing that.

A crowd of guests surrounded the couple. The Awesome Sister on the left held up her hand. "Okay, next question. This one is for Elaina. What is the one thing Alex thinks you should take a class in?"

The crowd laughed as Elaina eyed Alex playfully and pursed her lips. Alex turned to Elaina with a raised brow.

"Knowing him, he'd probably say cooking," Elaina said with a shrug. "I'm sure he's tired of my burned eggs in the morning."

Alex's sister shook her head. "Nope, you got another one wrong. Alex said, and I quote, 'Nothing because Elaina is perfect just the way she is.'"

A chorus of "aahh" came from the partygoers. Elaina pressed a hand to her cheek and glanced away from Alex. Alex reached over and pulled her hand away before pressing a kiss to her lips. Claps and cheers ensued.

Russell found himself grinning and clapping along. He wouldn't have believed it if he hadn't seen it. Elaina Robidoux blushing and in love. With Alex Tyson, of all people. Good for her.

"Okay, that's enough," one of Alex's sisters said, pushing her brother's shoulder. "We're going to stop this game if you two are going to start kissing after every answer. There's food in the kitchen, good music playing, and gifts to open."

"Don't forget the ring hunt," the Awesome Sister on Elaina's right called out. "We've hidden rings all over. Whoever finds the most at the end of the party wins a prize."

The crowd dispersed after that, with many going toward the kitchen and food. Russell crossed the room to Elaina and Alex, where other visitors stood around them to offer congratulations.

He held out a hand to Alex when he was finally able to talk to them. "Congratulations to both of you."

Alex's eyes widened, and he grinned. "Good to see you, Russell. I'm glad you made it."

"Of course. I had to come by and see the happy couple," he said.

Elaina watched Russell closely before turning to Alex. "Why don't you help Byron with the music? He'll have us listening to old-school stuff all night. Since we're stuck inside because of the rain, I'd at least like to liven things up a bit."

Alex smirked and shook his head. "That's my cue to walk away." He kissed Elaina's cheek. "This is a party. Don't talk about work too much."

Elaina's smiled up at him as if he were her sun and stars. "Just this one talk. I promise."

Russell waited until Alex walked away before asking, "Is something wrong?"

She shook her head. "Not at all. Ashiya is coming today."

Russell's heart flipped. He glanced around the room before catching himself. The knowing look in Elaina's eye meant she'd said that to see what reaction she'd get.

He shifted and shrugged. "Not surprising. She is your cousin."

Elaina leaned in. "And she just inherited a fortune," Elaina said in a low voice. "A fortune she's asked me to help her figure out what to do with."

Inherited a fortune? From her grandmother? Ashiya didn't want fame or fortune. He remembered her saying that repeatedly. If she had inherited a fortune, she'd feel burdened by it, and she'd worry about the additional troubles it would bring in her life. How was she dealing with things? Was she okay?

The thoughts raced through his brain in the milliseconds after Elaina spoke. He slammed down a mental door to block them. There he went, getting caught up in Ashiya again. Her fortune, her problems, didn't concern him anymore.

He shifted and crossed his arms. "What does that have to do with me?"

Elaina tilted her head to the side. "You're the person who's going to help her."

"Why would I?"

"Helping her helps Robidoux Holdings. Helping Robidoux Holdings helps you prove your loyalty and tells me whether or not you should get the CEO position."

"Elaina—"

She held up a hand. "This isn't a demand or an order. It's a request. Consider it. Talk to her. Get over your ego or whatever was hurt when you two ended your secret rendezvous, and think about what you want and how to get it." She lifted a shoulder. "That's all I'm saying. I'd love to help Ashiya, but I've got enough on my plate getting the company in order. That doesn't mean I want to hang her out to dry. Especially pitted against a new family she doesn't know. She's the major shareholder in the Legacy Group."

Russell's arms uncrossed, and he frowned. "The Legacy Group?"

Elaina nodded. "Exactly."

The Legacy Group started out as a homemade soap brand forty years ago. Ten years after that, the group expanded from making boutique soaps into hand soaps, shampoos and body washes that could be used daily. His mom loved their original soap, and it had been a staple in his house growing up.

That wasn't the only reason he knew about the company. Grant had always kept an eye on them. He'd watched their profits and growth, and mentioned on more than one occasion that he'd love to acquire the company. When Russell asked why he didn't try, his only response had been that he didn't want the hassle. A sentiment Russell never understood before. Now that he was aware of the animosity between the families he understood.

"So you're telling me that Ashiya's grandmother was the owner of the Legacy Group, and now it's hers?" He'd known so little about her. That reminder only hurt him all over again.

"It is, and she's decided to take over, but she needs help. If you can help her and convince her to bring the company under our umbrella, it'll go a long way toward proving to me that you have what it takes to be my CEO."

Alex called Elaina's name from across the room. She glanced over Russell's shoulder, and the calculating look in her eye melted away. The bright, warm smile that took over her face was so un-Elaina-like that he almost couldn't believe she'd just asked him to rekindle his relationship with Ashiya to help grow Robidoux Holdings. Alex and his mom were waving her over.

Elaina turned back to him and patted his shoulder. "Think about what I said. Now, if you'll excuse me. I promised my father-in-law that I'd try out this new cake he made. Enjoy yourself."

Russell stood there dumbfounded for a second as Elaina morphed into doting daughter-in-law and twined her arms with Alex's parents'. She had to be a chameleon. He should ignore her words. There was no way he could work with Ashiya again. That didn't stop what Elaina had revealed from snaking through his brain and wrapping around the part of him that knew becoming CEO of Robidoux Holdings would give him the power and connections to find answers to his brother's case.

His gaze scanned the crowd. He didn't even lie to himself and pretend he wasn't looking for Ashiya. That would have happened regardless of what Elaina said. Ever since they'd split, his eyes scanned a crowd for her. Usually so he could go in the opposite direction. He wasn't so sure he'd go in the other direction today.

He was relieved when he didn't spot her. Elaina's suggestion had been quick and to the point. Helping Ashiya could potentially benefit Robidoux Holdings. If he was committed to Robidoux Holdings, then how could he ignore this chance? And how was Ashiya handling all of this?

The last question kept circling through his mind. She didn't play the power games in her family. All she'd wanted was to make her store successful and live life on her own terms. Or at least, that's what she told him. He'd believed her when she said that, but he'd also believed her when she said she cared about him. That she wanted the same things he wanted. To find someone to love and settle down with.

Russell shook off the embarrassment that always crept in whenever he remembered the way he'd opened his heart to Ashiya, only to learn she was using him as a front to get back the guy she really wanted.

He spent the next half hour mingling. He spoke with India and Travis about plans for their new baby. Got updates from Byron, who was now the mayor of Jackson Falls, about the city council's collaboration with Robidoux Holdings on a revitalization project. And shot the breeze with fellow employees as they talked about how good it was to see Elaina happy and in love. The entire time, his body was hyperaware of the possibility of Ashiya showing up, but she never did.

The moment he noticed the rain had stopped, even if it was just for a moment, he went out the back door for some fresh air. The late afternoon was thick with humidity and the scent of the rain. He breathed in deep and walked off the porch toward a gazebo in the backyard.

He thought about what Elaina asked and what his cousin Isaac suggested. Maybe he should listen to them. Use Ashiya to get what he wanted the same way she'd used him.

He let out a humorless chuckle at the thought. "Might as well. Being the good guy got me nowhere before," he said to himself as he reached the gazebo.

He looked up from the ground into the gazebo, and his eyes met Ashiya's. He froze in place. She sat on a bench on the opposite side. A paper cup in her hand, sadness in her beautiful eyes.

The corner of her mouth lifted. "I always liked that you are a good guy."

ASHIYA WAITED FOR Russell to bolt like he typically did whenever faced with her. She watched as the surprise in his eyes faded and he glanced around searching for an exit. She forced herself to smile instead of letting the disappointment in her heart take over, begging him not to run away. She missed him so damn much, but considering the way she'd hurt him, she had no right to ask anything of him.

She sipped her soda and crossed her legs. "Good guys don't always finish last."

He shifted his weight from one foot to the other. His eyes darted back toward the house before he let out a breath and faced her. "That hasn't been my experience. Things went a lot better for me when I didn't give a damn about much."

She smiled and lowered her gaze to the fizzing dark cola in her cup. She remembered when he'd talked to her about that. The angry, I-don't-give-a-fuck phase he went through in his teens and early twenties after his brother disappeared. How he lived his life as if every day would be his last day. Until he'd met a woman, fallen in love, and had his heart broken. He'd stopped playing games after that. He'd only wanted to find someone he could love and trust. Ashiya had known then that she was in too deep with him. That she might hurt him, but she'd been too selfish to back away.

"Things are good for you now," she said without touching on his history. "From what I hear, you're stepping into the helm at Robidoux Holdings."

He watched her for several seconds before his shoulders relaxed and he took a small step into the gazebo. "Almost. There are still a…few things in my way."

He'd taken a step toward her, not away. The giddiness fizzled and popped inside her like the bubbles in her cup. She wanted to jump up and get closer to him. She also didn't want to show him just how happy it made her that he wasn't running away.

She forced what she hoped was an easy, I'm-chill look onto her face. "I know you'll overcome them. You always do."

His eyes met hers. "Not always."

Ashiya broke eye contact. He hadn't overcome her foolish pride. *"Don't go back to him. We've got something good. Trust this."*

He'd begged her to stay and she'd still walked away. She'd been such a fool.

"I heard about your grandmother. I'm sorry." He sounded sympathetic.

Though Ashiya wasn't eager to talk about her late grandmother or the inheritance she'd accepted on a whim, she also didn't want to go anywhere near the pain of their ruined relationship.

"Thank you. I wish I would have gotten to know her before she passed away."

"You didn't know her well?"

The confusion in his voice reminded her how little of herself she'd shared with him. She'd tried so hard not to fall for Russell. Tried and failed.

"I didn't. She and my dad weren't on the best of terms thanks to his marriage to my mom. I hadn't seen her since I was nine or ten."

His thick brows rose. "Really? Then why did she…" His voice trailed off, and he glanced away.

Ashiya chuckled. "Let me guess. The rumors of me inheriting a fortune have already gotten around."

He lifted a shoulder and tugged on his ear. "Elaina mentioned it."

Ashiya nodded. "I asked her for help. I don't know a thing about what to do now that I'm a major shareholder in such a large organization. My grandmother ran things with the help of my cousin, but he hates me on principle."

"Elaina mentioned you needed help." He met her gaze. "She asked me if I'd help out."

Ashiya's shoulders straightened. "She did?"

Ashiya had asked Elaina for help in confidence. It was bad enough she didn't know what to do with her newfound wealth and responsibility after growing up in and around the Robidoux family. She wished she could have asked India, but India had left the family and focused on her music. Byron knew what to do, but he was the mayor of Jackson Falls. Her parents were out of the question because asking either of them would cause another rift in their already strained relationship, so that left Elaina.

"She's busy with taking over now that Grant's left," Russell said, sounding somewhat apologetic. "That's why she asked me to step in and be your mentor. She doesn't know about our history."

He said *history* as if it were a shameful secret. She guessed for him it was shameful. She had kept them a secret.

"Let me guess. You helping will also help Robidoux Holdings because I've got so much ownership in such a large corporation?" She tried not to sound bitter, but sometimes her family could be a real trip.

"This isn't just about Robidoux Holdings. you asked for assistance, and she's trying to find a way to support you."

"Except I'm the last person you'd like to work with." The words were a statement. She knew how he felt about her. Hell, he'd tried dating India when she'd come back to town. That was the first time she'd wondered if Russell had pursued a relationship with her not just because he'd liked her but for the connection with her family.

He didn't answer. Ashiya glanced up, but he wasn't looking at her. His jaw was clenched, and he stared back at the house. She nodded slowly. Elaina might have asked him, but it probably came with a heavy dose of *Do this if you want to succeed in our family.*

Ashiya stood and took a few steps toward him. "You don't have to help me. I'll figure this out."

He met her gaze, and Ashiya's breath caught. He hadn't looked her dead in the eye in so long. She hadn't forgotten how his stare took her breath away. The way he looked at her as if she were the most important and beautiful treasure he'd ever discovered. She'd craved that so much after they'd split, and she realized that regardless of all her history with Stephen, he hadn't looked at her like that after the first few months they dated. Once she'd realized how much of a mistake she'd made, all she could do was hope Russell would look at her like that again. Hope to see the spark of desire that always let her know he was about to make her breathless in other, more decadent ways.

"It's not that I don't want to work with you," he said. "I just don't know if it's a good idea."

"Because of what happened between us?"

"That and because you aren't cut out for this. You said so yourself. You never wanted to be in charge of a major corporation or get involved in business the way your cousins did. I'm not interested in playing around with you again."

Ashiya's spine stiffened. He didn't think she could do this. The same indignation that had flared through her when Levi accused her of not being able to run the company roared to life. She closed the distance between them and poked a finger into his chest.

"Not wanting and not being able to do something are two different things. I can handle anything put in front of me."

He stepped forward, pressing into the finger against his chest. Ashiya sucked in a breath, surprised by the movement, and the hard look in his eyes.

"Oh really? Because when I came to you with everything you said you wanted, you backed away and went back to what was familiar. Why should I trust this will be any different?"

Her hand dropped from his chest. He reached out quickly and wrapped his fingers around her wrist. His hold was firm but didn't hurt.

"Why should I put my efforts in you again, Ashiya?"

The air sparked between them. The closeness of his body reminded her of their times together. Russell was a nice guy, but that nice guy exterior didn't hide the skilled lover within. He knew how to get her off. Knew how to touch her, kiss her, make beg for more. Heat flowed through her blood vessels, and her nipples hardened to tight peaks.

She tried to breathe. Tried to think, but her mind was filled with memories of how good it had been between them. She'd been such a fool for falling back on what she knew. Falling back on a relationship that had died years ago, but she'd tried to force it into something real because of her own insecurities and emotional baggage.

"Because I've learned from my mistakes," she said truthfully. She relaxed and leaned closer to him. His eyes dropped to her lips. Desire flared in her midsection. He used to nibble and suck on her lower lip when they kissed. The tender bites made her ache for his touch, and he'd known it. She ran her tongue across her bottom lip. His fingers tightened on her wrist. "If you put your effort, your trust, in me, Russell, I'll give you all of me."

His eyes jumped up to hers. He didn't believe her. The doubt in his eyes called her a liar. But there was something beneath the doubt. Desire. Desire and memories. He hadn't forgotten what they'd had. They were close enough that she could touch him, so she did. She eased forward just enough for the hard tips of her breasts to brush his chest. The pleasure of the light touch was so sweet and torturous, she had to bite her lip to keep from groaning.

Russell dropped her hand and jerked back. He took several long, heavy breaths and turned away. He stopped before walking out of the gazebo and glanced at her over his shoulder. The wall of defenses he put up whenever she was near masked all the longing and need that had brightened his eyes just moments before. "I'm sorry, Ashiya, but I can't play the fool for you again."

CHAPTER SIX

THE FOLLOWING AFTERNOON, Russell sat on his apartment's balcony overlooking the wooded area behind the apartment complex and called his parents. He called his parents at least three times a week no matter what was going on in his life. On days he didn't call, he texted. He never wanted his mom to worry about where he was or if he was okay. Even at the age of thirty-four, he didn't get upset when she checked in on him or asked what he was doing or where he was going. Not after what happened to Rodrick.

He settled back in the wooden rocking chair and sipped the soda in his hand while the phone rang. His mom picked up after the third ring.

His mom's sweet Southern drawl came through the phone. "Hey, baby, I was just thinking about you."

"All good things, I hope," he said with a smile.

His mom's delighted chuckle took him back to when he was a kid and he and Rodrick would sit at the kitchen table and tell her about how they'd leveled up on a video game while she made dinner. She laughed more often back then, and it had taken years after Rodrick's disappearance for her to start laughing again.

"I was just reminding your dad to send our travel plans to you. He said he was going to send them tomorrow, and I said he was going to forget. You know tomorrow is bowling night with him and the team. He won't remember after work. Make sure you remind him to send them to you."

"I'll text him for them tomorrow," Russell said. "Where are you all going this year?"

"Oh, we are finally taking that Alaskan cruise. You know I can't wait." His mom's excitement was palpable through the phone.

"That should be fun. You've always wanted to do that."

"I have, and I told your daddy we're doing all the excursions."

His mom went into details about their plans for the cruise. Russell listened and laughed as his mom updated him on all the adventures she hoped to have during their trip. He was excited for them. After his brother disappeared during his spring break trip his junior year of college, his parents had spent so much time trying to learn what happened to him. They'd begged the police for assistance, tried to get national news attention, but in the days before hashtags on social media could bring the spotlight on a missing twenty-one-year-old Black man, no one had cared outside of the local newspaper in the small town outside Raleigh, North Carolina, where he'd grown up and one mention on the local evening news.

His brother disappeared without a trace, and no one seemed to care except his family. Seven years after Rodrick's disappearance, his dad had convinced his mom to take a trip around the time of year when his brother disappeared. Getting out of town visiting all the places Rodrick would have enjoyed was their way of not spending the anniversary of the loss of their son agonizing over the lack of information and wondering about what might have happened.

"Sounds like you've got it all planned out," Russell said when his mother stopped to breathe.

"I do. I wish you could come with us this year."

"I wish I could, too. But things are hectic at work."

"Any word on the promotion?" Expectation filled his mom's voice.

Russell leaned his head back and suppressed a sigh. "I'm being considered, but I don't know if it'll work out."

"Why not? No one is better for the position than my baby," his mom said as if that were a truth universally known.

"That may be, but there are other things at play."

"Things like what?"

Like Ashiya, and Elaina's request that he help her. He'd considered it. That was why he'd stayed out in the gazebo with her instead of going back inside as soon as he'd seen her. He'd stayed only to be drawn to her. Being close to her was like a pull he couldn't ignore, and he'd remembered the difficulty of forming coherent thoughts whenever she smiled at him. Then she'd licked her luscious lower lip, and in that moment, he'd realized helping her would endanger him.

He couldn't say all of that to his mom. One: he was not in the habit of talking about his relationships with her. No need to have her thinking every woman he went out with would be her new daughter-in-law. Two: he didn't want his mom to know he still craved a woman who'd hurt him.

"Just office politics," he said.

"Whatever the politics are, play them. Remember people with money and power are the ones who get things done in this world. You're working hard and climbing the ladder at Robidoux Holdings. Maybe if you become a CEO, then the new detective with reopen your brother's case file."

Russell sat forward. "New detective?"

His mom sighed, and when she talked, the old pain of losing a son crept back into her voice. "Yeah. They've given it to another newbie at the sheriff's department. You know I call every year, and every year they give me someone new to talk to."

Russell gripped the phone. "What did he say?"

"The same thing. No case is ever closed until it's solved. They will continue to keep an ear out for leads. They'll let me know if any new information comes up. But we know it won't."

All the tension left his body. Another year, another new detective, another round of disappointment. Every year he hoped a new set of eyes would give some insight on what happened to Rodrick, but the case was colder than a glacier in Antarctica.

"Give me his name and number. I'll call as well."

"Thank you. Maybe he'll listen to you better than he listened to me."

"No matter what, Mom, I'm not giving up on this. If I have to drive down to Hilton Head myself and meet with him, I'll do that."

He hated not knowing what happened to Rodrick. The practical part of him said his brother was gone. They'd legally declared him dead ten years after his disappearance in an attempt at closure. They'd even had a headstone placed in the cemetery next to the family church. Still, the hopeful part of him wanted to believe Rodrick was still out there. That someone would eventually come forward and tell them how to bring his brother back to the family.

"I know you will." The pride in her voice made him feel a little better. "I'll send you the information after we get off the phone."

"Good." He would call this detective tomorrow.

"Russell." His mom's voice sounded hesitant.

"Yes ma'am?"

"I appreciate everything you're doing for me and your daddy, the way you keep looking for Rodrick and trying to find out what happened. But son, I also want you to live a good life. Find a nice woman. Get married. Have a family of your own. Your daddy and I won't be around forever."

"But you will be around for a long time," he said, forcing lightness in his voice he didn't feel. Living in a world without Rodrick was hard enough. He didn't want to imagine a world without his parents. "I'm dating, and as soon as I meet your future daughter-in-law, I'll let you know."

"What about that Ashiya girl you mentioned a while back? Whatever happened with her? You seemed to really like her."

"It just didn't work out. Look, Mom, I've got to get some things together before work. Send me the detective's number, and I'll remind Dad to send me your travel plans."

His mom's chuckle said she knew he was tired of her prying. "Okay, baby. You have a good night."

"You too, Mom. Love you."

"Love you, too."

He ended the call and stared at his phone. Three years after their breakup, his mom still remembered Ashiya's name. She didn't remember the names of any of the other women he dated. She'd never met Ashiya, but he'd talked about her once right when he thought they were getting serious. Right before Ashiya's ex confirmed that Russell was just the toy she'd used to make him jealous.

Russell wanted everything his mom wanted for him. A wife, kids, a family. He couldn't imagine life without his parents, but that didn't mean he wasn't keenly aware they wouldn't live forever. If something happened to them the way something happened to Rodrick, he'd be alone. They were all he had left, and he constantly felt an underlying desperation to start his own family. He just wasn't desperate enough to start one with someone he didn't love or trust. No matter how much he still thought of Ashiya and what they could have been, he knew he'd be a fool to trust her again.

ASHIYA LEFT PIECE TOGETHER in Lindsey's capable hands in order to make an appointment with Elaina at Robidoux Holdings. As much as it irritated Ashiya to know Elaina asked Russell to help her, she also understood her cousin's reasoning. Elaina was busy not only trying to put Robidoux Holdings back on track after the shake-up, but also overseeing the workings of a separate manufacturing facility she'd recently opened. Elaina really didn't have the time to mentor Ashiya on being a new company CEO, so she'd done the next best thing.

Understanding her reasoning didn't take away the embarrassment, though. Now Russell could add incompetent to the list of things he thought of her. In the brief time they'd dated, he'd looked at her as if she were the most fantastic thing he could've ever discovered. A sexy, smart businesswoman he could respect and admire. She hated how much she missed that gleam in his eye. Now he looked at her as if she were poison.

She arrived at the Robidoux Holdings building and was quickly ushered up to the executive suite and into Elaina's office. Elaina stood gracefully as Ashiya entered. The stylish white pinstripe pantsuit Elaina wore fit her perfectly, and her hair was pulled back in a loose but neat ponytail.

Elaina's discerning gaze traced over Ashiya before she raised a brow.

"Nice suit. Chanel?" Elaina asked.

Ashiya grinned and nodded. "It is. I found these vintage pieces in Hilton Head and decided to keep them instead of putting them in the store." As soon as she'd seen the orange Chanel skirt and matching jacket, she'd known she was keeping them. Bright colors were her weakness.

Elaina came around the desk and motioned toward the leather chairs arranged around a glass table. "I don't blame you. That almost tempts me to try brighter colors."

"You should. I mean, you look great in the neutral tones you tend to stick with, but you'd look fabulous in an emerald green or red." Ashiya settled into one of the leather chairs.

Elaina's eyes widened. "I get enough attention without wearing red."

"If they're going to notice you, might as well let them see just how fabulous you are," Ashiya said.

Elaina's lips lifted in a slight smile. "I appreciate the sentiment, but *fabulous* is not the word I'd use to describe me. Thank you for the subscription for the tea, by the way. I didn't get the chance to talk to you at the engagement party."

Ashiya knew the change in subject was on purpose. Elaina didn't like talking about herself and especially any reference to her being anything but the bitch most people took her for. She hoped her cousin would slowly get used to accepting compliments from others instead of deflecting.

"You're welcome. I enjoyed the party. Alex's family seems really great."

Warmth filled Elaina's brown eyes. "They are. It's

sometimes hard for me to believe there are actual normal, healthy families out there."

Ashiya chuckled. "It is a novelty for us."

"A good novelty. What about your father's family?"

Ashiya cocked her head to the side. "Answer that question yourself. These are the same people who disowned my dad for marrying my mom and haven't spoken to him since."

"Do you know why your grandmother left everything to you?"

Ashiya sighed and shrugged. "I think to make up to my dad. Her personal assistant says my grandmother followed me and was proud of what I accomplished. I don't know what I did that was so great for her to leave everything to me."

"You own your own business, and your store was featured in several travel magazines."

Ashiya waved off Elaina's praise. She was proud of what she'd done with Piece Together. Nothing could take that pride away from her. Still, it wasn't the same as being in charge of a large-scale corporation. "Again, it's just a small consignment shop. I was planning to give my inheritance away."

"What changed?"

Ashiya thought of her cousin's words, and her hands balled into fists. "They don't think I can do this. They expect me to mess up or ruin the company."

Elaina smirked. "Never underestimate a Robidoux."

The arrogance-laced confidence in Elaina's voice washed away Ashiya's righteous indignation. "Except I'm not quite a Robidoux."

Elaina waved a hand. "Don't be ridiculous. You're Aunt Liz's daughter, and she is a Robidoux despite what she changed her name to after marriage. Never forget that. You can do this."

"But can I do it without help? Let's be real, Elaina. I'm not cut out for this." She indicated Elaina's office. "The most I did for Robidoux Tobacco was my summer internships on the philanthropy side. Now I'm supposed to help run a multimillion-dollar beauty company."

"Who in this family knows fashion and beauty trends better than you?" Elaina's voice was direct and practical. "The first thing you have to do is stop acting as if you're some tragic case who flunked out of school. You're smart. You know you're smart. Stop whining and step up to the plate."

Ashiya sat back in her chair. Coddling was not what she'd get from Elaina. Still, she wasn't ready to hear confidence from her cousin. It's why she'd come to Elaina. If anyone didn't believe Ashiya could handle things, it would be Elaina.

"I still need a mentor or guide. I don't trust my dad's family to help me out."

"I agree with that. But you know I can't leave Robidoux Holdings right now. It's why I've found a solution."

The phone rang on Elaina's desk. She stood, walked over and picked up. "Yes. Good. Let him in."

"Who's that?" Ashiya asked.

"Your help," Elaina said with a sly smile.

Ashiya turned to the door as it opened, and Russell walked in looking like a CEO centerfold in a dark blue suit that fit his broad shoulders perfectly. Ashiya's heart flipped in her chest, and she fought hard not to sigh. Damn, she had it bad for this guy. She'd been so stupid to toss back everything he'd offered her.

Russell glanced from Elaina to Ashiya sitting in one

of the chairs. "I didn't know you had someone here. I can come back."

Elaina shook her head. "No, come in. This is why I called you over."

Ashiya stood. "Don't worry, Elaina. I already spoke to Russell, and it would be unfair to pull him away from Robidoux Holdings, too."

Eliana shot her an irritated look. "I'm his boss, so I know what he has time for. Plus, helping you helps the family."

"Still, I wouldn't feel right working with him… I mean, pulling him away. I know you can't leave the company, but if you can at least be willing to answer some of my calls if I have questions, I'm sure I can figure things out."

"Nonsense," Elaina shot back. "There is no way I'm watching you go to Hilton Head by yourself and get eaten alive by your father's family. You need someone there who we all can trust. I trust Russell."

Ashiya's cheeks heated. Great, now Elaina had spoken out loud about how much help she would need. Silly her to believe her embarrassment in front of Russell couldn't be amplified.

"Hilton Head?" Russell asked in a sharp voice.

"Yes," Elaina said. "I know I didn't mention the travel part before, but Ashiya is going to have to be down there until she gets a handle on her role in the company. Of course, Robidoux Holdings will cover your travel and living expenses."

Ashiya shook her head. "It's okay, Elaina, really. I'll hire a business consultant to help out. Someone neutral to me and my dad's family. Maybe you can give me a recommendation."

Russell turned and faced her fully. "No need. I'm willing to go with you and help out."

ASHIYA COULDN'T STOP her jaw from dropping at Russell's quick agreement. He'd been adamant at the party about not working with her. What in the hell changed in forty-eight hours?

"You will?" she asked.

"Of course, I will," he said confidently, as if he hadn't spent three years treating her like the enemy. "Elaina is right. Helping you helps Robidoux Holdings. Plus, a consultant may be useful, but no one will look out for your best interests in the same way we will."

Ashiya blinked several times. "But you said—"

"I thought it over and realized I was too quick to disagree. I'm happy to help."

He smiled the smile that usually made her want to immediately slip out of her panties, but this time there was no warmth or desire in his eyes. Instead there was something else. Resignation, maybe. For some reason, she didn't think his agreement had anything to do with wanting to help her.

"Great," Elaina said in a no-nonsense voice. "Why don't you go to your office and talk about the plans. I've got a video conference in a few minutes."

Having effectively been dismissed by Elaina, Russell nodded. "Sure. Ashiya, follow me."

She nodded slowly. "Okay. Thanks Elaina."

"Of course. You're family. I know Russell is the right person to help you."

Ashiya tried to smile but doubted she was successful. Elaina either didn't notice or didn't care. Ashiya followed Russell out of the office and down the hall. She expected him to get on the elevator to go to a lower level, but instead his office was a few doors down from Elaina's in the executive suite.

It was the first time she'd been to his office. His was similar to Elaina's with the glass table, leather chairs, and sleek modern desk, but his was smaller, and pictures sat on his desk of his parents, along with one of a younger Russell with another young man who looked similar. His older brother, Rodrick. He'd mentioned his brother to her once when they were dating. That he'd gone missing and they were still trying to find out what happened to him.

"Have a seat," Russell said, pointing to one of the leather chairs.

"Look, Russell, you really don't have to do this. You made it pretty clear the other day that you don't want to work with me. Don't feel obligated to do this just because Elaina wants you to."

"I'm not doing this for Elaina." He settled into one of the leather chairs and looked up at her. "I've got my own reasons."

Reasons like spending more time with her? Giving her a second chance? Realizing the two of them belonged together? Her heart loved all of those suggestions. Her brain, on the other hand, realized she was getting way ahead of herself when she noticed the frosty look in his eye.

"What are those reasons?"

"I need to go to Hilton Head. I would have asked Elaina for the time to travel there anyway. Since that's where your family is, I decided she was more likely to be okay with me taking off for a while if I was going to help you."

The disappointment weighed heavily on her shoulders. She slowly sank into one of the chairs. "Oh. Do you mind if I ask what you're going for?"

"Personal reasons."

She watched and waited for more. Nothing came. She smiled and leaned to the side. "Personal like dating?" She went for teasing with her tone. He used to smile, and his eyes would go soft when she teased him.

"Personal like personal," he replied dryly, looking away from her. "What exactly are you expected to do as part of your grandmother's company?"

His swift cut and change of subject were brutal. She'd hurt him and knew she had no right to wish for his smiles again, but she was also stubborn as hell. He was going to help her and would be the only person in Hilton Head she knew well. That was enough for her to have some small spark of hope.

"She was the majority shareholder in the company. She left all of those shares to me. My cousin is the chief financial officer, but my grandmother was still company president and chairman of the board. Now that I own all her shares, I'm automatically a member of the board. My great-aunts think my grandmother wanted me to step in and take over running things. My cousin and probably the entire board of directors doesn't want me there."

"If you're on the board, you don't have to take an active part in running the company. You can sit back and let others handle things while your shares earn money."

"I could, but I don't want to do that. If I'm that heavily invested, then I want to know what's going on. If I sit back as a silent member, then that leaves the door open for others to plot and swap shares to outrank me, or worse, eventually push me out. I've got to show them that I'm not someone to be ignored."

"I'm surprised."

"Why?"

He lifted a shoulder. "Because before you never wanted

to be a part of the cutthroat world of corporate America. You said you stayed out of the fights at Robidoux Tobacco and opened your store to live life on your own terms. Now you're ready to fight head-on with your father's family for the same thing."

"I wasn't going to take it, but when they said I couldn't do it, I also couldn't sit back and let them win."

His wry smile made her heart flip. "I guess you are a Robidoux after all."

"I guess." She met his eyes. "When we see something we want, we go after it. Even if it's something we lost or let go of, once we realize the value, we'll fight harder to get it back."

Her eyes didn't waver. She wanted him to hear the double meaning. Wanted him to understand that no matter what might have happened or the mistakes she made, she wanted him back.

Russell blinked and glanced away. "Just send me the information on your family's company and when you plan to go back down." His voice was brisk and dismissive, but she'd seen the spark of desire before he looked away.

"I'm going at the end of the week," she said.

He nodded, rubbed his hands over his pants, then stood. "That works out for what I need to do as well."

Ashiya suppressed a smile and the spark of hope glowing hotter in her chest. He still felt something. He might not want to, but he did. As long as she knew there was something still there on his end, she wouldn't give up. She would get him back, and this time she would keep him.

She stood and held out her hand. "Thank you for your help, Russell."

His eyes darted to her hand and then back to her face. He reluctantly shook her hand. "You're welcome."

When he tried to pull back, she tightened her hold. She took a step closer until the heat of his body brushed against hers. "I shouldn't say it, but I am. I'm glad to have you back in my life, even if it's just for professional reasons. Believe me when I say I won't mess things up this time."

His eyes widened, and he stared back. She let his hand go, turned and walked out before he would come back with something that would challenge her confidence. Because at the moment, she felt pretty good about making Russell hers again.

CHAPTER SEVEN

RUSSELL MANEUVERED HIS car through the picturesque streets on Hilton Head Island. He chuckled while talking to Isaac on the phone and listening to his cousin tell a story about his latest dramatic client. The client was driving Isaac up the wall with all of the ridiculous reasons he had for not making a decision about which house to buy.

"Wait, so you're telling me he ruled out the latest house because the bathroom was painted green?"

"Yes! Bruh, this guy is about to make me lose my mind," was Isaac's frustrated reply.

"How was I supposed to know green was his unlucky color? The house before, he said felt like it had cameras hidden. He's wasting my time, and I'm about to cut him loose."

"Tell him you can't meet his needs and move on."

"I should. The only reason I haven't is that his budget is high. I can make a really good commission on this sale. Once I do that, then it's easier to break into the more high-end houses."

"I get it. Still, know your limits. Don't do everything just for the money."

Isaac sucked his teeth. "You're one to talk. Remind me again where you're headed and why?"

Russell glared at the console where Isaac's name was displayed. "Stop. You know why I'm here. I can't get the police to give me any respect over the phone. If I'm here in person, I can put more pressure on the new detective to find out what happened to Rodrick."

"Alright, I hear you, but it doesn't mean you have to help Ashiya while you're down there. You could put pressure on the police without working with her."

Something Russell had reminded himself of a dozen times a day since agreeing to Elaina's request. He'd made the trip to South Carolina every time a new detective was put on the case in the hopes that seeing a real life person still interested would spark some sort of motivation to find the truth. He'd convinced himself being here long-term helping Ashiya would give him the chance to check in with the detective frequently. He didn't want to admit that the proximity to Ashiya had anything to do with his agreement.

"I told you, Elaina said helping her is a way for me to prove my loyalty to her and the company."

Isaac grunted. "Whatever. You still like her."

"I don't still like her," Russell shot back, then cringed at the almost desperate plea to his voice.

Isaac laughed. "Okay, I believe you." He didn't sound at all like he believed Russell.

"Listen, doing this helps me with two major problems. I'll get to prove my loyalty to Elaina and, and being here will hopefully put pressure on the police and find answers to what happened to my brother. Those are the only reasons I'm willing to work closely with Ashiya."

When Russell spoke to the new detective, he'd gotten the same runaround they'd given his parents. The detective promised to review the case file and get back to Russell if anything new came up. He hadn't gotten off the phone confident about receiving any updates anytime soon. Coming to Hilton Head, was the best way to put pressure on the police department.

"I hear you, bruh," Isaac said, a little more serious than before. "We all want to know what happened to Rodrick. The fact that he disappeared without a trace on spring break and not one person from that party knew what happened to him is beyond fucked up. I know you're trying to get answers."

"That's all."

"But…"

Russell sighed. "But what?"

"But while you're down there, you're also going to be working close with Ashiya and no matter how much you want to pretend like you're not interested in her, we both know you're still feeling her. Just be careful if you start messing around with her again."

"I'm not going mess around with her or anything like that."

"Still," Isaac warned. "We've all been there. We have good intentions to leave a woman alone, but when she's got that fire…it's hard to let go."

There was not a damn lie Russell could detect in that statement. His GPS directed him to take an upcoming turn. "Look I'm almost at the house. I'll give you a call later this week after I learn more."

"No problem. Talk with you soon."

The call ended, and Russell thought about Isaac's words while following the robotic instructions of his GPS. Ashiya not only had the fire, she was also the heat, fuel and oxygen. Her flirty personality, sexy voice, the way her body curved in all the places that made his mouth water. So much about her made him weak in the knees. He had to be careful working with her. Especially after the way she'd held on to his hand in the office.

"I won't mess things up this time."

Damn if her confidence wasn't sexy. Knowing she wanted him was a turn-on as well. He shouldn't follow up on where the part of him that still longed for her tempted him to go. When was going back to the person who'd broken your heart ever a good idea?

He wanted her. He knew that. But what would make this time different from the last? Just because she was done with her ex, Stephen, didn't mean a damn thing. Mind over body. He just had to remember to be smarter than his dick.

A few minutes later, he arrived at the estate Ashiya had inherited from her grandmother. He'd agreed to meet her there before going to the condo Robidoux Holdings rented for him while he was in town. Her cousin, who currently ran the company, was coming by later that afternoon to update her on what was happening. Ashiya asked him to be there for the initial meeting.

He rang the doorbell, and a few seconds later a Black woman with short natural hair wearing a light blue button-up shirt and black pants answered the door. Her brow furrowed as she quickly glanced him up and down.

"Can I help you?" she asked in a clipped tone before looking over her shoulder.

"Um, yeah. I'm here for Ashiya Waters."

The sound of raised voices drifted through the house. The woman glanced back at him. "She's busy right now." She moved back as if she were going to close the door in his face.

Russell took a step forward and held up a hand. "She's expecting me. I'm Russell Gilchrist."

The woman's dark eyes narrowed on him as she gave

him a confused look. Then the voices continued, and she sighed. "Russell who?"

"Gilchrist. I'm working with her."

Her eyes widened, and she snapped her finger. "You're the person helping her deal with the inheritance." She reached over and grabbed his hand. "Good, because she needs you right now." She jerked on his hand, hauling him in the house, and slammed the door behind Russell.

Russell's jaw dropped. He planted his feet firmly on the floor to stop her from pulling him farther. "What's going on?"

The woman stopped pulling but didn't drop his hand. She let out an impatient sigh. "Her cousin is laying into her, and I don't think she was ready for this."

The voices continued to come from the back of the house. Russell honed in on them. He couldn't make out the words, but he could tell a man was berating someone. A woman's voice jumped in but was quickly drowned out by the man's. Russell's heart thudded. That was Ashiya's voice.

He immediately hurried down the hall in the direction of the voices. What had she said? Ashiya's cousin was laying into her? If he so much as laid a finger on Ashiya, he'd best be ready to lose his whole damn arm. A fierce protectiveness rushed through him and drove his footsteps down the hall. As he drew nearer, he was able to make out the words.

"If you think you're about to come down here and take over, then you've got another think coming. I refuse to stand by and watch you ruin this company." The man's voice was angry.

"I have no intention of ruining anything," Ashiya shot back in a firm but calm voice. "Obviously my grandmother wanted me to be involved. I will at least see how I can be of help—"

"Don't even pretend as if you care about your grandmother," her cousin's accusatory voice cut in. "You're no better than your mom. Here to try and take everything."

"Don't you dare talk about my—"

"You can't do this," the man said with finality. "I won't let you do this. I've got the backing of the board. No one will support you. The best thing for you to do is leave now."

Anger boiled inside of Russell. Who the hell did this guy think he was? He knew nothing about Ashiya. He didn't know how smart she was. How determined she was. The way she didn't let anything get in the way of what she wanted. He was fucking lucky to have her there, and he'd better realize that quick.

Russell got to the almost closed door where their voices came from. He didn't knock or introduce himself. He pushed the door so hard it slammed against the wall. Ashiya gasped and pressed a hand to her chest. Her wide eyes filled with relief when they met his.

The guy, her cousin, jerked around and faced Russell. He was tall, broad, with dark skin, and eyes that would have shot daggers if they could. He wore a dark gray shirt with black slacks that matched the ominous look in his face.

Russell crossed the room to Ashiya's side in a few determined strides. He let his eyes roam over her for any signs that her cousin had put his hands on her. Thankfully, her peach shirt and blue-and-ivory-patterned skirt were neat and in place, nor was there a hair was out of place on her head. After his quick perusal of her body, he met her eyes. She seemed frustrated and tired, but she didn't seem afraid.

Good. If there had been any hint of fear in her eyes, he was going to punch her cousin's teeth out of his mouth.

"Russell—"

"Who the hell are you?"

Ashiya and her cousin spoke at the same time. Russell studied Ashiya for another second for any signs of distress. She nodded and gave him a weak smile. He felt a modicum of tension leave his body. She was fine.

He spun toward her cousin and straightened his shoulders. "I'm Russell Gilchrist. I'm here to assist Ms. Waters during this transition."

The guy's eyes narrowed. He pointed a finger at Russell. "There won't be a transition. She doesn't belong here, and—"

"You don't get to decide if she belongs here or not," Russell said with a wave of his hand. "From the way I understand it, Ms. Waters is now the majority shareholder in the Legacy Group. Therefore, she can do what she wants. No matter the will of the rest of the board, she has the last word. Including firing you, which is something I recommend she do immediately."

The guy's eyes widened. Ashiya stepped closer to him. Russell continued before either of them could speak.

"Now, before you say something more you'll regret that will influence her decision about your tenuous role at the company, I suggest you pack your stuff and leave." He balled his hands into fists. He let all the rage coursing through him after listening to the guy berate Ashiya as if she were a kid enter into his voice. "Now."

To his credit, her cousin didn't back down or cower from the lethal tone of Russell's voice. Russell silently waited him to say another thing. Her cousin's eyes flicked to Ashiya and then back to Russell. Without another word, he turned and stalked out.

Ashiya pressed a hand to her forehead. "Thank God that's over."

Russell whipped around to face her. He placed his hands on her shoulders, and was surprised to realize his hands trembled. "Are you okay? Did he hurt you? Do you need anything?"

ASHIYA HAD BEEN more irritated than afraid of her cousin. Her Uncle Grant could rant and rage ten times worse than Levi Galliard ever could. One thing she'd learned from watching her mom and late Aunt Virginia deal with Grant and men like him was to let them go ahead and vent out all of their frustrations and then cut them to the quick once they were through. Which was exactly what she planned to do with Levi. Despite all his threats of getting the board against her and telling her what she couldn't do, she knew very well what she could do. She could come in and fire his overconfident ass.

A part of her really wanted to do that. The only reason she hadn't done so immediately was Brianna's insistence that the her Grandmother Gloria and her sisters wanted the family together. Firing Levi, no matter how tempting, wouldn't bring her closer to her family or The Dragons. At least not immediately. Plus, she needed Levi's knowledge about the company to keep the things stable.

Still, she'd gotten all prepped and ready to remind Levi that she could fire him immediately when Russell came through the door in all of his white knight, slay the bad guys, save the girl glory. Ashiya was a bona fide sucker when it came to fairy tales. She was well aware that they were unrealistic and had some pretty fucked up storylines, but that didn't stop her from sighing happily at the end. Nor did that stop her heart from fluttering like hummingbird wings at the protectiveness in Russell's eyes.

She'd never played the damsel in distress, and what she was about to do would probably have Elaina rolling her eyes so hard they'd fall out of her head, but at the moment all she wanted was for that look to remain in Russell's beautiful hazel eyes.

"I'm okay," She let her voice waver. With a sigh, she let her shoulders slump beneath his touch. "It was just all so much."

She waited from him to pull away as if her touch burned him the way he typically did. Waited for his eyes to ice over and suspicion to enter his gaze. Instead, concern erased his anger.

"He had no right to yell at you like that." Steel lined Russell's voice.

"He's upset," she said, keeping her voice contrite.

"Being upset doesn't mean he gets to treat you that way."

Ashiya placed her hand on his chest. His heart thumped heavily beneath the muscles. It took everything in her not to pull him closer. "Thank you for stepping in like you did."

The gratitude heavy in her voice was not part of her damsel act. She meant it. Few people fought for her unconditionally. Russell had always promised to have her back. Hope burned brighter knowing he continued to do so.

His body stiffened beneath her hand. She saw the doubt creep in his eyes. Maybe the hand on the chest was too much.

"Ms. Waters, do you need anything?" Brianna's voice came from the door.

Ashiya pulled back from Russell before he could let her go. His fingers lingered on her shoulders before dropping away. Embarrassment made her face hot at being caught trying to entice Russell with a helpless act. She turned away quickly before Russell could see her blush. "I'm fine."

Her foot twisted and she stumbled. Russell immediately wrapped an arm around her shoulder. "Get her some water, please."

"Of course," Brianna said and hurried away.

Ashiya looked up into Russell's face. She knew she had to look dumbstruck. That's how she felt. Dumbstruck and elated. His arms were around her again.

She smiled up at him. He cleared his throat and looked away, but he didn't pull away. "Have a seat." He led her across the room to one of the couches.

Ashiya sank onto the cushions, and he sat next to her. She bit her lower lip to keep the giddy grin from taking over her face. No matter what he might say, he still cared about her. No way would he be like this if he didn't.

He moved to slide away. Ashiya wrapped her hand over his to stop him. When his eyes jerked up to hers, she held on tighter. "Thank you for stepping in like that."

"I was worried he would hurt you."

She frowned. "Levi? No, he reminds me of Uncle Grant."

Russell scowled. "Then he'll definitely try to bully you."

She lifted a shoulder. "He might try, but his bark is worse than his bite. Uncle Grant is scarier."

The dark look that had been in his eyes earlier when facing Levi came back. "Don't underestimate him. You should fire him."

She shook her head. "I don't want to."

"Why not?" he asked as if she were crazy.

"He's worked for the company for most of his life. He's like the male Elaina, from what Brianna has told me. He knows the company in and out. If I want things to remain stable, then I need him."

Russell shook his head. "Not if he disrespects you."

"I agree. This is all still a shock to him, and he's lashing out. If he doesn't calm down and see reason, then I'll let him go. Besides, I doubt he'll keep up the temper tantrum now that he knows I have you on my side." She squeezed his hand. "Thank you again for agreeing to help me. I know this isn't what you wanted, but I do appreciate you."

He must have realized his hand was still in hers after the squeeze, because he pulled away. "Helping you helps Robidoux Holdings."

He gruff words might have been spoken to dampen her spirits, but the half-hearted way he spoke them had the opposite effect. She would get him back. She just had to be patient.

"That doesn't mean I shouldn't thank you."

An awkward silence grew between them. He glanced at his watch. "I should go. You've already had a hard day with your cousin, and I need to find my rental property. We can talk tomorrow."

Ashiya slid closer to him and grabbed his arm. "No, please stay here."

His eyes widened. "What?"

She scrambled for words that wouldn't make him immediately bolt. "I mean, there's no need to pay for a rental. This place is huge, and since we'll be working together, you might as well stay here."

He was pulling his arm away before she even finished talking. "I don't think that's a good idea."

"There's an entire guest suite on the other side of the house. I promise I won't come over there, and I will leave you alone to come and go as you please. Plus, I don't like staying in strange places by myself. I feel like my grandmother's ghost is watching me in every room. I'd feel safer is someone else were here besides me."

She lowered her eyes after the admission. Every word was true. She was afraid to stay there alone. The house was too big. Too quiet with just her there. The staff didn't stay the night. The place was unfamiliar. She'd gotten through the nights so far with sleeping pills to keep away the nightmares of the last time she'd been all alone in a strange place, and woke up foggy-headed, wishing Russell were near.

She hadn't planned to ask him to stay. It wasn't until this moment that she considered asking him. Even if she already knew the answer he'd give.

"I'm sorry. I know that's too much. You don't have to stay here with me." She tried to infuse her voice with confidence, but it trembled.

A long silence passed before he said, "I'll stay."

Her head jerked up so fast she almost put a kink in her neck. "You will?" The relief in her voice made her cheeks heat with embarrassment again. She cleared her throat. "I mean...are you sure?"

He took a long breath and looked back at the door. "No, I'm not."

"Thank you," she said sincerely.

Russell looked back at her. He held her stare for several long seconds. Ashiya didn't try to mask her feelings. Staying alone in a strange place scared her. Having Russell next to her made her feel safe. She needed him, and she wasn't too proud to let him know that even if it meant a rejection.

He sighed, stood, and ran his hands over his pants. "I'll get my bags out of the car."

CHAPTER EIGHT

RUSSELL TOSSED AND turned through most of the night. He finally fell into a fitful sleep around five a.m. He dreamed about running in and saving Ashiya from her cousin, who in the dream had morphed into some sort of green-eyed, gray-skinned monster trying to eat her. He'd not only slayed the monster and rescued Ashiya, but afterwards pulled her into his arms. They'd fallen onto the floor and had passionate, carpet-burn-for-days, sex.

He'd woken up drenched in sweat, chest heaving, dick hard, and a wild cocktail of lust, embarrassment and anger boiling in his system.

Why had he agreed to stay here? Scratch that. He knew exactly why he'd agreed to stay here. When had he ever been able to resist that pleading look in Ashiya's eyes?

He *knew* better. Knew she was okay and that her cousin hadn't harmed her. Still, the moment she'd looked up at him with those big, beautiful eyes and offered one of the many guest rooms, he'd caved.

He was such a fucking idiot. Had he not just told Isaac that he wasn't going to get involved with her again? He could practically hear his cousin's *told you so* laughter when he found out. Which meant Russell couldn't let him find out. He would tell Ashiya this morning that he wasn't going to stay here anymore. Robidoux Holdings had secured a place for him, and he was going to stay there.

After showering and dressing, Russell went in search of Ashiya. She was typically an early riser. He remembered that from when they dated. She was always bright and cheerful first thing in the morning without the aid of caffeine. Instead of her morning brightness irritating him—he wasn't ready for a coherent conversation until after a cup of coffee—he'd enjoyed seeing her smile and hearing her infectious laughter. Waking up with Ashiya next to him had started his day off better than any cup of joe ever could.

The smell of coffee led him to the kitchen. There he found the same woman who'd answered the door the day before. Brianna, if he remembered correctly. She'd brought Ashiya water the night before, showed him to his room on the opposite end of the house, and then disappeared. He wasn't sure what her role was or if she lived there. She was dressed in tan slacks and a black button-up shirt and held a coffee mug in one hand and her cell phone in the other.

"Good morning, Mr. Gilchrist," Brianna said in a crisp, professional voice. "Would you like some coffee? We also have tea if you prefer."

"Coffee is good." He glanced around the kitchen. "Where's Ashiya?"

Brianna put her phone and mug down and pulled another mug from the cabinet. "She's still asleep."

Russell froze. "Asleep?" he glanced at his watch. It was nearly eight in the morning.

"Yes. She doesn't get up before ten."

"Ashiya? You're mistaken. She's an early riser."

Brianna poured coffee into the mug, then turned to him with a curious look. "Are you sure about that?"

The way she asked the question made his cheeks heat. He had a feeling Brianna wanted to know what was up between him and Ashiya. Admitting how he knew she was an early riser would only feed her curiosity. He wasn't there to give anyone insight on his personal relationship with her.

"When we've worked together in the past, she always seemed like a morning person," he said. "I wouldn't expect her to sleep in."

"Oh." Brianna's shoulders slumped a little, and for a second, her professional demeanor slipped into one of disappointment. "In the few days she's stayed here, I've had to wake her up. I was on my way to her room now to do that."

He declined cream and sugar, and Brianna handed him the cup of coffee. Russell narrowed his eyes. "Do you stay here, too?"

"Oh no. I live in Bluffton. It's a town across the river. I was Ms. Gloria's personal assistant. Though Ashiya hasn't hired me for that role. Her grandmother asked me to step in and help her out as she gets used to taking over things around here."

Russell breathed in the divine smell of coffee before taking a quick sip. "You come over and wake her up in the mornings."

"That's not an official part of my duties, but Ashiya said it's okay for me to make her get up if she'd not up before ten. Besides that, I've been going over the various assets her grandmother left to her, getting her up to speed on where her grandmother left off with various projects, and answering her questions about the family."

Russell took a long sip of the coffee. That wasn't like Ashiya. Not only wasn't she one to sleep past eight in the morning, but it didn't take a lot to get her going. He hated the kernel of worry that wormed its way into his midsection.

The urge to find her bedroom, wake her and ask what

was going on was damn near a push on his back. He glanced at Brianna, who watched him intently. If he did go searching for her, it would only make Brianna even more curious about the nature of his relationship with Ashiya. After he'd charged in the night before and threatened her cousin Levi, he was sure rumors would spread about him being more than a business partner and consultant to her. He didn't need that for a few reasons. One was that he shouldn't get into the habit of being Ashiya's savior, but the biggest reason was to protect her from personal attacks from her cousin. He had no doubt Levi would use a relationship between him and Ashiya as a reason to further discredit her.

"I've got to go out and run an errand," he said. He'd let Brianna deal with the new non-morning-person Ashiya and go visit the detective about his brother's case. "Will you let Ashiya know? I'll be back by lunch, and we can go over some of the company information."

Brianna nodded. "I will. That's probably a good idea anyway. She's more focused in the early afternoon."

Russell frowned, but kept his concerns to himself. If something was wrong, he'd find out about it later. "Thank you."

"Do you mind if I ask where you're going? Do you need directions or anything like that?"

Russell had the address of the police department memorized.

He shook his head and put down the coffee mug. "No. I know exactly where I'm going."

ASHIYA SIPPED COFFEE from the bright red mug in her right hand while she flipped the pages of the latest Legacy Group quarterly reports with her left. It was her third cup and she still felt as if there was cotton in her head. A side effect of the sleeping pills. She hated not getting up early and getting a jump start on things, but without them, she'd either be unable to fall asleep or she would have gone in search of Russell and done something stupid like ask him if he'd hold her until she drifted off.

Neither was a good choice, so sleeping pills won out. She hated that at her age she was still plagued by nightmares of being alone in an unfamiliar place. Therefore, she'd deal with the grogginess until the house felt familiar and she could sleep all night.

The door to the library opened. Ashiya didn't glance up. Brianna had been coming in and out for the last few hours bringing her more paperwork to review, coffee to drink, and updates from the board in preparation for the next meeting in a week.

"I don't understand the reports from the marketing division," Ashiya said, still going over the numbers. "The promotional campaigns they launched went well, but something is bothering me after reviewing the last three quarterly reports."

"What's bothering you?" Russell's deep voice answered.

Ashiya jerked upright. The pages of the report fell to the coffee table as her eyes flew to his. He wore a light gray suit with a blue shirt and dark tie. The suit's fit made her want to trace her hands over his broad shoulders and taunted her gaze to linger on his long legs. He was dressed as if he were going to have a day in the office instead of helping her review reports.

"Why are you so dressed up?" Ashiya asked.

Since she'd barely dragged herself out of the bed, she'd thrown on a pair of gray leggings and an oversized T-shirt. She'd put on makeup and wrapped a colorful scarf around her hair to try to look decent, but that was it. Sure, Russell was there in a professional capacity to help her, but she hadn't expected full suit and tie to start.

Russell looked down at his clothes then back up at her. "Why are you so underdressed?"

Her shoulders straightened. "We're just going over reports."

"But we're still working," he said dryly. "You look as if you're going to a slumber party."

Ashiya put a hand to the scarf over her hair. "No, I don't. You're the one dressed as if you're going to a funeral," she shot back.

He ran a hand over his tie. "I dress like this every day."

And if he dressed like that daily, then she'd have a hard time not jerking on that tie to pull him in close for a kiss. Russell was too sexy when he dressed up. Then again, Russell sitting across from her in basketball shorts and a T-shirt wouldn't be much better. He was just as sexy in them as he was in a suit. She loved the way the mesh material clung to his ass and, when they shifted just right, hinted at the girth of his perfect penis.

She pulled her mind away from thoughts of Russell's nether regions. She'd gotten him to stay. If he caught her salivating over him, then he'd leave faster than she could blink. She had to convince him to give them another chance carefully and delicately.

"You dress like that to go to the office at Robidoux Holdings. We're meeting here in the study."

"You're saying you want me to put on pajamas like you?" he asked, sounding dubious.

Ashiya crossed her arms over her chest and glared. She started to give another sly remark but held back. The ridiculousness of their conversation struck her, and she laughed. "You're right. I'm underdressed. I woke up late and didn't feel like getting all dolled up for this. I'll do better next time."

His lips twitched as if he were holding back his own laugh before he finally let them lift in a half smile. "And I'll admit I'm a little overdressed." He came further into the room and sat in the wingback chair next to the couch.

"Where did you go?" She tried to keep her voice light even though she was dying to know where he'd been. "Brianna mentioned you were going out somewhere."

"I had to see someone." He picked up one of the papers on the desk and looked at it.

Ashiya could tell by his dismissive tone that he didn't want to tell her exactly who he had to see. That didn't mean she would give up. "That still doesn't tell me where you were."

He glanced up at her. "Not here."

"Who did you meet?"

"Nobody you would know." He looked back at the report.

Her eyes narrowed. Did he know someone in Hilton Head already? Was it a woman? Had he agreed to come here just so he could spend more time with her?

"You don't know who I would know. Besides, you're here to help me. Not to go off and meet up with someone."

He dropped the report and gave her an irritated look. "Are you saying I need to report who I'm seeing to you?"

She leaned her elbow on the arm of the couch and propped her chin on her hand. "Yes," she said with a smug smile.

Russell shook his head and focused back on the papers on the desk. "I wasn't aware that was part of the requirements of this assignment."

She didn't like the way he dismissed her request. His reporting his every move to her wasn't a requirement, but she didn't like the idea of him sneaking off to meet some unknown person without telling her. What if he really was seeing someone else?

"I'm just making make sure you're not meeting someone behind my back who wants to get rid of me."

The look he gave her said he knew she was being ridiculous and he wasn't amused. "Really, Ashiya, why would I do that? I'm here to help you, not to undermine you."

She smiled sweetly. "Then tell me who you're meeting."

"You don't need to know all that."

"Yes, I do. If you won't tell me, then I'll ask Jeanette to get one of the private investigators at her firm to find out, so you might as well let me know now." Jeanette owned Lady Eyes Private Investigations and had worked for the Robidoux family previously.

She cocked her head to the side and gave him a try me smile. She really wouldn't get a private investigator. She knew Russell wouldn't undermine her efforts with the Legacy Group. The dubious look he gave her said he also knew she wouldn't go that far, but the way he shook his head said he realized wasn't going to stop bugging him.

Russell leaned back in the chair and met her eye. "Fine, I went to the police station. I had to meet with the detective in charge of my brother's case. A new person was assigned, and now I want to make sure they don't just ignore his file like the seven before him."

All playfulness seeped out of Ashiya. While her imagination had run wild having her believe he'd met up with a woman who would make it harder for her to get him back, he'd been doing something that had to be difficult. His brother's disappearance was a wound that would never heal as long as his family didn't have answers.

Ashiya sat up straight and placed her hand over her heart. "I'm sorry."

His brows drew together. "For what?"

"For pushing. I didn't mean it when I teased you about potentially selling me out. I know you wouldn't do that. I was trying to be silly."

The tension around his mouth and shoulders eased. He shifted in the chair. "I knew you were teasing. You know I couldn't stab you in the back like that. I said I would help you, and that's what I'm here to do." His full lips twisted into a wry smile. "I also forgot you could be nosy as hell."

That was the third or fourth smile he'd given her this morning. The slow melting of his defenses around her was like a love shot to her heart. Maybe, just maybe, the easy teasing that used to be between them would come back.

"I am nosy. It's part of being a member of the Robidoux family. You always have to know what's going on in case someone comes for you. Maybe that's why trust is hard for me."

"You trusted me once."

She had. With everything in her. She'd never doubted a word Russell said or an action he took. He'd never betrayed her trust, but she'd shattered his.

"I still do. I messed up your trust in me. I said I would do better this time. I won't tease you about going behind my back again."

He glanced away. "Don't apologize. I was being intentionally vague about where I went."

"Your brother's case is here?"

He nodded. "This is where he came for his spring break trip."

He'd told her his brother never came back from spring break his junior year of college. He hadn't said where the trip was, only that he continued to press the police to find out what happened to his brother. When he'd told her, she hadn't pushed for more information because she'd stupidly been trying to hold back a piece of her heart. Her relationship with Russell was supposed to have been a bridge in the gap in yet another breakup with her ex-boyfriend, Stephen. Too late she realized her heart had decided to go against her brain's original plan.

"I'll talk to the police," she said.

Russell's head jerked back. "What? Why?"

"Because I now have some level of pull with all of the shares I've inherited. It's the least I could do with this power and money I've gotten."

It was also the least she could do considering how she'd hurt him. She didn't just want a second chance with Russell. She wanted to make him happy. She might not be able to bring his brother back, but if there was anything she could do to help him find answers, then she'd do it.

"You don't have to do that."

"I want to do something." She reached over and placed her hand on his knee. The gesture was an automatic reflex from the days when they were together, and she'd reach out to touch him for comfort or in support whenever she wanted. "You're helping me. At least let me help you. Maybe when they see that the head of the Legacy Group is also behind the investigation, they'll do more."

His leg shifted. "But—"

She pulled her hand away. "No buts. I'm doing this." In his conflicted gaze, she saw his need to not believe in her fight with the gratitude for her offer. He might not want to accept her help, but he was smart enough to use every advantage available to him. She changed the subject before he could let his doubt in her convince him to continue to refuse her offer.

"Now, help me look at the marketing groups' spending reports and compare them to the overall quarterly reports." She picked up the last report she'd reviewed. "I think the numbers are off, but maybe I'm missing something."

Russell stared at her for several seconds. Ashiya glanced back at him and smiled. His brows drew together before he pulled off his suit jacket and slid forward in his chair. "Show me what's bothering you."

CHAPTER NINE

TWO DAYS LATER, Ashiya had to admit that she and Russell worked well together. Before, their relationship didn't include discussions about work. He might ask her about her day at the shop, and she'd ask how his day went, but other than that they'd spent their time meeting in small intimate restaurants, going to late-night movie showings, and making love until the early morning.

She knew they were compatible personally, but she was surprised by how compatible they'd turned out to be professionally. No one looking in would have been able to tell Russell could barely look at her just a few weeks ago. He helped her review the quarterly reports and spending statements and answered any questions she had with patience.

"So, I'm not wrong about the numbers looking funny?" Ashiya asked after they'd finished reviewing the last three years of spending statements out of the marketing division.

Russell frowned at the paper in his hand and shook his head. Since their first day, he'd discarded the suit and now met her in the library wearing a polo shirt like the gray one he wore today and slacks. He always kept the top button of his shirt unbuttoned, and frequently Ashiya caught a glimpse of the gold chain he wore around his neck. A cross hung from the chain. She knew that because she'd love watching the cross swing against his chest whenever he walked around with no shirt on.

"No," he said. "But whoever is behind the spending reports hid this really well. The numbers on the spending
reports don't match up with the revenue statements. In
each report, the slight shift in profits is explained. Indi-
vidually you wouldn't think anything is wrong, but when
you look at it as a whole, there are thousands of dollars
missing. Again, not enough to draw a lot of attention in
an organization this big."

"But enough over time to make someone a nice bit of
extra money."

Russell dropped the report in his hand and nodded.
"Any indication that your grandmother knew about this?"

"Not that I know of. Brianna hasn't mentioned anything, and she worked with my grandmother every day.
If my grandmother knew about this, then she might not
have let Brianna know."

Russell rubbed his chin and eyed the reports spread out
before them. "But your cousin Levi was also taking over
and handling things for your grandmother."

"He was," Ashiya said with a sinking feeling in her
stomach. She didn't want to think Levi would do this, but
it wasn't as if he'd left the best impression on her.

"When did he start taking over?"

Brianna answered from the door. "He started taking
over for her two years ago." Brianna came into the room.
"That's when your grandmother stepped down from being
directly involved and let Levi handle everything."

Ashiya sat up straighter. "That's around the time the
numbers started fudging."

Brianna pressed her fist against her chest. "You can't
believe Levi would play around with the numbers. He
wouldn't."

Russell grunted and pointed to the reports. "He had to

have noticed this. If it's been going on for two years and he didn't notice, then that's even more reason to fire him."

Brianna stepped forward. "I know he didn't start out on the right foot with you all, but despite his…personality flaws, he does care about the company. Almost as much as your grandmother."

"If he cared then he wouldn't let things go on this long," Russell countered. "He needs to go."

Ashiya let out a deep breath. "I really don't want the first thing that I do is to fire my cousin."

"Talk to him first," Brianna said. "Ask him directly. Levi won't lie."

Ashiya raised a brow. "He might if it means not going to jail for embezzlement."

Brianna shook her head. "It's not him. I know it's not."

Russell stood. "Everyone lies." His eyes flicked to Ashiya quickly, then away.

Ashiya's face heated as she met his gaze. They might be working well together, but since that first day, Russell had kept things professional and hadn't softened any more towards her. They'd come to a resolution that day, but it didn't mean he trusted her. He was right—everyone lied at some point—but she hadn't lied to him. She entered their relationship with the wrong intentions, but her feelings were real, and she'd never cheated on him.

"Maybe so, but we should also hear both sides to the story," she said firmly. "Otherwise we could make rash assumptions."

Russell had never given her the chance to tell her side of things. He'd come to see her once after they'd split up, but Stephen had been at her place while she was out. The look on Russell's face, full of pain and betrayal, when she'd arrived had twisted her heart. He'd left without talking to her. Stephen refused to tell her what he'd said to Russell. His only comment was that he'd told Russell the truth, that they belonged together. The smug smile on his face had made her stomach churn.

Russell's jaw tightened. He glanced out the window. The sky was still bright, but it was late afternoon. "It's getting late. We should call it a day."

"I'll order dinner," Brianna said.

Ashiya nodded. "Do that. We can talk some more about the upcoming board meeting while we eat."

"You want to keep working?" Russell asked.

Not really. She was tired of looking at the funny numbers and wondering what they meant for the Legacy Group, but for the past two nights, Brianna had ordered dinner, and Russell made up an excuse to leave. Once they were done with work, he didn't want anything else to do with her. At this rate, she'd never get the chance to thaw the block of ice around his heart. If she had to use work to entice him to eat dinner with her, then she would.

"I do. The board meeting is in a few days. I don't want to just be prepared; I want to be overly prepared."

He lifted a shoulder. "Fine. We'll talk more while we eat. I've got to use the bathroom, so order whatever you want."

Ashiya let out a breath and bit her lower lip to keep from smiling. He hadn't argued. He wouldn't be running away from her tonight.

"This morning you said you planned to stop at six." Brianna looked from her watch to Ashiya.

Ashiya jumped up from her chair and went over to Brianna. She lowered her voice even though Russell had walked out. "I am, but I want him to stay for dinner. If I hadn't brought up work, he would have left to eat some-where else."

Brianna frowned and pointed over her shoulder toward the door. "Is there something going on with you two that I need to know about?"

Ashiya shook her head. "Nothing that you need to worry about. Not right now, anyway. But I will need you to find an excuse to leave either right after the food comes or in the middle of dinner."

"You do realize I'm hungry and you're asking me to miss eating."

Ashiya gently tugged on Brianna's arm. "You can take your food with you. I just need a reason to eat with Rus-sell without someone around."

Brianna's eyes narrowed, but she smiled. "Nothing going on that I need to worry about, huh?"

"Seriously. Just do this for me."

Ashiya needed time with Russell that didn't revolve around reports or her inheritance. He was doing his best to make sure he only interacted with her when it came to the Legacy Group, which wasn't giving her much of an op-portunity to rekindle his feelings. She tried to be patient, but that wasn't her best trait. Plus, his "everyone lies" com-ment struck a nerve. She had to find a way to talk things out about what happened between them.

Russell came back into the room before Brianna could answer. "Did you order?"

Brianna pulled her phone out of her pocket. "Not yet. Ashiya and I were just talking about what to order."

After a few minutes of discussion, they decided to order burgers and fries from a nearby diner that used a food de-livery service. They went over the members of the board and the last few board meeting minutes while they waited.

Brianna's cell phone rang after the food arrived and they were unpacking things in the kitchen. She frowned down at her phone screen. "It's Levi's grandmother." She pressed the button and put the phone to her ear. "Hello Ms. Galliard." She paused and listened. "I'm helping Ashiya right now. No, we're wrapping up." There were a few seconds of silence when a small smile lifted the corners of Brianna's mouth. "Of course. I'll come that way now. No problem. Bye."

Ashiya raised a brow. She'd asked Brianna to disappear when the food came, but she hadn't expected her to go so far as to use Levi's grandmother as her excuse. "What did she want?"

Brianna slid her phone into the pocket of her slacks. "She wants my input on the surprise party she's throwing for Levi's birthday next Saturday. She says no one knows him as well as I do." The pleasure in Brianna's voice was surprising.

"You're really going to help?" Ashiya didn't think this was preplanned. Brianna seemed genuinely surprised and delighted by the invitation.

"I am," Brianna put the takeout container with her burger in a bag and lifted it from the counter. "I'll see you tomorrow."

With that, she rushed out of the kitchen as if there was a fire beneath her feet. Ashiya and Russell watched the direction she went for a few seconds.

"Does she…" Russell's voice sounded questioning.

"Like Levi?" Ashiya finished. "I think so. Though I don't know why or what she sees in him."

Notwithstanding the way Brianna defended Levi, there was the way her eyes softened when she talked about him, and the pride in her voice when she told Ashiya about the good things he'd done for the Legacy Group.

Russell turned back to her. "Are you sure she didn't know about the funds and is protecting him?"

Ashiya opened her mouth to deny, then snapped it closed. She pursed her lips and considered. "I mean, I don't get the I'm-going-to-stab-you-in-the-back vibe from her. She seems to want me to succeed because that's what my grandmother wanted."

"That doesn't mean you should trust her right off the bat. She could be a puppet of Levi's."

Ashiya took a deep breath. "I really don't think so, but…" She glanced at the door again.

"But what?"

"I am a member of the Robidoux family, and I know that what's on the surface can hide a lot underneath." Her instincts told her she could trust Brianna, but she couldn't rely on instincts alone.

He grunted. "You would know that."

Ashiya's back stiffened. "What's that supposed to mean?"

"Nothing. Just exactly what you said. What's on the surface can hide a lot." Bitterness entered his voice.

"Yeah, but you're saying the words as if you've got something else you want to say."

He stared at her for several tense seconds. "There's nothing else to say." He looked away and picked up his takeout tray. "Since Brianna's gone, I'll eat this in my room and respond to my emails for Robidoux Holdings."

Ashiya rushed over and placed a hand on his arm when he moved to turn away. No way was he going to toss those words out and then disappear on her again. "There's a lot to say."

He shook his arm until her hand fell away, then faced her. "No there isn't, Ashiya. The only thing we need to talk about is your inheritance and finding out where the money went."

He shifted to go around her. She reached out and grabbed his arm tighter. "Yes, there is a lot to say. Say it. I can handle it. I know you're mad and hurt, and—"

He jerked away and glared. "When was the last time you talked to Stephen?" His voice was flat, accusatory, and frustration blazed in his eyes.

Ashiya lifted her chin. "It's been over a year."

His lips twisted in a skeptical smirk. "I don't believe that."

He tried to walk away, and Ashiya hurriedly stood before him and blocked his way. "Six months after you and I broke up, he asked me to marry him. The same day, another woman showed up to say she was pregnant with his kid. They got married last year. He called me to invite me to the wedding."

At first, she couldn't believe Stephen had the audacity to call and invite her to his wedding. Then she reminded herself that was just what his ego would want. Stephen would love nothing more than to have Ashiya at his wedding. He'd probably imagine her teary-eyed and jealous as he married someone after years of "not being ready" with her. She'd wished him well and hung up the phone.

A line formed between Russell's brows. "Were you disappointed? When you found out she was pregnant?"

Ashiya crossed her arms over her chest. "I was relieved."

"Relieved?"

"Yes. The day you walked away, I knew I'd made a mistake. I tried to tell you, but you wouldn't even talk to me.

So, I did what I always did and decided to give Stephen another chance. Finding out he'd gotten someone pregnant was the wakeup call I needed. I made a huge mistake staying with him for as long as I did. I never should have walked away from you. Finding out the person I hurt you for was not worth it was what I deserved."

His hard expression didn't soften. The only reaction was the flaring of his nose with his deep breaths. This was the confession and truth she'd wanted to tell him for so long, but he never gave her the chance. Every time she'd imagined telling him, she'd hoped he'd do something other than stare at her as if she were some specimen under a microscope.

She took a step toward him. "Russell, I—"

"I've got work to do." He turned away and walked out of the kitchen without a backwards glance.

RUSSELL FLIPPED ONTO his back in the king-sized bed, kicked off the covers, and stared at the ceiling. His pajama pants twisted around his legs, a fine sheen of sweat covered his chest, and he couldn't find a comfortable spot anywhere in the damn bed. With a frustrated sigh, he jumped up and flipped the wall switch to turn on the ceiling fan.

He lay back on the bed and watched the fan blades spin. As the circulating air chilled the sweat on his body, his mind whirled. What possessed him to ask her about Stephen in the first place? If he was really over Ashiya—the way he should be—then he shouldn't care about when she last spoke with her ex. He shouldn't feel even a grain of happiness knowing she wasn't with him anymore, or that the guy had turned out to be just as much of an asshole as he'd expected him to be. That all the I-told-you-so thoughts and feelings he'd had about Ashiya's decision to go back to that guy had turned out to be true.

The petty side of him was happy. Not happy about Ashiya being hurt—no one deserved to be lied to—but happy he'd been right. He'd known he was the better choice for her, and Stephen wouldn't make her happy. Once he put the pettiness aside, he was left with something else. Something he didn't want to acknowledge, even though ignoring the feeling was next to impossible.

Expectation.

What did all of this mean? Did it have to mean anything? Why was he even questioning the meaning behind anything she'd said?

He turned to his side and closed his eyes. The questions didn't stop. He flipped to his other side. A vision of Ashiya in the kitchen when she'd told the story filled his mind. The look of honesty in her eyes. The regret mixed with vulnerability as she admitted to being played by the person she'd thought had loved her.

"Fuck!" he groaned and sat up.

He wasn't going to sleep like this. He was hot and thirsty. He'd get a glass of water, grab one of the files on the company out of the office, and come back to bed. He might as well do something productive to get his mind off of Ashiya. Maybe an hour or two of reviewing the company reports would cure his insomnia, too.

He stood and walked out of the bedroom. The lights were on in the kitchen. Russell blinked against the sudden brightness from the dim hall into the lit kitchen. He glanced around, but no one was there. Ashiya must have left the light on. He headed for the fridge. The pantry door was open, and he pushed it closed and automatically turned the lock.

He opened the fridge and reached for a bottle of water. The sound of a shriek made him freeze. Frowning, he turned around and scanned the kitchen. The scream came again followed by banging on the pantry door.

Russell's pulse skyrocketed. He ran from the fridge to the pantry, unlocked the door, and jerked it open. Ashiya rushed forward, slamming into his chest. She shrieked and punched him in the chest.

"Ow!" Russell slid back and rubbed the spot she hit.

"Why would you lock me in there?" she yelled. Her eyes were wide and frantic. Terror made her voice shake.

Russell held his hands in front of him in a "chill" motion. "I didn't know you were in there. I just closed the door."

"I know you hate me, but that wasn't necessary." She brought a hand to her forehead. Her fingers trembled. Her whole body trembled.

His initial shock faded, and worry rushed in. He slid closer to her. "Ashiya, I'm sorry."

She hit his chest again. "Don't do that."

He grabbed her wrist to stop her from hitting him. "Ashiya, it's okay." She froze and glared at him. Her trembling didn't stop. Her pulse raced erratically beneath his fingertips. "I didn't know you were in there. Seriously. I'm sorry."

She took several shallow breaths. She closed her eyes and took several deep breaths. "I don't like being locked away."

Her words struck him as odd. Why would she be locked away? He would never lock her away.

"I wouldn't do that to you. I saw the open door and closed it on my way to the fridge."

She nodded stiffly. Her eyes stayed closed as she

worked to control her breathing. A tear slipped from one eye. "I'm sorry—"

He pulled her against his chest and wrapped an arm around her. "No, I'm sorry. I didn't know. It's okay. You're out."

She stiffened in his embrace. Something that had never happened before. She'd always melted into his embrace. Looked up at him with those beautiful eyes and smiled her radiant smile. He'd never seen her afraid, and he didn't like it. Nor did he ever want to be a source of fear for her.

She pushed back. Russell loosened his grip but didn't let her go. He dreamed of having her back in his arms so much despite knowing he couldn't ever let that happen again. Now that she was there, he wasn't ready to release her. Slowly, she raised her chin.

Time stopped the second her eyes met his. Russell forgot about all the reasons he shouldn't want her in his arms. Forgot all the times he reminded himself that she was bad news. Forget the pain he'd felt when she'd left him and only remembered the way her lips felt against his.

Her body softened. Her fingers spread against his chest. Could she feel the pounding of his heart? The sweet scent of her filled his senses. She always reminded him of cinnamon and honey. Like the most decadent of desserts. The softness of her body in his arms infected his brain.

His head lowered. She lifted onto her toes. Anticipation tightened his muscles with each second they drew closer. Her sweet lips brushed against his. Desire roared through his bloodstream like lava.

"I knew you were going to hook up with her again." Isaac's taunting voice screamed in his mind.

Russell jerked back. Ashiya's eyes popped open. What the fuck! Just that quick and he was ready to kiss her.

Nah, it would have been more than that. He wouldn't have stopped with a kiss.

He dropped his arms and shuffled back. Ashiya wavered, then regained her balance. Her lips were parted and taunted him to pull her back and finish the kiss. Her breasts rose and fell with her deep breaths. They drew his eye and made his hands clench with the need to cup them, run his finger over the hard nipples visible through her thin T-shirt. His already swelling dick thickened even more.

He had to leave. If he didn't walk away right now, he'd pull her into his arms and not consider all the reasons making love to her right now was a bad decision until the harsh light of morning woke him.

He ran a hand over the back of his head. "Yeah, so... see you in the morning." He turned and hurried out of the kitchen as if the devil himself was on his heels.

CHAPTER TEN

ASHIYA DECIDED SHE wouldn't bring up the almost-kiss from the night before with Russell. As much as she loved seeing desire burn in Russell's eyes, and had tossed and turned when she'd gone back to her room until the sleeping pill she'd taken finally kicked in, she also knew bringing up the kiss would make Russell run faster than a gazelle being chased by a lion.

Knowing he wanted her was enough for now. If they continued to work together, she'd have more chances to get closer to him. If she didn't push, maybe he'd accept his feelings and even be okay with giving them a second chance.

So, when he hesitantly entered the office the next day, she didn't smile at him like she wanted to. She continued to review the board meeting minutes in her hand and casually asked, "Can you review the subcontract agreement my grandmother approved six months ago for Hanover Company to make the new line of shampoo? I marked up some items I had questions on, and I'd like to get your opinion."

Russell cautiously entered the room like a gazelle waiting for the lioness to pounce. Ashiya didn't look up even though she felt his gaze on her. After a few tense seconds, he cleared his throat.

"Uh, yeah, sure. Where is it?"

Ashiya picked up a folder with the contract and held it

up, again without looking his way. Russell took the contract and sat in a chair opposite her. Ashiya glanced over at him and suppressed a smile.

"Thank you," she said.

His eyes lifted to hers. "Sure."

She broke eye contact first and went back to reviewing the minutes. It took everything in her not to keep stealing glances at him. Not to focus on the glint of the gold chain revealed in the opening of his butter-yellow polo shirt, how tempting his thighs were in his blue slacks, or the grace of his long fingers as they slid across the papers, and imagine them doing the same over her skin.

Several minutes later, once she'd read and re-read the minutes twice more to give Russell time to realize she wasn't going to bring up the kiss and to control her reaction to him just sitting and breathing, she put down her paper.

Russell looked up from the contract. "Are you ready to go over your questions?"

She nodded. "Yes."

For the next few minutes, Russell answered her questions about the contract and gave her insight on how the subcontractual agreement not only helped the Legacy Group meet the demand for a new product line but also kept an underperforming factory afloat.

Ashiya leaned an elbow on the arm of her chair. "I guess Grandma had a soft spot."

"Why do you say that?" Russell sat back in his chair. He'd relaxed during their work discussion. The wariness in his eyes faded, and interest replaced it.

"Well, it would have made sense to lay off the workers and automate the manufacturing of the shampoo. Instead, she not only agreed to letting them manufacture the new shampoo, but also gave them the go-ahead to make a generic version of another soap. This saved jobs and gave the facility an extra cushion in case the new shampoo doesn't pan out. I don't think she wanted to let them go."

Russell glanced over the agreement, then nodded. "I think you're right. The agreement is profitable, but profits would have been higher laying off the workforce and automating production." He met her eyes. "She obviously put people ahead of profits."

"That makes me feel better. That's the type of leader I want to be. I'd like to make decisions that benefit our workers and the bottom line. I wouldn't want to only be focused on how to cut corners and make more money. Since my grandmother already laid that foundation, then it should be easier for me to keep it going."

The more she learned about the Legacy Group, the more she realized her grandmother was a smart businesswoman who cared. Many of her decisions took profit into account, but also the well-being of the people who worked for the company. From the person working in the facilities up to those working in the executive suite, no employee was taken for granted. Even more surprising, her cousin Levi either suggested or oversaw many of the improvements in the years he'd taken over at the company. That didn't fit her idea of a person willing to embezzle funds from the company.

"Your grandmother obviously didn't want to put profits over people, but remember the meeting minutes. There were board members who were against the agreement. Your cousin Levi typically voted with your grandmother, and his vote was often the swing. If he disagrees with you in the future, there's no guarantee he'll give you the same loyalty he gave your grandmother."

She let out a heavy breath. "True. I just hope he wouldn't

vote against me to the detriment of the company. Being mad at me shouldn't be a reason for him to not continue to make the Legacy Group successful."

"Jealousy and greed can turn any person. I still think you should fire him."

Ashiya shook her head. "Not yet. If he turns out to be stubborn, and stupid, then I'll let him go. For now, I'd like to focus on getting him on my side. My grandmother obviously trusted him. He has to have some kind of redeeming quality."

"Don't get your hopes up on that."

She wasn't, but after reading up on his actions, she believed Levi knew the Legacy Group better than anyone, and losing his knowledge and experience would hurt the company. Somehow, she'd have to find a way to work with her cousin. If she could get him to let go of the frustration of her grandmother leaving everything to her and not him, then maybe they could work together.

That was a big maybe.

"I'm not being naive. Figuring out Levi is going to be hard, but it's not impossible," she said with more confidence than she felt. "That's why we're going to his birthday party this weekend."

Russell sat up straight. "What?"

Ashiya had considered the idea soon after Brianna was asked to help her Aunt Gertrude plan for the event. Since coming to Hilton Head, she'd spent most of her time reviewing Legacy Group information and preparing for the upcoming board meeting. She hadn't spent time with her family since the funeral.

"Levi's party is the perfect chance for me to learn more about Levi and the rest of my family. If I can build a bridge with Levi, maybe the two of us can work together to run the company."

Russell raised a brow and gave her a skeptical, you're-better-than-me look. "I think that's asking a lot. Don't forget there is still the question of the embezzled funds."

"I haven't forgotten about that. Going to his party also gives me the chance to question him about that. If he is involved, then I won't hesitate to fire him."

No matter how much she wanted to work with her cousin, she wouldn't keep him if he was doing anything to harm the Legacy Group. She might not have wanted her inheritance, but she'd agreed to accept the responsibility. She wouldn't let it be destroyed under her watch.

Russell nodded. "I'm glad to hear that."

"As much as I want to get closer to my dad's family, I won't play the fool." She leaned forward, rested her arms on her knees and smiled at Russell. "So, will you come with me?"

He broke eye contact and crossed his right ankle over his knee. "If it's a family thing, I don't need to go."

"But you're my business consultant. You'll also need to learn more about the family and maybe even talk to Levi without it being in the middle of a shouting match. I'll feel better if you're there with me."

He hesitated before saying, "Fine. I'll go."

She straightened and clapped her hands. "Thank you."

Russell shook his head, and his lips lifted in a half smile. Ashiya's heart swelled. If he'd looked at her like that three years ago, she would have sat on his lap, wrapped her arms around his neck and kissed him. He'd cup the back of her head with one hand and run the other over her hip and thigh. Then she'd wiggle just enough to feel the rise of his dick against her ass.

The half smile on Russell's face drifted away. Ashiya stopped clapping and pressed her clasped hands over her racing heart. Tension sucked the air from the room as memories from the night before, rushed in and took advantage of their moment of weakness.

She wanted his lips on hers again. So much so she was on the verge of saying to hell with moving slow and hopping on his lap for old times' sake. But she couldn't push. Not if she wanted Russell to admit how he felt for her.

Ashiya cleared her throat and stood. "I'll go review more of the meeting minutes."

Russell held up a hand. "Why were you in the pantry last night?"

Ashiya froze, and her lips parted. She hadn't expected him to broach the subject of the night before. Not this soon. She'd assumed he would want to forget everything and pretend it never happened. At least until it happened again. The spark in his eye the moment before was a sure bet it would happen again.

She lowered back to the edge of the chair. "I was getting a snack."

"That late?"

The question in his voice made her chuckle. She hadn't been there to lure him into her arms. "Is there something wrong with getting a late-night snack?"

He shook his head. "No. You just...you weren't typically a nighttime snacker."

Fair enough. She was adamant about not eating after eight. Whenever she ate late, either she couldn't fall asleep because of acid reflux or she'd toss and turn with weird dreams.

"I need something in my stomach when I take a sleeping pill," she said with a shoulder shrug.

"You're taking sleeping pills?" His questioning tone seemed to not be about her taking the pills but for the reason.

She nodded. "Only since I've been here. It's hard for me to rest in a strange place. That combined with the stress of taking over the company, I knew I wouldn't be able to sleep without them."

"That's why you're sleeping in. You were always an early riser." He nodded, and he spoke the words as if he'd just solved a mystery. Had he worried about her sleeping in instead of being the perky morning person he used to know?

"I don't take them until later in the night, and then I struggle to get up in the morning." She held up a hand when he opened his mouth to respond. "I know I can't keep this up. I can't skip morning board meetings because I'm groggy from a sleeping pill."

He cocked his head to the side. "That isn't what I was going to say."

"Oh, what was it?"

"You're up this morning. Did you not take one last night?"

Ashiya dropped her eyes to the items on her desk. "No."

She should have, but she'd been afraid that sleep, even a chemically induced one, would bring back the nightmares. Though logically she'd known she wouldn't be left there for too long. Russell was the only person who could have closed the door, and even though she wasn't his favorite person in the world, she knew he wouldn't leave her locked in the pantry all night. In the moment, memories of being locked away for two days with no one coming no matter how loud she screamed had risen to the surface and chased away all logic.

She hated the fear. Tossing and turning, reliving the

memory of being in Russell's arms, was better than the potential of having nightmares. She'd take being groggy because of fantasies of the way he'd looked at her, how his lips had come within centimeters of touching hers, any day. Surprisingly, she'd eventually fallen asleep at four and snatched a few hours of sleep.

She tugged on her ear and avoided eye contact. "I guess I was worn out after overreacting about the pantry."

"I'm sorry about that." Regret filled his voice.

She waved away his apology. She'd overreacted and was embarrassed to have him see her like that. "It's fine. I know it wasn't on purpose."

"Why did you —"

Ashiya's cell phone rang. She let out a relieved breath and snatched it up from the table. "It's Brianna. I should take this."

Russell hesitated a second before nodding. "I've got some things to check out."

"You do that. I'll find out the details on Levi's party and let you know." She accepted the call and put the phone to her ear before he could reply. "Hello?"

She ignored Russell's stare and focused on Brianna's update about her meetings with the board members. She was thankful for the interruption. If he asked her why she'd panicked, then she'd have to tell him some reason. She didn't want to lie to Russell again, but she couldn't tell him the truth.

It was her fault she'd gotten locked away for two days. Anyone who knew the story would understand, but revealing her weakness would only make her vulnerable. She'd kept the secret for so long, she could almost pretend as if it never happened. That, and she never wanted anyone to judge her parents for what happened.

What would the good people of Jackson Falls say if they knew George and Elizabeth Waters had accidentally left their daughter locked in a basement in a strange home over a weekend? In true Robidoux fashion, she and her family kept that little mistake, as her mom called it, to themselves.

Russell finally stood and walked to the door. He stopped before leaving and looked back at her. Ashiya smiled and waved him out, but the smile felt brittle. His eyes narrowed before he turned and left. Leaving her with the impression that the conversation they'd started wasn't over.

CHAPTER ELEVEN

RUSSELL LEFT ASHIYA to her call with Brianna and decided to use the time for his other reason for being in Hilton Head. Besides the visit with the detective at the start of the week, he hadn't had the chance to do much else in his search for Rodrick. He couldn't blame Ashiya—he was here to help her—but that didn't stop guilt from twining through his midsection because he'd let his incessant attraction for her widen the cracks of his defenses.

He'd braced himself for her to bring up what happened the night before. Braced himself for her to force him to confront what he already knew: that he still wanted her. Ashiya had tried to get him to talk to her and admit that they could try again so many times since they'd split, and each time he'd shut her down quickly. Almost kissing her the night before would have been the perfect opportunity for her to prove her point. Instead, she'd focused on work and kept things professional until he'd been the one to broach the subject. Only to have her thrown off guard again.

There was so much he didn't know or understand about her. She'd held so much of herself back when he'd fallen in love that now he wanted to discover all of her secrets. Right now, learning everything about her, held more pull than staying away from her.

He turned past the sign offering newly constructed

homes into a neighborhood of beautiful houses with perfectly manicured lawns. He leaned forward and read the
gold numbers on the matching mailboxes before finding
the number 264. He pulled up to the curb in front of the
two-story, Craftsman-style home.

A blue Range Rover sat in the open two-car garage. A
young white boy who looked to be between the ages of six
and eight played with several toy trucks on the walkway
in front of the house. He stopped playing and glanced at
Russell with wide, curious eyes.

Russell cut the engine and got out of the car. He smiled
and walked around the car to his passenger side, though
he didn't go into the yard. "Hi, is this were Melissa Chandler lives?"

The boy nodded so hard his blond curls bounced.
"That's my mom. I'll get her." He jumped up from his
mountain of toys and ran up the brick stairs and into the
house. "Mom! There's a guy out here."

Russell left his car and walked to the bottom of the
stairs. The sun shone brightly down on this little slice of
suburbia. A small part of him felt guilty for coming unex-
pectedly like this. A bigger part of him knew the element
of surprise could work in his favor.

Melissa Chandler was one of the people to last see his
brother. She'd attended the same party that Rodrick had,
and his brother had mentioned meeting a girl named Melissa and hanging out with her and her friends. Russell had
never met her before, just heard her name as someone the
police had investigated who didn't have answers. Since he
was in the area for a long time, he'd decided that visiting
some of the people himself who'd seen Rodrick last might
jog memories more than the same round of questions from
an uninterested detective.

The boy came back to the door, a short blonde woman on his heels. The woman smiled warily as she caught sight of Russell. She opened the glass door but didn't step out on the porch.

"May I help you?" she asked in a Southern belle drawl.

Russell nodded. "Are you Melissa Chandler?"

"I am. Do I know you?"

Russell shook his head. "No, but you did know my brother, Rodrick. My name is Russell Gilchrist. My brother Rodrick attended a spring break party with you about fifteen years ago and never came home. I was hoping you would give me a few minutes and let me know if you remember anything about that night."

Her mouth parted with a silent inhale. After a quick blink of her blue eyes, she nodded and came out of the house onto the porch. "Oh, yes, Russell Gilchrist. Detective Mitchell mentioned you."

Russell was surprised that she expected him. "He did?"

"Yes. He called me a few days ago. Every few years the department assigns a new detective, and they call and ask me questions about that night." She lifted her shoulder in a what-you-gonna-do fashion.

Russell waited a beat for her to continue. When she just continued to smile a sweet, innocent smile, he continued. "And what do you tell them?"

"The same thing. I don't remember much. They keep saying I went to the party with your brother, but it wasn't like that. Me and several friends met up with a group of other college students in town for spring break. We all went together. I didn't know half of the people in the group."

"You don't remember Rodrick?" Russell asked.

Rodrick hadn't called to check in every day when he'd been partying during spring break, but Russell remembered a quick call with Rodrick when he mentioned meeting up with a girl named Melissa later that night. He'd told that to every detective, and every detective came back with the same story: the only Melissa they could find at the party didn't remember his brother.

Russell slid his cell phone out of the pocket of his slacks and pulled up a picture of his brother. He held up the phone face forward and walked closer to the steps so she could see it better.

"This is Rodrick. It was taken right before he came down here for spring break. Are you sure you don't remember seeing him that night?"

Melissa's eyes dropped to his cell phone and her body froze. The edges of her smile wilted, and something flashed in her eyes. A second later she glanced at him and shook her head. "I'm so sorry. He looks vaguely familiar, but that could also be because the detectives have shown me his picture so many times. You really have no idea what happened to him after all these years?"

Russell pulled his phone back. Disappointment weighed heavily on him. From her initial reaction he'd thought she'd remembered something. He wanted to demand she look at the picture longer. Beg her to study it and go through everything that happened that night. He couldn't do either. He was a strange man who'd shown up at her house unannounced. If he pushed and she got upset, this entire visit could go sideways.

"No, we don't. My parents and I are still trying to find answers."

"I'm so sorry to hear that." Her words rang hollow. As if she were giving the condolences out of politeness and not because she truly felt that way.

"It's been really hard on my mom. Having her son disappear without a trace or a word."

Melissa's gaze slid from him over to her son playing with the trucks. A line formed between her brows, and she pressed a hand to her heart. "I can only imagine how she must feel." That time she sounded more sincere.

"Which is why if you remember anything or know of anyone else I can talk to, I'd appreciate it. All I want is to find out what happened to my brother."

She let out a shaky breath and met his eyes again. "I wish I could help you, but I really don't know what happened to your brother. It was such a long time ago."

"What about other people at the party? The detective mentioned a Bryce Viognier. Would he know any—"

"Bryce, no!" Melissa held out a hand and shook her head. "He wouldn't know anything."

Russell frowned. "But he was also at the party."

"Yeah, and Bryce was drunk as a skunk at that party. He's always had a drinking problem, and it's only gotten worse as the years have gone on," Melissa said, sounding disgusted. "If you do talk to him, good luck with him remembering what happened the day before, much less fifteen years ago."

Once again, disappointment dipped Russell's shoulders. The idea of talking to a man so drunk he couldn't remember the previous day wasn't very encouraging. Still, he would try to find Bryce and talk to him. Detective Mitchell mentioned Bryce lived in a houseboat at the pier and was rarely in town because he often took his boat up and down the coast. Russell hoped to talk to him before he left town again.

"Anyone else you can think of?" he asked. "Any bit of information a person could have would help."

Melissa gave him an apologetic smile that didn't make Russell feel any better about making this impromptu trip. "Sorry. Most of the kids moved away or were from out of town."

"But you decided to stay? Are you from this area?"

She nodded. "I am. I planned to move away, but I was lucky and got a job with the Legacy Group. There's no place like home."

"The Legacy Group? Then maybe I'll see you around. I'm working with the new chairwoman."

Melissa's smile fell. "You are?"

"I am. I'll be in town for a while. If you do happen to remember anything, you'll be able to reach me easily."

Melissa toyed with the edge of her blouse. "Good to know." Once again the sincerity had left her voice.

He forced his lips up into a smile. "I won't take any more of your time. See you around, Melissa."

She stayed on the porch and watched him as he walked away. He couldn't tell if she were lying or not. Remembering what happened at a spring break party fifteen years ago would be hard for anyone. He wished he had something more concrete than a quick call with Rodrick about meeting a girl named Melissa to go on. She might not even be *the* Melissa Rodrick mentioned.

He lifted his hand and waved as he drove off. Melissa waved back but didn't smile. The disappointment of another cold lead sat heavily across his chest. He wouldn't let the disappointment discourage him. As long as he kept looking, then he had to believe that one day he'd find out what happened to his brother.

CHAPTER TWELVE

AFTER SPENDING THE next day and a half tap-dancing around the almost-kiss with Russell, Ashiya was ready to let off a little steam at Levi's birthday party. Though when she arrived and noticed Levi's party was almost as elaborate as a Robidoux party, she wasn't sure how much steam she'd realistically be able to let off.

Her Aunt Gertrude had rented the local country club, and the clubhouse was transformed into a black-and-gold wonderland fit for a king. Round tables were covered with black tablecloths. Gold, LED-light-filled balloons everywhere from the tall centerpieces to the various backdrops gave the place a warm, cheerful glow. People mingled around the space, laughing, sipping champagne, and a few were already on the dance floor, dancing to soulful music.

Ashiya glanced around the room before looking at Russell at her side. "Looks like one of my family's parties."

"I was just thinking the same thing."

They'd followed Brianna's instructions and dressed in black or gold to fit the theme. Russell's dark gold button-up shirt stretched across his broad shoulders. Black tailored pants accented his perfect ass and long legs. His gold chain peeked out occasionally, when he turned just the right way and stretched the edges of his collar. The man was too fine for his own good. Ashiya longed to rip open his shirt, expose the chain, and run her hands over his chest.

Not to mention he smelled divine. His spicy, clove-inspired cologne mingled with his natural scent for a direct attack on her libido. Not salivating over him as they'd ridden together in the car had taken a massive amount of willpower on her part. That and his ability to not bring up the *almost-kiss* in the kitchen had her rethinking her strategy. If she didn't do something soon, he would continue to pretend as if it never happened.

"Are you ready?" he asked.

To pull him into a dark corner and have her way with him? Yes. But since that wasn't what he meant, she focused on the reason for coming. Getting to know her family while subtly interrogating Levi about the suspected embezzled funds.

"I am. If I'm going to build a relationship with my family better, this is the best place to start." She spotted *The Dragons* sitting at a head table across the room. The three women observed the crowd and leaned in often to whisper to each other.

Ashiya straightened her shoulders. Her stomach churned just enough to remind her that she might not have as much fun as she hoped tonight, but she wouldn't make any headway if she didn't try. "I'll start by saying hello to my great-aunts."

Russell's gaze followed hers. "I'll go with you."

She gave him a bright smile, hoped he didn't see the nervousness in her heart reflected in her eyes, and headed that way. He followed behind her. She couldn't prove that he watched her as they crossed the room, but a part of her could always tell when Russell's eyes were on her. She added an extra swish to her hips so the short hemline of her vintage gold cocktail dress brushed across the backs of her thighs. Russell let out a soft cough and moved to walk beside her. Ashiya's smile broadened. He'd been watching.

"Hello, Aunties," Ashiya said cheerfully. "You ladies look beautiful."

Her Aunt Helena's starch-white hair looked freshly cut and tapered. She wore a black twenties-style flapper dress with a black shawl draped over her shoulders, an electronic cigarette perched in one hand. Aunt Maggie's gold suit dress sported a huge crocheted flower on one shoulder, and a wide gold hat covered her dark hair. Aunt Gertrude had also gone for a black dress, sequined and with a deep V that complemented her pushed-up cleavage. A black feather fascinator adorned her honey-gold hair.

Maggie held out a peppermint toward Ashiya. "I'm glad you came."

Ashiya took the candy. "Of course I would come. It's a great way for me to get to know my family."

Helena lifted her electric cigarette and eyed Ashiya. "Seeing as how you've been in town for days and haven't come by, I didn't expect you tonight."

Ashiya blushed under the reprimand. Yes, she'd been busy, but she also hadn't expected her aunts to want to see her often since she was the stray child who'd swooped in to snatch the family fortune. She'd remember to take the time to visit them in the future.

"I've been busy going over the company information. But I do plan to visit more often." In the face of their dubious looks, she turned to Russell at her side. "This is Russell Gilchrist. He's working as a consultant to assist me as I step into the lead as chairwoman at the Legacy Group."

The ladies' gazes swung to Russell and sized him up. "This the one who told you to fire my Levi?" Gertrude asked.

Russell coughed and pressed a hand to his chest. Ashiya let out a tight laugh and patted his shoulder. "That was just one of many suggestions."

"Mmm-hmm," Gertrude said. Though she kept the sweet smile on her face, her eyes were like razorblades. "He looks more like a boyfriend than a consultant."

Ashiya dropped her hand from his arm. "Russell has worked with my family for years and has experience with large corporations. This is strictly a business partnership."

"That doesn't mean he's not your boyfriend," Maggie said, slipping a mint into her mouth with a knowing smile.

"I'm not," Russell said firmly.

Helena's white brows rose. "I've heard that tone before. There's something going on between you two. Don't let that be the reason you're trying to fire Levi."

"No one is firing Levi," Ashiya said. "In fact, where is the birthday boy? I'd like to congratulate him myself."

Helena's eyes narrowed, but she pointed. "He took a call and stepped out. Go get him and tell him to get back in here."

Ashiya nodded. "I'm on it."

She turned to leave, and Russell turned with her.

"Not you, young man," Helena said, pointing her electric cigarette at him.

Russell pointed to his chest. "Pardon?"

Maggie tapped the table. "You stay. We'd like to get to know the *consultant* helping our new chairwoman."

Russell threw her a save-me look. Ashiya smiled sweetly and nodded. "I'll be right back."

She hurried away before he could say more. He might as well get used to The Dragons' fire if he was going to help her. Working with her at Legacy meant dealing with them since they were also shareholders and regularly attended board meetings.

Ashiya wound her way through the crowd, looking for Levi. She saw Brianna and made a beeline to her side.

"Have you seen Levi? You look great, by the way!"

Ashiya was used to seeing Brianna in her button-up shirts and slacks every day. She hadn't expected her to go all glamorous on everyone. Brianna's gold chiffon, one-shoulder dress clung to her breasts and revealed a sliver of midsection before stopping just above the knee.

Brianna smiled sheepishly and slid her hand over her short corkscrew curls. "Thanks. I'm just glad I finally got a chance to wear this dress. It's been in my closet for years." She pointed over her shoulder. "Levi went outside. He was on the phone. I just tried to get him to sit at the head table so we can start with the toasts, but he said the call was important."

"Who's toasting?"

"Some of his friends and your aunts."

"None of my cousins?"

Brianna raised a brow. "Your grandmother and your aunts really want to bring the family back together, but that doesn't mean I'd put your cousins in charge of toasting Levi. It'll turn into a roast instead and… I'm trying to keep this party fun."

Ashiya chuckled. If Levi was anywhere near as overbearing with her cousins as he was with her, then she could imagine what they'd say. "Smart. I'm going to talk to Levi."

"Good luck," Brianna said with two thumbs up.

Ashiya froze in place. "Am I going to need it just to talk to him?"

Brianna's eyes widened, and she shook her head. "No.

I know you two started off on the wrong foot, that's all. Levi's really sweet. Once you get to know him."

Ashiya bumped Brianna's shoulder. "I think you're a little biased."

Brianna's eyes dropped, and she smiled. "Maybe so. Still, remember what I said."

Ashiya left Brianna blushing and went outside in search of her cousin. He wasn't immediately outside the clubhouse. She walked to one side of the building, and his voice traveled to her.

"We need to get this figured out before my cousin discovers the missing money," he said.

Ashiya stopped short at the edge of the building and cringed. Damn! She really hoped he wasn't behind the embezzlement. She didn't want to fire Levi, but she couldn't keep him around if he was stealing from the company.

"Give me a call tomorrow. I've got to get back in this party before my grandmother kills me," Levi said. A few seconds later, he rounded the corner. He saw her and froze before a scowl took over his face.

Ashiya crossed her arms over her chest. "I really hoped you weren't behind the missing money."

His eyes widened. "You've noticed it already." Disbelief filled his voice.

Ashiya's head cocked to the side. "I'm kind of offended that you're surprised."

"Honestly, I didn't think you'd notice. It's so subtle," he said. "I thought you'd take the reports at face value. If you looked at them at all."

She uncrossed her arms and put her hands on her hips. "So, you're admitting you took the money." She couldn't believe his audacity. It was one thing to steal from her grandmother's company, another to be so blasé about doing so.

He shifted, legs widening in a defensive stance. In his black dress shirt and dark pants with that what-the-hell-did-you-just-say glare in his eyes, he would have been intimidating if Ashiya wasn't so pissed. "I didn't take the money. I'm trying to find the person behind the embezzlement."

"I'm supposed to believe that?"

He sliced a hand through the air. "I honestly don't care what you believe. I've already started my own investigation into the missing money."

Ashiya eyed him, but his gaze didn't waver. "Then why did you say you needed to clear this up before I found out?"

"Honestly, if I found the person and you didn't even notice, then proving to the board why they should trust me over you would be easier."

His bluntness proved he was ruthless. She also appreciated his candor. If she hadn't noticed, that would have been a good way to push her out. "But me noticing foiled that plan."

"Not quite. As long as I find the person first, then I still look more capable than you." He moved to walk past.

Ashiya stepped to the side and blocked him. "I've got one better. How about we work together to find the person?"

He took a step back and eyed her as if she'd proposed something outrageous. Considering their strained relationship, working together was kind of far-fetched. "Why would I work with you?"

"Because I still don't trust you. You could be lying right now." He opened his mouth, and she held up a hand. "Which means I have enough grounds to fire you for the fact that this happened under your watch."

His eyes narrowed. "You're searching for a reason to get rid of me."

"No. I'm trying to work with you to prove you aren't the asshole I think you are and find the nice guy Brianna seems to think you are."

His shoulders relaxed, and the glint in his eyes softened. "Brianna is smart but naive."

"Maybe, but working with me to find this person means keeping your job. It also means I'll get a chance to know my cousin."

"Why do you want to know me?"

"Because apparently it's what my grandmother and the aunties want. I'm here to take people at face value. If you really aren't behind the embezzlement and want to find the person, then work with me." She held out her hand. "Otherwise, turn in your resignation on Monday."

Levi glanced at her hand, then met her gaze. After a few tense seconds, he wrapped his hand around hers and shook. "Fine. I'll work with you."

CHAPTER THIRTEEN

A FEW DAYS after the party, Russell walked into the kitchen and froze. Ashiya paced back and forth from the fridge to the island. She had one of the legal briefs for the Legacy Group in her hand. Her full lips moved as she silently spoke to herself. Her high heels clicked on the floor, and even though he hated himself for doing it, he noticed how much of her legs was revealed by the short skirt of her navy-blue fitted dress and the way the material clung to her curves.

He'd noticed her a lot in the past few days. Working with her hadn't been as bad as he'd assumed. In fact, he enjoyed working with her way more than he should. Though she didn't have a background in the corporate world, she did know enough about business and was savvy enough to pick up on the intricacies of navigating a much larger organization. His attraction to her, which he'd prayed for years would die and go to hell, had come back to life in full force.

The almost-kiss the week before hadn't helped. Neither had going to that party with her over the weekend. Watching her charm her aunts, try to get to know her various cousins, and dance in that ridiculously small gold dress had reminded him of all the reasons she'd stolen his heart in the first place.

"What are you doing?" His voice came out harder than

he'd intended. He was doing exactly what Isaac predicted and that irritated him.

Ashiya stopped mid-stride. She stared at him with wide, worried eyes. "I can't do this."

The panic in her voice made him hurry toward her. "Do what?"

"This!" She pointed to the brief in her hand. "Go there?" She pointed toward the front of the house. "I can't do it."

He immediately understood. Today was her first day touring the Legacy Group's facilities, and she was attending the first board meeting as chairwoman. They'd spent the days since the party preparing for this. She might not have the history with the company that her cousin Levi did, but she'd absorbed enough data to be familiar with the items on the agenda.

"Yes, you can." He went to the coffee maker and grabbed a mug from the rack next to it.

"No. I can't." She hurried over to him. "I'm serious, Russell. What was I thinking? I never wanted to be in charge of a multimillion-dollar company. I spent my life staying out of being considered for this type of role."

He poured coffee into the mug. "You didn't want to be a part of the Robidoux family holdings, but that doesn't mean you can't take charge and help run Legacy. You've already proven you have what it takes." He kept his voice calm.

"How? How have I proven anything?" she asked doubtfully.

Russell faced her and stared her in the eye. "The first day you reviewed the financial reports, you spotted the missing money. You understand the Legacy Group's place in the market, and you've already told me some ideas you've had on ways to improve marketing and profitability. Don't you dare say you can't do this."

She blew out a breath and ran a hand through her hair. "That's talking to you in here. I can talk to you because I'm comfortable around you. I know you won't judge me. That entire room of board members wants to judge me." She turned and leaned back against the counter.

"Let them. You're still the majority shareholder, and you've got me by your side. You'll be fine."

Her lips lifted in a smile he didn't want to admit made his insides twist into a knot. "I do have you." The gratitude in her voice, combined with a hint of longing, was a jolt to his already agitated libido.

A jolt he did not need at this moment, when he was trying to convince her that she could handle the upcoming board meeting. He cleared his throat and glanced away. "Once you get through this meeting and we find out who's embezzling the money, I can go back to Jackson Falls and Robidoux Holdings, and you can take over running things without me."

He said the words as a reminder to himself. This situation was only temporary. He would not be by Ashiya's side forever. Once this ended, so would any personal connection he would have to her.

Ashiya's shoulders slumped. "I know. That's the point. You're consulting me so that I can stand on my own. I'm still going to hate it when that day comes."

"Why is that?"

"Because it means you won't be by my side anymore." She placed a hand on his arm and stepped closer him. "Seriously, Russell, thank you for helping me. I couldn't have done this without you."

Her eyes were serious. Her tone was sincere. There was no hint this was one of her attempts to flirt with him, so why did his heart rate speed up so much?

"Yes, you could have. You would have hired a consultant who would have given you the same advice as me."

"Maybe, but I'm still glad you're the one helping me." She hadn't dropped her hand. Her beautiful eyes looked up into his and pierced straight to his soul. "I know I can't hope for anything more than this between us, so of course I never want this time to end. I'm not looking forward to feeling the way I felt when you walked away the last time."

Russell struggled for words. He'd meticulously avoided letting the conversation slip back to their old relationship since she'd told him she no longer had contact with Stephen. He didn't want to rehash something that was over, and he'd hoped she'd understood. But the look in her eye made him think she'd also spent the past few days thinking about what it would be like for them to try again.

He had to snap out of this. Ashiya knew all his switches and just what to say to wrap him around her little finger. He'd been twisted in knots by her before.

"Ashiya, I—"

"I know. This isn't like last time, and I shouldn't have brought it up," she said in a soft, sad voice that wrapped around his heart and gave the slightest of pulls. "Even though I know that, and I'm nervous about today's board meeting, having you in my corner reminded me how much I messed up before. How I could have always had you in my corner. If I'd done things differently."

Her hand slid down his arm before trailing away. "I'm sorry for making this awkward." She took a step back. She pulled the corner of her full lower lip between her teeth and glanced down.

That damn move. Why did she have to do that? The sight of her biting her lower lip, the sweet but sexy look in her eye, the softness of her voice. That shit got him every time.

Russell put down his coffee, took a step forward, and placed his hand on her waist. The movement was automatic. Something he'd done so many times when they'd dated. He realized he'd reacted to her two seconds before he also realized he shouldn't have made a move.

Her lashes lifted. Her eyes filled with wary hope. "Did I…make it awkward?"

There was a glint in her eye. She hadn't tried to bait him before, but his response was just enough to awaken her instincts. She knew how to pull him. Frustration warred with his desire. Frustration that an ounce of vulnerability on her part could get him to react so easily. His hand tightened on her waist. "You know exactly what you're doing."

Ashiya pressed forward. Her breasts brushed his chest. "What am I doing?"

"Ashiya," he said in a low, warning voice. *Step back. Let her go.* His brain screamed common sense at him. His body ignored all good sense.

Her hand slid up his arm and clutched his shoulder. Her soft breasts pressed further into his chest. "Russell?"

Let her go. Let her go. Right now! Step away before you do something stupid!

His grip on her waist loosened. Ashiya's eyes widened, then narrowed. She lifted onto her toes and pressed her lips against his. Fuck, her lips were so luscious. Her taste, so sweet, decadent and familiar was like morphine in his veins. Dulling his senses and taking him to a state of euphoria he hadn't felt in way too long. She let out a soft whimper. Desire surged hotter than the sun. Just like that, he was lost.

ASHIYA HADN'T MEANT to kiss him. Even though he'd retreated after the party, her plan was to be more subtle. to let him feel comfortable with her. But wasn't there some saying about the best-laid plans not going the way they should? Because the moment he'd mentioned leaving, she'd realized her time was finite. If he went back to Jackson Falls, they'd be over. The idea of not having him this close, of losing his support again, made her feel as if she were falling.

Russell's strong arm wrapped around her waist as he pulled her completely into his embrace. Ashiya relaxed and let Russell take over. His head slanted, and his tongue slid across her lower lip. Ashiya opened and let him deepen the kiss.

Russell's hands roamed over her body. One glided down her back, over her hip, and cupped her ass in a demanding squeeze. His other arm wrapped around her upper back, where his hand pressed against her spine and pressed her hard against his body. He hugged her close while his lips and tongue made her light-headed with his kisses.

Ashiya wrapped her arms around his neck and held him tight. She couldn't believe she was here in his arms again. She didn't want to let him go. And with each sensual tug on her lips, need burned through her. Her nipples hardened into tight peaks; wetness pooled in the swelling folds of her sex. She'd always loved his kisses. The way he thoroughly kissed her was only a precursor to the way he savored other parts of her body. Memories of his mouth on her neck, breasts and clit drew a long, deep moan from her.

Russell's body shivered. He broke away, and Ashiya whimpered, but he didn't pull back. Instead he turned her until her back pressed against the wall. His hands gripped her ass and he trailed kissed across her cheek, over her ear, and down to her neck. When he bit, then sucked hard, she arched her back. The pleasure and pain she'd missed so much, both exquisite and raw.

She wrapped one leg around his. Her dress slid up her

legs, and he jerked it the rest of the way up to gather around her waist. The thin material of her wet satin panties slid across the front of his slacks. His hips shifted forward. The heavy weight of his hard dick pressed into the heat of her clit. Pleasure exploded like stardust over her nerve endings. Ashiya gasped, and her head fell back.

Russell let out a deep, rumbling groan. "Mmm-hmm."

His hips twisted again, this time more firmly against her sex. Ashiya shifted her hips to meet his. They moved in tandem. Him pressing forward into her, and her meeting each one of his thrusts. Pleasure built like steam in a cauldron. Ashiya had lost control. She chased the feeling, knew that she'd longed for this, dreamed of this for so long that she was close to exploding with pleasure. She didn't care. Not when the person taking her over the edge was Russell.

"Russell... I..." she gasped as he thrust forward again.

He bit her neck. Just hard enough to make her breasts ache even more. "You what?" His voice was low, decadent, cocky. He knew how to make her his.

"Fuck, I need you," she gasped. "Please, Russell." She was begging and didn't care. Not when her panties were soaked and she was on the brink of climaxing.

She reached for his belt buckle. He squeezed her breast with one hand, his thumb making quick circles across her hard nipple. His other hand wrapped around her wrist. She sucked in a breath. If he pushed her away, she might cry. He brushed her hand aside only to loosen his belt.

Yes! Thank God! This is really happening!

A sharp gasp came from the door followed by the sound of something loud hitting the floor. Ashiya and Russell froze. Both of their heads whipped around at the sound. Brianna watched them with wide eyes. A silver mug spilled coffee onto the floor. They all stood still and stared for several tense seconds before Brianna placed her hands over her eyes.

"Sorry! My bad! I didn't mean to...intrude." She spun on her heel and ran from the room.

Ashiya's head fell back against the wall. Russell stared down into her eyes, his expression unreadable. She waited for the passion in his eyes to cool. For shock, frustration, or worse disgust, to cloud his gaze. Instead, he closed his eyes, took a long breath, and slowly pulled away from her. Ashiya longed to pull him back, but the moment was gone.

Russell cleared his throat and fastened his belt. His eyes didn't meet hers. "Um... I'll... I've got to get something before we go." With those dismissive words, he turned and left the kitchen.

CHAPTER FOURTEEN

THANK GOD FOR BRIANNA. During the car ride to the office, without her keeping up a nonstop discussion on the board's agenda about their current status in the beauty care market, Ashiya wasn't sure if she and Russell would have made it. The tension between them was thick as molasses and just as sticky.

She couldn't believe he'd kissed her. Not just kissed her, but damn near ravished her. Yes, *ravish* felt like the right word.

If she couldn't believe it, then she knew he had to be flabbergasted. He wouldn't look at her and directed all his comments related to the company and upcoming board meeting directly to Brianna. As if she couldn't already guess he regretted kissing her, the way he ignored her proved it.

Ashiya was immensely thankful for the board meeting. No matter how much the thought of being picked apart by the board members made her feel as if she were facing a firing squad, the idea of listening to Russell lay out all of the reasons kissing her was wrong would hurt worse than anything the board members could dish out.

They arrived at the Legacy Group offices, which were located in the main building of an office park in Bluffton instead of on the island. The company owned all four floors, and many of their subsidiaries were in spaces around the park. Russell opened the door for her and Brianna.

Brianna smiled and nodded. "Thank you."

"You're welcome," Russell replied with his own warm smile. His gaze darted to Ashiya. Then he quickly looked away.

Ashiya's smile felt brittle and forced, but she kept it there. "Thanks."

All she got in return was a stiff nod. Suppressing a sigh, Ashiya followed Brianna into the spacious lobby. She'd come up with her counterarguments for all the reasons the kiss between her and Russell was wrong later. Right now, she had to ignore the unsatisfied ache between her legs, face the firing squad and convince them to spare her.

You're the chairwoman, Ashiya! They can't get rid of you. You run this.

She gave herself the mental reminder, squared her shoulders, and tried to emulate the cool confidence she'd seen so many times in her cousin Elaina.

Brianna led her and Russell to the front reception desk. A man in his early twenties had just hung up the phone. He smiled up at Brianna. Then his eyes widened, and he jumped up from his chair.

"Ms. Winters! You're here," he said, his voice cracking.

Brianna's head tilted to the side. "I am. I'm giving the new chairwoman a tour of the offices before the nine-thirty board meeting." Brianna motioned to Ashiya, who'd come up on her left. "This is Ashiya Waters. Ms. Waters, this is Anthony Sims."

"Nice to meet you, Anthony." Ashiya held out her hand.

Anthony swallowed hard before taking her hand in a weak shake. "Same here. Uh…" He quickly pulled his hand back and gave Brianna a worried look. "I was just about to call you. The board meeting was moved up an hour. The rest of the board just arrived and went up."

Ashiya's jaw dropped. "What?"

Brianna's mouth pressed into a thin line. "Who moved the meeting?"

"Levi did, didn't he," Ashiya said, disappointed. She'd hoped that after she and her cousin agreed to work together at the party, he would stop being petty in other areas, too. Moving the board meeting was a direct move to make her look bad.

Anthony waved his hands and his head. "No. It wasn't him. It was Brian Hill."

Brianna closed her eyes and let out an annoyed breath. "Brian," she said in a frustrated whisper.

Ashiya frowned and mentally went through the names of all the board members. Brian Hill was one of the longest-standing members of the board. He worked at one of the subsidiaries and had been an early investor in her grandmother's company. From what she'd learned, he was one of the members most against her taking over the company.

"You know what," Ashiya said with a confidence she didn't feel. "We'll just tour the offices later. Let's go up and join the meeting."

Brianna ran a hand over her hair and nodded. "You're right. Let's go."

She turned in the direction of the elevators. Russell placed a hand on Ashiya's arm right as she started to follow. His touch was like lighter fluid to the simmering embers of her desire. Maybe he felt it too, because he snatched his hand back quickly after.

"Brian may be trying to play a power move, but remember you still have the upper hand. You're the chairwoman and majority stakeholder. What you say goes. No matter how much they may not like it. You've got this."

The confidence and support in his gaze almost brought tears to her eyes. Her throat clogged up, and gratitude surged in her chest. She wanted to lift onto her toes and press a kiss to his lips again.

Nope. No time for that. Right now it was time to focus on the board meeting.

She nodded and straightened her shoulders. "I know, and I'm ready. Despite what they think about me, I know who I am. They've decided to mess with the wrong one today."

Russell's smile was like the sun in her sky. He nodded and placed a hand on the small of her back. She grinned with exhilaration and confidence as they followed Brianna to the elevator.

ASHIYA'S CONFIDENCE ONLY lasted through the introductions. Had she compared the board to a firing squad? That was her first mistake. They were much worse. Instead she seriously related to the monsters in the movies chased by villagers with torches and pitchforks. There were two or three moderately friendly faces, Levi being one of them, on the eleven-member board of directors, but the rest were like an angry mob. And Brian Hill was their leader.

"No disrespect, *Ms. Waters*, but you have to understand our discomfort," Brian said in a tone that implied all disrespect.

Brian Hill was thirty years older than Ashiya, with a receding hairline and an untrustworthy gleam in his eye. He reminded her of a rat, and right now she was the item he wanted to chew apart.

"Despite your discomfort," Ashiya returned in a calm voice that belied her inner quaking, "I want the same things as you and the rest of the board. I want the Legacy Group to succeed. My grandmother and her sisters worked hard to build what started as a small soap company into a major corporation with multiple beauty products in various markets. The last thing I want to happen is to watch that disappear."

Brian sneered. "If you were so proud of your grandmother's company, then you would have worked here from the start the way Levi did. I trust his judgment."

"Which is why I'm keeping Levi on staff. I also trust my cousin's judgment and his experience with Legacy. I'm not here to shake things up."

"But you're already talking about things you want to change." Brian flicked the list of Ashiya's suggestions. Some of the other board members grumbled and nodded.

"I've brought suggestions that I'd like the board to consider," she said calmly. With every prick of his poisoned tongue, she wanted to yell back her frustration and tell him to go fuck himself. If lashing wasn't exactly what he wanted her to do she'd go off. But, she was here to prove she could run the company, not buckle under pressure.

"That's why I also brought in Russell Gilchrist as a consultant. He's worked closely with my family's company, Robidoux Holdings, and is very aware of the inner workings of a corporation larger than this. I'm not coming in blind or unprepared."

Brian snorted. "I don't care who you brought. It doesn't change the fact that your grandmother decided to leave control of our futures with a thrift store owner. Just do us all a favor and go back to your little shop where you belong. We don't want or need you here."

Stay strong. Be the bigger person. Don't let your feelings show.

Ashiya tried the internal pep talk to soothe the burn of his insult. The low murmurs of agreement from the other board members were like coarse salt in the wound. Why had she agreed to do this? Even if she could do the job, was she really cut out for this world? Maybe she did need to pack up her stuff and go.

"That's enough, Brian," Levi's voice snapped through the room.

Brian jumped and blinked in Levi's direction. Ashiya and Russell also froze before staring across the table.

"Levi," Brian said with an incredulous laugh. "You know just as well as I—"

"I said that was enough," Levi said. "Despite what you may think, I trust my Aunt Gloria's judgment. I also believe in Ashiya's abilities. I've looked at her proposals, and they aren't bad. Besides, everyone here also knows you like to yell and intimidate but don't contribute anything else. Keep your mouth shut and let Ashiya go over her proposals."

Brian's lips pressed into a thin line. Levi looked at Ashiya and nodded. Ashiya took a deep breath. She didn't know why Levi stood up for her, but she was eternally grateful.

"Thank you, Levi," she said. "If everyone will please turn to page three."

For the next hour, Ashiya went over her suggestions on ways they could improve marketing and product positioning. There were more questions, many of them skeptical, but she was able to answer them all. In areas where she struggled, Russell backed her up with his experience. She wouldn't say she'd won them all over, but by the end of the meeting, the board had at least put down their pitchforks and let the fire on their torches die out.

After the meeting, she, Levi, Brianna and Russell remained in the board room. Ashiya turned to her cousin. "Thank you for standing up for me earlier."

Levi waved off her thanks as if the idea of receiving gratitude from her made him itch. "Brian deserved it."

"But you've said the same thing." She remembered that vividly.

Levi shrugged before sliding a hand into the pocket of his tailored gray suit pants. "I may have, but you're family. If my mom and The Dragons have taught me anything, it's that we can talk about family, but no one else is allowed to."

There was a very similar saying on her Robidoux side. No matter how much they might fight each other, they would drop everything and fight whoever came for their family member. She wouldn't say she and Levi were going to be close, but she had hope that their tenuous agreement to work together might be successful.

She crossed her arms and grinned at Levi. "So, I'm family now."

Levi's lips twisted in a disapproving frown. "Biologically we're family. Don't get sentimental about it."

Ashiya didn't care. She continued to grin. Brianna bumped Ashiya's elbow. "I told you he wasn't so bad."

Levi looked ready to argue, but a knock on the door stopped him. The four of them turned to the door. A petite blonde woman in a white silk shirt and a tan pencil skirt stood there.

"Excuse me, Mr. Galliard, but it's time for your next meeting," she said.

Russell sucked in a breath. Ashiya glanced over at him. His body had stiffened. His eyes narrowed. Ashiya looked from him back to the woman. What was that about?

"Thank you, Melissa," Levi said. "Before you go, come in and meet our new chairwoman and her business partner."

Melissa came into the room. When her gaze landed on Russell, her smile faltered for a second. "It's nice to meet you both."

"I've already met her," Russell said.

Ashiya swung around toward Russell. "How?"

Since they'd cleared up where he'd gone that first day, she'd let go of the idea of him seeing another woman in the area. Had she been too quick to relax her judgment? How could he kiss her if there was someone else?

"I visited her a few days ago." Russell didn't take his eyes off of the woman. "Related to my brother's disappearance fifteen years ago. Rodrick attended the same party as Melissa and wasn't seen again. I hoped she would have some memory about that night that could help me. But unfortunately, she didn't."

Ashiya turned back to Melissa. Relief was short-lived as the blood drained from Melissa's face. Nobody looked that guilty when simply trying to help someone find their long-lost relative. Did she and Russell have something going on?

"Is that true, Melissa?" Levi asked.

Melissa nodded and pushed her hair behind her ears. "It is. I wish I could remember more. It was just such a long time ago."

Levi turned to Russell. "Melissa is my administrative assistant. I couldn't get through a day without her. I trust her completely and can vouch for her."

Russell's intense stare remained on Melissa for another second, before his gaze softened and he smiled a charming smile that didn't reach his eyes. "That's good to know. I'd hate for your star employee to turn out to be a liar."

CHAPTER FIFTEEN

"Do you really only know her through the case?"

Russell glanced over at Ashiya as they took the elevator down to the first floor. They'd completed the tour of the offices. Done the shaking of hands and introductions. Everyone there seemed happy to be working for the Legacy Group and nervous but excited about Ashiya taking over where her grandmother left off. He hadn't gotten any weird vibes from anyone, but that didn't mean a thing. Someone was slowly taking money off the top, and they had to figure out exactly who was behind it.

Ashiya peeked at him from the corner of her eye. Her voice was nonchalant when she'd asked the question, but the way she bit the corner of her lower lip and tugged on her ear gave away her feelings. She was jealous. He pressed his lips together to hold back the stupid smile that wanted to take over his lips.

Damn her, and damn that kiss. Damn him even more for wanting more even though he knew jumping back on for a ride on the Ashiya train was a bad idea. Except he was having a hard time focusing on the bad and just remembering how good they were together.

"Know who?" He intentionally played dumb.

Ashiya crossed her arms over her chest. "Levi's administrative assistant, Melissa. Is it really through your brother's case?"

He nodded. "Yes." He tried to sound unbothered. To not show how this little spark of jealousy in her made him want to back her against the wall, kiss her thoroughly, and remind her that she was the only woman in his thoughts.

She faced him fully then, an expectant look on her face as she stared at him, waiting for more.

He shrugged. "What?"

Ashiya rolled her eyes. "And she doesn't remember anything?"

"That's what she said."

The doors to the elevator opened just as Ashiya turned to Brianna next to her. "What do you know about her?"

Brianna looked up from her phone and followed Ashiya and Russell into the lobby. "Melissa? She's okay. She's worked for the Legacy Group for about eight or nine years. She started out as an admin in the finance department and eventually worked her way up to the executive offices. She knows the ins and outs of the company almost as much as Levi."

Levi's trust in Melissa wasn't enough to make Russell feel any better. He couldn't shake the idea that Melissa was *the* Melissa his brother mentioned and remembered more about that night than she let on. Without any concrete evidence, there wasn't much he could do to prove it or make her talk.

"I also asked her about a guy named Bryce Viognier," Russell said. "He was there that night and might remember something. But she said he's not reliable."

Brianna frowned. "That's not surprising."

Russell turned to Brianna. "Why do you say that?"

"Because that's her son's father. They dated since college but never got married. I think they officially broke up about a year ago. He drinks a lot, and when he's not drinking, he's taking his boat up and down the coast. According to her, he's kind of a bum."

The drinking part matched what Melissa had told him, but he hadn't mentioned her relationship with Bryce. "She left out the part about him being her kid's father."

Brianna lifted a shoulder as if not surprised. "I mean, they had a tumultuous relationship from what I hear. Now that they're broken up, I doubt she'd volunteer that information to a stranger."

"Maybe so," Russell said. "She told me he's sailing right now. Otherwise, I would have gone to talk to him."

Brianna shook her head. "He's back in town. I saw him at the post office yesterday."

Russell straightened. "He is?" When Brianna nodded, he glanced at his watch. "Ashiya, you go back with Brianna."

Ashiya's eyes widened. "Why?"

"I need to pay Bryce a visit. I want to talk to him about that night and see what he knows."

She stepped forward. "Then I'll go with you."

He shook his head. "There's no need for that. I can handle this."

"And I promised you that I'd try to help out where I can. I won't say anything. I'll just be there as a second set of eyes and ears. Besides, it's always better to have someone with you when you do things like this. What if he is drunk or belligerent? You'll need a witness if things go weird."

He was about to argue. After what happened between them in the kitchen earlier, he didn't need to be alone with Ashiya, but her logic made sense. Things had gone well with Melissa, but he hadn't forgotten the moment when he'd wanted to push for more information but worried she might consider him a threat. He needed to work out his wa-

vering feelings for Ashiya, but if having the chairwoman
of one of the town's biggest companies with him could
convince the guy to talk more, then he was willing to use
that to his advantage.

"Fine. Brianna, can you get back okay?"

Brianna nodded. "Sure. You two take the car. I'll call
for a ride."

"Are you sure?" he hated leaving her stranded there.

Brianna let out a chuckle. "I live here and have gotten
around without help before. I'll be fine. You go do what
you need to."

"Thank you." He turned to Ashiya. "Let's go."

Once they were in the car, he began to regret his decision. The delicious smell of her perfume drifted to him,
and he was hyperaware of her sitting next to him in the
small space. On the ride there, they'd had Brianna to keep
both of their minds off what happened that morning in
the kitchen. Now there was no one, and the radio station
wasn't helping, playing a throwback of Janet Jackson saying she didn't want to stop just because people watched.
He understood how Janet felt. He'd almost said to hell with
Brianna watching and shoved Ashiya's underwear aside
to finish what they started.

He hit one of the preset buttons, and even though he
didn't recognize the rap song on the radio, it was better
than what played before. "You did well today. In the board
meeting," he said after a moment of awkward silence.

"Thank you. I remembered your pep talk this morning."

He could barely remember what he'd said that morning
before the kiss. His brain was filled with the memory of
her soft lips on his, full breasts on his chest, the way his
hand still perfectly cupped her ass.

He cleared his throat and shifted. "I wasn't expecting that of Levi."

"Neither was I. But I'm glad he stepped in. Things got better after that. It felt nice to have him step up for me."

"Don't get too comfortable with him. Until we figure out the embezzlement, we can't trust him."

It would take a little more than Levi speaking up for Ashiya once for Russell to relax toward the guy. Not after seeing the way he'd reacted when Russell first came to town.

"I know, but my gut tells me that it's not him. I don't want it to be him." She said the last part almost wistfully.

"Why not?"

"It would be nice to have more family. I mean, I love India, Byron and Elaina, but I've never gotten to spend time with my dad's side. If my grandmother wanted to bring me back into the fold, that has to mean something. Maybe there is hope for reconciliation."

The optimism in her voice touched a part of him. A memory of one late-night confession came to mind. The two of them a tangle of arms and legs in the bed. Her head on his chest. She'd run her fingernails through the hair on his chest while he'd trailed his hands up and down her back.

"I've spent so much of my life trying not to compete with my cousins that I had to also keep a buffer between us. I thought I could be closer to India, but even she disappeared for years without a look back. They were the closest thing I had to siblings, but it was still kind of lonely."

The loneliness in her voice that night had sounded so similar to the loneliness he'd lived with for years. *"After Rodrick...disappeared, I didn't have anyone to talk to.*

Sure, there was Isaac, but it wasn't the same as having my brother."

She'd shifted in the bed and looked up at him. *"I'm so sorry, Russell."*

"So am I." He'd brushed a finger across her lower lip. *"You don't have to feel lonely anymore. Whenever you need to talk. Call me."*

Her smile had sent such a rush of emotion through him, he'd known he was in love. He'd lowered his head and kissed her. The memory also stirred up the emotions from that night. The feeling that he'd found her. The person he wanted to spend the rest of his life with. The person he wanted to love and protect forever.

He reached over and placed his hand on hers. "I hope things work out with you and your cousin."

Ashiya sucked in a breath. She placed her other hand on his. Reality rushed back. He pulled his hand free. He was falling again. Fast and hard. What was worse, he didn't want to stop the descent.

Ashiya rubbed her hands on her lap. The nervous gesture made the edge of her navy dress rise a few centimeters up her thighs. "So, Melissa really didn't tell you that Bryce was her ex?"

Russell jerked his gaze away from her amazing legs and focused on the road. "No, she didn't."

"I guess she doesn't have anything to do with the case, but it still seems odd."

"A lot of things about that conversation seem odd. I know Levi trusts her, but I don't. I think she knows something, and I need to find out what."

"Then we'll find out. Together."

Their eyes met. Something squeezed in the vicinity of his heart. The side of her mouth lifted with a small, confident smile before she turned away to look out the window. Russell gripped the wheel and listened as the rap song went off and switched to a song about second chances.

BRYCE'S BOAT WAS docked at the Safe Landing Marina thirty minutes away along Battery Creek. Russell parked in the marina's guest parking area and asked in the main office about the location of Bryce's boat. Ashiya hurried to keep up with Russell's long, determined strides. Her heart clacked against her rib cage with the same fierceness as her heels along the dock. Her stomach was a tangle of knots and she had to remind herself not to fidget nervously. She knew how much this meant to Russell, and therefore she felt just as invested in learning something.

She took in the rigid set of his wide shoulders. The firm set of his jaw. Both indicated he was just as anxious about what they'd discover. If anything.

Two men stood on the dock next to the boat they'd been directed to. They were both in their mid to late thirties. One had dark blond hair, and the other had long red hair pulled back into a ponytail. The men stopped talking and watched as she and Russell approached.

"Can I help you?" The blond man asked. His voice was curious but not unwelcoming.

"I'm looking for Bryce Viognier." Russell looked from the man who'd greeted them to the other.

The smile on the blond man's face stiffened. His shoulders straightened and he faced Russell fully. "I'm him."

Russell held out his hand. "My name is Russell Gilchrist. I'm looking for information about my brother, Rodrick."

Bryce glanced down at Russell's hand but didn't take it. The smile on his face slowly faded away. He took a long breath before addressing the redhead. "I'll catch up with you later, Paul."

Paul raised a thick brow but nodded. "No problem, Bryce. See you later." He gave Russell and Ashiya a wary look before going back in the direction they'd come.

Bryce motioned with his head toward the boat. "Come on in. Let's talk." He turned and stepped up onto the deck.

Russell moved to follow. Ashiya grabbed his arm. He turned to her with a frown. "What?"

"What do you mean, what?" she said in a low voice so Bryce wouldn't overhear. "We're not getting on that thing."

"Why not?"

"Because we don't know him." She eyed the boat skeptically. She hadn't missed the way his welcoming smile disappeared as soon as Russell mentioned his brother. She did not have a good feeling about this.

Russell's shoulders relaxed. "I get it. That's why I already texted my parents when we were in the office to let them know I'm here and I told the detective on the case I planned to talk to the people who were at the party that night. Not to mention Brianna knows we were coming. If anything happens, people will know where we were and why."

"Still." She eyed the boat. The chances of something happening to them were slim, and there were several people who knew where they were.

He reached over and took her hand. "I've got you. I won't let anything happen to you."

Her heart turned into a big ball of melted ice cream. "Fine, but just know I've got a pocketknife." She patted her purse.

Russell's eyes dropped to her purse, widened, then

jumped back up to meet hers. "Why do you have a pock-etknife?"

"Why wouldn't I?"

He shook his head. "Then I guess you've got my back," he said with a lopsided smile. "Come on. Let's go."

She followed him onto the deck. Bryce was rummaging inside a red cooler. He pulled out a beer and turned toward them with it held out.

"Want one?"

Russell shook his head. "No, I'm driving."

Bryce held the beer out toward Ashiya. She held up a hand. "No thank you. I'm not really a beer drinker."

"Suit yourself." Bryce popped the tab on the beer and took a sip. "So, what did you want to ask me?" he sat on the top of the cooler and pointed towards two chairs next to a small table.

Ashiya made a move for one of the chairs, but Russell spoke before she took a step. "Do you remember my brother from that night?"

Bryce took a longer sip of his beer. "I remember I've been asked about your brother every year for the past fourteen or fifteen years."

"Can you tell me about that night?" Russell asked, sounding calmer than Ashiya would have been, considering Bryce's blasé tone.

"I can tell you the same thing I've told the police. I barely remember your brother," Bryce said in an unapologetic voice.

Ashiya's interest spiked. "But you do remember him?"

Bryce's assessing gaze slid to her. He took a sip of his beer, burped silently, then shrugged. "I met a lot of people. When the detective showed me the picture, he looked familiar. But that's all I know."

"Is that all Melissa knows?" Russell asked.

Bryce froze with the can halfway to his mouth. The metal crunched as his grip tightened. Beer oozed out over his hand. "What did she say?"

"That she doesn't remember my brother at all. But I hear that you two were dating back then."

Bryce grunted. "Melissa never was good at considering the big picture. Always impulsive and always wanted things her own way. I learned that too late." He grumbled and finished off the beer.

"Did you see my brother with anyone else that night? Was he talking to someone? Did he leave with someone? Anything you can remember could help us find out what happened to him."

Bryce shook his head and stood. "Look, I'm really sorry about your brother, but I can't help you."

"Can't or won't?" A note of frustration filled Russell's voice.

Ashiya stepped closer to Russell and put her hand on his arm. Tension vibrated through him. Imagining the pain and anxiety he must feel made her heart fracture.

Bryce tossed the empty can into a bag tied to the cooler. "I can't. I can't tell you what happened to your brother. Spring break is a wild and crazy time. I was drunk during most of it. I'm sorry." He reached into the cooler and pulled out another can.

Russell's arm clenched beneath Ashiya's palm. "You're sorry. Melissa is sorry. The detective is sorry. Sorry doesn't help me, and it doesn't bring back my brother." Pain made Russell's voice tight and hard.

Ashiya squeezed his arm, but he turned and stormed off the boat. Ashiya gave Bryce a half smile. "If you remember anything else."

"Yeah, yeah, I'll call you," Bryce said, sounding weary.

As he cracked open the next can and took a long sip, she turned and left the boat. She had absolutely no confidence that they'd voluntarily hear from Bryce again.

CHAPTER SIXTEEN

THE SOUND OF a beat dropping stopped Russell in his tracks on his way to the kitchen. The music continued and came from the back of the house. He glanced around as if he'd find the answer to the sudden sound of hip-hop music vibrating in the normally quiet house.

After the visit with Bryce, Russell had gone straight to his side of the house to decompress. He couldn't believe absolutely no one remembered his brother from that night. His brother's cell phone's last location was at the party. It was the only thing the police had found. Rodrick had been there, but not a single person who'd attended knew anything.

He refused to accept that he'd never find out what happened to his brother. Refused to accept that Rodrick was gone without a trace. If he had to track down every single person who attended that party to get a hint of what happened, he'd do that.

Ashiya hadn't followed him to his side of the house and had given him the space he needed. He remembered she was perceptive like that. She never pushed him when he was lost in thought. She'd wait him out and then listened without judging when he was ready to talk. It was one of the reasons he'd fallen for her before.

One of the reasons he was having a hard time not falling again.

The beat of the music picked up. Answers about the

source of the music wouldn't come if he continued standing in the hall. He followed the sound of the bass. As he got closer, he recognized the lyrics of "Lucid Dreams" coming from the back lanai. Russell opened the double doors and blinked several times. The back lanai had been converted from a basic functional outdoor space to a festive, celebratory space.

Red, yellow and blue balloons floated from the backs of the patio chairs. Tiki torches mounted around the space added to the golden glow from the porch lights. Red and yellow confetti covered the tables, and a large speaker changed colors with the beat of the music.

Ashiya stood behind the gas grill under the pergola on the side of the lanai. She'd changed into cutoff shorts and a white tank top. A Superman apron protected her clothes. She swayed and rapped along with the music while flipping something on the grill. The mouthwatering aroma of burgers drifted to him.

He shook his head to make sure he wasn't imagining things. When the scene didn't change or magically disappear, he walked out and over to her.

She looked up from the grill. Her bright smile hit him dead in the chest and pushed him farther down the hill of falling back in love with Ashiya.

"Hey, I hope you're hungry." Her hips moved to the beat. She flipped what he could see was a burger with one hand and picked up a champagne flute with the other.

"I am," he answered slowly. "What's all this?"

She sipped her champagne then threw out her arms. "A celebration!"

"What are we celebrating?" He was not in the mood to celebrate, but her enthusiasm and smile were working really hard to improve his disposition.

"Surviving my first board meeting," she said as if the answer were obvious.

Russell let out a laugh. The board meeting felt like something that happened a month ago. He'd gotten so caught up in the bitter disappointment of not learning anything new about his brother that he'd forgotten about the one win of the day.

Ashiya took another sip of champagne and licked her lips. His stomach clenched as if she'd run her tongue across his abdomen. He'd forgotten about that kiss, too. Almost.

He glanced around at the balloons and confetti. "This is what you've been doing while I was—"

"Sulking. Yep." She put down the champagne flute and picked up a plate.

Russell crossed his arms over his chest. "I wasn't sulking."

"It's okay. You have every right to sulk. I wanted to sulk after meeting with that guy. He knows something. I feel it."

"I agree with you," he said, his mood souring again.

"He can lie today, but we'll get the truth tomorrow. Even if we have to hunt down everyone who was at that party. I've got the resources now to help you find them. So that's what we're going to do."

"I didn't ask you to help me track my brother down."

"I know, but I already told you I want to help." She lifted a shoulder and used a spatula to take the burgers from the grill to the plate in her hand. "Just accept my help and get over it."

He couldn't stop his smile any more than he could stop the warmth spreading through his chest. There she went being irresistible again. This was why he'd avoided her for so long after they'd broken up. He had a hard time fighting his attraction to her.

"What made you decide to grill? We could have ordered food."

"I really want a hamburger, but I didn't want anything greasy. Brianna reminded me of the grill out here. I thought I'd give it a try." She pointed to the table. "There's buns and other fixings over there."

She turned the dials on the grill to shut off the gas and came around. Russell followed her over to the table where sliced tomatoes, lettuce, onions and pickles along with ketchup and mustard and a variety of cheeses sat on plates. He tried, and failed, to keep his eyes off the way the fringe on the cutoff shorts brushed the back of her thighs.

"Who else is eating? Is Brianna inside?"

Ashiya shook her head. "No, she had something to do. It's just us. I hope you don't mind."

"I don't mind." He meant the words. Ashiya's light was enough to lift his mood, but he wasn't in the headspace to entertain a lot of people. Since Brianna had eaten with them almost nightly since he'd arrived, Russell was pretty sure Ashiya had sent her away. Instead of being annoyed by the thought, he was pleased. Once again, Ashiya knew what he needed.

"Good! Let's eat. I've got chips inside. I'll be right back."

She put the burgers down and rushed inside. A few minutes later she returned with a variety pack of chips in one hand and the bottle of champagne in the other. They made their burgers and settled down to eat. The conversation flowed smoothly while they ate. They focused mostly on the board meeting and the next steps she would take to win over the board. From that it flowed to his work with Robidoux Holdings and his hopes to make similar changes there once Elaina accepted him as the new CEO.

"She's running things on her own right now and relying on the rest of the various directors. She's doing a good job, but she also wants to focus on her own investments. Eventually she'll have to fill the position," he said after they finished eating and were sitting back, enjoying the view of the river and the warm evening breeze, and popping the second bottle of champagne.

Ashiya was relaxed back in her chair. Her sexy legs were stretched out and crossed at the ankle while she dangled the champagne flute from one hand. "Elaina just needs time to trust you. You were Uncle Grant's person, so of course she's leery."

"I respect your uncle and I hope he feels the same, but at the end of the day, my loyalty is with Robidoux Holdings and whoever runs it."

She glanced at him from the corner of her eye. "Was respect the reason why you dated India?"

Russell's spine straightened. "I didn't date India. I went on a few dates with her."

Ashiya twirled a finger at him. "You liked her. For a second there she was falling for you."

"Was that what prompted you to call me and go in?" he asked without any heat.

Shortly after he and India both decided that they weren't right for each other, he'd gotten a call from Ashiya. She'd accused him of trying to make her jealous by dating her cousin. And to warn him that he shouldn't get too invested because India's heart was pulled in another direction. He'd been so surprised at her audacity to say something to him about his dating life that he'd gotten angry and reminded her of the way she'd broken his heart.

"I didn't go in. I was trying to warn you."

"Is that also why you tried to push her in my direction?"

he asked. "India mentioned you saying I was the most eligible bachelor in town."

Ashiya shrugged and met his eyes. "You were."

He leaned forward and rested his forearm on the table's glass surface. "Still, if you didn't want me with your cousin, then why did you push her toward me?"

Ashiya looked away first. "You're a good man. You deserve a good woman. I know you hated me, and India was in search of a nice guy."

"And what if we would have worked out?"

She shifted in her seat. She took another sip of her drink. "I would have dealt with it."

"Would you?" He didn't believe a word of that. "Because that conversation said you wouldn't have."

She sat up straight and crossed her legs at the knee. "I wanted you close. Even if you weren't with me." Her confession came out in a quiet voice.

His heart impersonated a jackhammer against his rib cage. He was slipping and falling. He wouldn't be able to get up. Pursuing meant trouble. He asked anyway. "Why?"

"Apparently I hold on too long. Usually to the wrong thing. Or the thing I really want." Her lips lifted in a sad smile. "I was trying to let you go even though I really didn't want to do that."

He wasn't sure how to respond to the vulnerability in her sweet voice. He knew how he was supposed to feel. Superior, smug, scornful. He should be happy that she'd realized what she'd messed up. Instead his happiness came from a far different place. The place that hadn't let Ashiya go no matter how much he'd ignored her calls, limited contact with her, and tried to forget her.

The music changed. Her recognized the song as wone with a new line dance associated with it. Ashiya's smile brightened and she put down her champagne. "I was dancing to this with Byron's daughter Lilah a few weeks ago. She had to show me there was a dance when I told her I didn't know."

She jumped up from the table and swayed her hips to the music. Russell watched her as she sang along. He knew her dancing was to deflect from the direction their conversation had gone. In all the time they dated, Ashiya flirted with him, seduced him and teased him, but he realized she never was vulnerable with him. She'd always held back a part of herself. He'd been so lost in her that he hadn't noticed until it was too late.

Opening up wasn't easy for her. He wasn't satisfied with just the tiny morsels she'd given. He was starving for more of her, and if he went with the urge in his heart and body, he wouldn't be satisfied if she wasn't just as open with him as he was with her.

He watched her dance. Took in her delight and joy with just getting lost in the music. She was pulling him back in with just a smile, a gesture and a confession. Each one packed enough of a punch to throw his entire world into a tailspin. He'd sworn up and down that there was no way in hell he'd ever give Ashiya another chance.

Well, the devil was laughing at him now.

Russell pushed up from the chair. He came up behind Ashiya and put his hands on her hips right in the middle of her left foot slide. She froze and looked at him over her shoulder, her beautiful eyes teasing.

"You want to dance?"

He shook his head and picked up their conversation where she'd tried to drop it. "I don't want you to let go of me. Not just yet."

CHAPTER SEVENTEEN

ASHIYA'S HEART, MIND, everything froze in the seconds after Russell spoke. She'd opened herself to him again, expecting to be shut down like before. She'd planned this impromptu celebration for the board meeting not only to distract him from the visit with Bryce, but to also find a way to avoid going over all the reasons the kiss earlier that day shouldn't happen again. Especially when she wanted that kiss to happen again, and again, and again.

"What do you mean?" Her voice came out as a shaky whisper. She was afraid to move or speak louder out of fear he'd realize what he'd said and move away.

He pulled her back against his front. His head lowered, and his lips brushed her ear. "I meant exactly what I said. Don't let go of me."

Her breaths came in short, choppy bursts. The momentary stun from his words melted away as desire slid across her skin like warm rain. Questions rose. Did he really mean what he said? Was he truly ready to give them a second chance? Was that really his erection she felt growing against her ass?

"Russell—"

His warm lips pulling on her ear cut off her words. Liquid heat shot from her ear down her body and straight to her sex. His tongue replaced his lips and traced lightly down the sensitive outer shell of her ear. Ashiya gasped.

Her hand reached back and clutched the hard muscles of his thigh. She arched her neck to the side. His teeth nipped at her ear and she whimpered. Russell knew exactly what to do to turn her into a puddle of need.

"Tell me you missed me." His warm breath caressed her ear. He snaked an arm around her waist and pressed his hand into her belly. "Because I sure as hell missed you."

The emotion that rushed through her from those words was like an avalanche, smothering her in so many feelings she didn't have the time to sort out. *Missed* him? That word wasn't strong enough. She'd *yearned* for him.

"I missed everything about you," she said with a low moan.

His fingers pressed harder into her midsection. His lips went from slow and languid against her ear to urgent and needy. He licked and nipped his way from her ear to her neck. His lips closed in on the soft spot over her pulse, and he sucked softly. Her knees buckled. Desire tightened her nipples. Warm wetness slid between her legs.

Russell's hand ran from her stomach to her breast. He cupped the heavy weight and squeezed. The material between his hands and her flesh dampened the caress, and Ashiya wanted more. With shaky hands, she reached for the hem of her shirt.

Russell took over and tugged her shirt up and over her head. Ashiya unbuttoned her shorts and shoved them to a heap at her feet. He groaned his approval before he jerked down the cup of her bra. Warm air brushed her hard nipple before he took the tip between his thumb and forefinger. He pinched with just enough pressure to make her sex clench. The sensation swept through every inch of her body. Her head fell back against his strong shoulder. Russell's other hand pulled down the strap of her bra, releasing her other breast, but he didn't pull the straps down far enough to allow her to freely move her arms. The loss of control only fueled her need.

His warm hands cupped her breasts while his fingers alternated between tracing over her nipples and pinching and tugging them. She bucked against him, rubbing her ass against his dick and relishing in every sharp breath he sucked in.

"You have no idea how much I missed you," he said in a shaky voice.

"Show me," she demanded. "Show me everything you missed about me.

One hand left her breast and slid down her torso, across her stomach, and brushed the edge of her panties. She didn't think it was possible for her breathing to get any faster. Anticipation and need pumped with each beat of her heart, driving her so fast she could have been running a sprint.

She bit her lip when he tugged her panties down her hips. The damp material slid down her legs. Ashiya hastily kicked them out of the way and pulled her arms free of the straps of her bra before taking it completely off. Russell didn't waste any time. He jerked her body back against his, took one breast in one hand, and slid his other hand between her legs and cupped her sex.

Her legs opened wide. Russell didn't hesitate. His finger slid across her clit like sweet perfection before pushing inside her. The breeze carried away the long, low moan Ashiya let out. She reached back, forced her hand between then, and cupped the hard length of his dick in her hand.

"I missed you, too. So. Damn. Much," she said in a shaky voice.

Russell spun her around. Her arms wrapped around his

neck, and his mouth covered hers. Their tongues glided across each other as they kissed. She drew everything from him—all his need, desire and longing—and savored each emotion. She'd craved him so much since letting him go.

"Inside," she said against his lips.

Russell nodded, grabbed her hand, and hauled her from the porch to the house. She tried to hide her grin as he made a beeline for his bedroom. But when he kicked open the door and swung her back into his arms as soon as they crossed the threshold, she didn't bother to hold back her delight. He could see all her joy. All her need. She would never let Russell doubt her feelings for him again.

His lips covered hers in a heady, urgent kiss. Ashiya pulled on the waistband of his pants as they stumbled to the bed. They fell back on the mattress. Ashiya immediately pushed him over onto his back and straddled his waist. He loved it when she was on top, and she loved the way he looked at her when she rode him to ecstasy.

"Condoms?" *Please, God, let him have a condom.*

His body froze. Dread turned her body cold. Well, she was on birth control.

"In the bathroom," he said.

Relief nearly had her fall over on his chest. "Go get them." She rolled off him. Russell jumped up from the bed.

Just to be sure he didn't let regret or thoughts of what they were doing stop him, Ashiya sat up against the pillows, knees bent, and spread her legs wide. Russell rushed out of the bathroom, took one look at her open and ready for him, and his jaw dropped. The heat that blazed in his eyes let her know if any doubts had tried to creep into his brain, they were gone.

He was across the room in two seconds. His body covered hers and his lips took hers in a searing kiss before he lowered himself and eagerly pulled one nipple into his mouth. Ashiya lifted her hips, pressing the wet heat of her need against him, then groaned in frustration.

"Take off your fucking clothes," she said in a rough voice.

He pulled back and jerked off his shirt. The gold chain that had taunted her so many times before hung around his neck, the cross resting right in the space above his pecs. He reached for the back of the chain.

Ashiya shook her head and waved a hand. "No. Leave that on."

Russell grinned and got his pants off in a blink. When he pulled her back, the warm weight of the gold cross against her breasts and the heavy press of his erection against her slick heat almost took her over the edge.

"You have no idea how much I missed you," he said in a desperate whisper.

Ashiya rolled him over onto his back again. She took the condom out of his hand and made quick work of covering his length. Her lips lifted with a greedy grin. She loved the hell out of his dick. It was perfection. Perfect length, just enough of a curve to hit every spot, and so deliciously thick. The only thing that kept her from taking him in her mouth was that her body ached for him more. She adjusted herself over him and slid down in a sure motion.

Russell clenched his teeth. His fingers dug into her hips. Ashiya pressed her hands against his chest and then raised and lowered her hips. They both groaned. She started slowly, savoring each filling stroke, but that only lasted a few heartbeats. Passion, longing and lust took over. Her movements became hurried.

She opened her eyes and looked down at him. His eyes were open and on her. Just like before, he watched her. Desire and adoration swam in his gaze. No one ever looked at her like that when making love. As if she were not only giving him pleasure but gifting him with something so precious and perfect that he wasn't sure he was worthy.

He slid a hand up her thigh and pressed his thumb against her protruding clit. Ashiya crashed over the edge. Her movements jerked and her rhythm was thrown off as the orgasm rocked her. Russell grabbed her hips, flipped her onto her back, pushed in deep and owned her with hard, fast thrusts. The ripples of her orgasm continued as she cried out. Russell's body tensed. He pulsed hard and oh so deep inside her, before falling heavily on top of her. Ashiya didn't care if she had to lasso the moon there was no way she'd ever let Russell go.

CHAPTER EIGHTEEN

ASHIYA WOKE UP slowly at five in the morning. She hadn't woken up that early since coming to her grandmother's home. Any other day she'd still be knocked out from the sleeping pills. She turned her head, took in Russell's sleeping profile on the pillow next to her and smiled. A dose or two of Russell worked better than any sleeping pill on the market.

She wanted to roll over into his arms. Wake him with a gentle kiss on his jaw while her hand roamed down his chest to slowly squeeze his dick until it hardened in her palm. He'd groan and grin before pushing her onto her back and giving her a morning pick-me-up that was ten times better than coffee.

Instead, she eased from the bed and hurried out of the room. As much as she wanted to wake up in his arms and have a repeat of the awesome night they'd shared, she didn't want to see regret in his eyes. Nor did she want to have the awkward morning-after discussion. The way he'd held her, kissed her, and made love to her the night before was the same way he'd done it when they'd dated. There was so much joy and hope in her heart about them finally getting another chance that she wasn't ready to shatter her happiness with all of the reasons they shouldn't be together.

She tiptoed to her room and quickly showered and dressed. Russell still hadn't stirred by the time she left the house and got behind the wheel of her car. She called Brianna as she eased out of the driveway.

"Good morning, Ashiya. Is everything alright?" Brianna asked, sounding worried. Not too surprising since Ashiya hadn't gotten up early since coming to town.

"Everything is fine. I'm just up early, and I don't feel like being stuck in the house. I thought that maybe I could go by the Legacy offices again this morning and meet a few more of the employees."

"That's a great idea. Do you want me to call Levi and let him know you're coming? He mentioned you sitting in on some of the meetings he's having in the next few weeks."

Levi had made the offer right as Ashiya began her tour of the facility the day before. Her cousin hadn't seemed enthusiastic about the idea of her butting in on his meetings, but he also seemed ready to accept that she had ideas, wasn't going anywhere, and ultimately had the power to do whatever she wanted since she was a majority shareholder.

"Let's do that," Ashiya agreed. "I'm going to find someplace to get coffee and breakfast, and then I'll meet you at the office later."

"I'm already up and almost dressed. Let me know where you're going, and I'll eat with you. That way I can give you an update on what's on the schedule. His morning is slightly busy."

"You know Levi's schedule?"

"Melissa was in a habit of sharing his schedule with me, and I shared it with your grandmother. She still does that."

"Did my grandmother sometimes sit in on meetings?"

"Not as much, but Levi would come over and give her an update on any major discussions of the day."

"Good to know. If there was a standing meeting he had with my grandmother, go ahead and start arranging them with me. If we're going to work together, we might as well start sooner rather than later."

Since she'd decided to do this, it was time to get into the habit of owing a major corporation. She would only learn so much by staying at home reviewing reports and getting updates from Brianna. If she wanted Levi and the rest of the board to take her seriously, and if she was going to find out the source of the missing money, then she would have to be involved.

Hours later, Ashiya was in dire need of another cup of coffee, and she wished she'd chosen three-inch heels instead of the six-inch heels she'd grabbed on her way out. To say Levi's schedule for the day was packed was like saying the interstate during rush hour was slightly busy. There was barely time to breathe or catch up on anything between the meetings.

Ashiya sat back and listened for the most part. Levi always introduced her as the new owner, then dove right into the meetings. Discussions were on everything from a fragrance blend for a new shampoo line, to marketing another brand of soaps to teens, and adding a new wrinkle-reducing compound to a face wash. Ashiya knew the Legacy Group had gone from a small soap-making business to a larger health and beauty organization, but to see and hear the decisions that went into the multitude of products was amazing.

At two, Levi looked at his watch and ended the last meeting. Ashiya, Brianna and Melissa followed him back to his office. Though Ashiya's feet were killing her, she tried to look upbeat and not let it show that she was tired and starving.

"We've got about an hour and a half until my conference call with public relations," Levi said once they entered the executive suite.

"Good, we can finally eat!" Ashiya said, pressing a hand to her stomach.

Three sets of eyes turned to her. Her cheeks burned with embarrassment. "I mean, you do eat? Don't you?"

Melissa chuckled and shook her head. "I put protein bars in his desk, but the man lives on coffee and fumes." She pulled out her phone and checked it. "I'm going to grab a sandwich from the cafeteria before meeting with finance on the budget for the new face cream. I'll be back in time for the three-thirty meeting."

Levi nodded. "Okay. I promised my grandmother I'd stop in. Since I've got dinner with the Douglass Industries CEO, I'll drop in now and check on her. If I'm a few minutes late, start without me. I'll catch up when I get in."

Melissa nodded. "You've got it." She smiled at Ashiya and Brianna before leaving the executive suite.

Ashiya stared at Levi. "Are you seriously not going to eat?"

He slid his cell phone in his back pocket and grabbed a set of keys out of the top drawer of his desk. "There's always something to eat at my grandmother's house."

"Do you think she'll mind if Brianna and I come along?" The idea of food drove her to ask the question rather than the idea of spending more time with the aunt who seemed least excited about her.

Levi, for his part, only showed a second of irritation on his face. Maybe he was getting tired of her tagging along. Ashiya just smiled the innocent, go-along-with-this smile that typically got her whatever she wanted.

He shook his head. "She won't mind. Let's go."

Levi was right. Aunt Gertrude didn't seem to mind that

he'd brought her along. If anything, she seemed slightly excited that Ashiya decided to intrude. She immediately had them settled in the sunroom on the back of her modest two-story brick home. Her backyard was large with a basketball goal in one corner and an outdoor grill and patio in another. Tall trees around the edge of the yard blocked her home from prying eyes. Levi was also right that she always had food ready. As soon as they were seated her housekeeper came in with trays of sandwiches, fruit and cheeses and a basket of chips.

Gertrude sat in one of the four white wicker chairs around the wicker-and-glass coffee table that filled the brightly colored room. Sunlight brought out the highlights in her honey-gold hair as she spread out the edges of the leopard print caftan she wore and leaned forward in her chair.

She waved one thin hand at the food. "You kids eat. I bet you haven't eaten since earlier this morning, have you, Levi?"

"I get through the day," Levi grumbled, but reached for one of the sandwiches on the tray.

Gertrude looked at Brianna sitting next to Ashiya across from the table. "Why don't you make him eat?"

Brianna lifted one shoulder. "I can't make him eat, Ms. Gertrude. No matter how much I fuss at him." Brianna gave Levi a glare that was more flirtatious that furious.

Levi was focused on his sandwich and missed Brianna's look. "No one can force me to do anything I don't want to. Besides, Melissa keeps me stocked with smoothies and protein bars."

Gertrude grunted. "I don't like that girl."

"What's new, Gigi," Levi said in a slightly exasperated voice. "Melissa is a good assistant. That's all I care about."

Ashiya perked up at the mention of Melissa. Although Melissa had been very helpful and professional today, Ashiya still didn't have a great feeling about the woman. She knew it was because of Russell's doubts and didn't care. "Why don't you like her?"

"For one thing, her parents are trash," Gertrude said flatly.

Levi sighed. "Gigi, stop."

Gertrude raised a brow innocently. "What? They are. Mean as hell, and they don't care who they step on to get what they want. They spoiled the hell out of that girl, and now she thinks she's important, when all she is is an over-priced secretary."

Ashiya leaned forward. "Oh really?" She was not against gossiping on an average day. When the gossip could possibly help her find answers to a problem for Russell, she was even more interested.

Levi held up a hand. "Stop it. We're not bashing Melissa today." His voice sounded like he'd had to stop several "Bash Melissa" conversations. "You called me over here for a reason. Tell me what it is. I've got a meeting this afternoon."

Gertrude grunted and pouted again but waved her hand. "Fine. I wanted to let you know that your cousin Cameron is coming home."

Levi's head whipped around to his grandmother. Brianna's hand froze on the way to pick up another sandwich. Ashiya looked between the three of them. From the self-satisfied smirk on Gertrude's face, to the shock on Brianna's, and the barely concealed annoyance on Levi's.

When they were quiet for way too long for her curious mind, she spoke up. "Who's Cameron?"

Gertrude turned to Ashiya with a gleam in her eye that

said she was more than happy to tell her. "He's one of Maggie's grandkids."

"He's a bastard," Levi said before chomping on his sandwich. Gertrude slapped the back of his head. He flinched and grunted. "Well, he is."

"You don't like him because he's just like you," Gertrude said.

Levi shifted in his seat. "He's not the least like me. He's lazy, doesn't give a damn about anyone but himself, and thinks he's better than everyone in the family."

"Well, do you blame him?" Gertrude said. "Maggie's son treated him almost as bad as Gloria did her George."

Someone who was given her dad's treatment. Apparently that was a trend in this family. Ashiya shifted forward in her seat. "Why?"

Gertrude placed a hand up to the side of her mouth and said in a stage whisper, "He's an outside baby."

Ashiya frowned and glanced at Brianna and Levi. They didn't appear confused, so she focused back on her aunt. "A what?"

Levi shook his head, his scowl deepening. "What my grandmother is trying to say is that my uncle stepped out on my aunt and had a kid with a woman across town."

"Oooh." Ashiya leaned back. That was messy. Despite all of the scandals and drama on her Robidoux side, the closet thing they had to an "outside baby" was her cousin Byron pretending to be Lilah's father when he wasn't. Biologically speaking. He'd adopted her the year before.

"What I want to know is, why should I care if he's coming back?" Levi asked.

Gertrude looked at him as if the answer were obvious. "Because he's finally gotten his life together. Maggie wants you to give him a job at the company when he's in town, and I told her I'd talk to you."

"No." Levi said without missing a beat.

Gertrude grunted, then looked at Ashiya. "Ashiya, sweetheart. You know how badly your grandmother wanted to get the family back together."

"Gigi, don't," Levi said in a tense voice.

Aunt Gertrude didn't stop. "He's really a good kid. He got into some mischief when he was younger but what kid with a chip on his shoulder doesn't? See if you can find a place for him at the company."

Levi glared at her. Her aunt gave her a pitiful, pleading look that immediately made her feel guilty for even thinking about saying no. Now she understood her aunt's enthusiastic response to her joining Levi for lunch. She had an ulterior motive and figured Ashiya could help her out.

Ashiya lifted her shoulders slowly and spoke hesitantly. "Um… I'd have to meet him first. Get to know who he is. I'm still figuring things out and don't want to make any rash decisions."

Gertrude blinked twice. Her shoulders slumped a little, but she nodded. "Fine. It'll be a while before he's here. Don't let Levi poison your mind before that."

"He won't," Ashiya said. "I like to make my own judgments about people."

"Good." Gertrude nodded firmly. "I was worried when you came, but I know your grandmother always hated that she never got to know you. She reached out to your mom a few times when you were younger, but she always said that you were busy with something and couldn't visit."

"Who? My mom?" Her mom said her dad's family never reached out to get to know them. Once she and her dad checked out on their marriage and he was away, Ashiya also believed that his family wouldn't want anything to do with her.

"Yes. Your grandmother even sent birthday cards every year, but after there was no reply, she stopped. I was surprised when she gave her money to you, but knowing that she wanted to make things right made sense. She was the most sentimental of the four of us."

Gertrude said the last part as if that were a shame. Maybe it was, in her eyes. She had wanted Levi to ultimately take control.

"That can't be true," Ashiya said, her mind still reeling with the news that her grandmother had tried to contact her before she died. "I never knew any of that."

"It's the God's honest truth. Ask your mom. She'll tell you. By the way, Levi, that Hamilton girl is back in town, too. Didn't you used to date her? She was nice. Bring her back around."

Ashiya drifted out of the conversation as Levi tried to convince his grandmother not to invite his ex-girlfriend to the house for dinner. Her mind couldn't focus on more gossip about her cousin, his obvious discomfort, or the way Brianna seemed to deflate at the woman's mention.

Had her mom really hidden her grandmother's attempts to contact with her? Elizabeth always said Ashiya was owed access to the fortune her father's family had. It made no sense for her to keep Ashiya in the dark. But knowing her mother, and the entire Robidoux family, she couldn't completely dismiss what Aunt Gertrude said. Now she had another mystery to solve on top of everything else. Why would her mom intentionally keep Ashiya from her dad's side of the family?

CHAPTER NINETEEN

RUSSELL INTENTIONALLY DIDN'T return to the house until after eight that evening. When he'd woken up, alone, he'd been disappointed but assumed Ashiya had gotten up to go to the bathroom or maybe even to her room for something. When he'd realized she'd left the house completely without saying a word to him, the doubts kicked in.

Why had she left? Did she regret what happened? Had she changed her mind about wanting to start over now that he'd caved?

He'd felt as foolish and unsure as a kid in his first relationship. Which only pissed him off. A phone call to Brianna gave him the answers he needed. Ashiya decided to go to the office and learn more about the company she inherited with the help of her cousin and not him. Satisfied that she was safe, he'd decided to view the day to himself as a blessing rather than succumbing to the feeling of being dismissed after serving his purpose for a night.

When he entered, the house was quiet. Not many lights were on. Ashiya's car was in the garage, so he knew she was there. Unless she'd gone out with Brianna or her family again. He'd stopped trying to tell himself he shouldn't be upset that she'd left without talking to him, or that he should be happy she decided to put space between them. He was confused, frustrated and off balance. She was playing games with him again, and this was exactly why he didn't need to be with her. Knowing that didn't make the situation any easier to accept.

If she wanted to run and hide and pretend as if the night before didn't matter, then let her. They'd made no promises. Hadn't agreed to get back together. He didn't owe Ashiya anything.

The thought fueled his steps as he walked through the house on the way to his bedroom. The glowing blue light from the television in the downstairs living area stopped him in his tracks. Ashiya sat on the couch with a glass of wine in her hand. She stared in the direction of the television, but she didn't seem to be engaged with what was on screen. Her brows were drawn together, her body tense as if she would jump up at any second, while her fingers tapped the glass in her hand.

Thoughts of ignoring her vanished as he crossed the threshold into the room. "Ashiya? You okay?"

She blinked and jumped. When she looked at him, her eyes were confused and sad, before she focused on him and smiled as if he'd just made all her cares melt away. "Russell, where were you? I was worried."

The concern in her voice drew him closer. Beckoned him to immediately tell her his exact whereabouts for the day. Ridiculous. He didn't owe her an explanation.

He took a step closer. "I was out trying to follow up with people at the party my brother attended and checking in on some projects with Robidoux Holdings." So much for not owing her an explanation.

"Oh, you've helped me so much, I forgot that you actually work for Elaina. Have you eaten? I ordered food." She moved to stand.

Russell shook his head and held up a hand. "I did. Don't worry about it."

"Oh." Her frown came back, and she sounded sad.

"I grabbed a sandwich at a deli while doing work before coming back here," he explained.

She slid over on the couch and patted the seat. "No worries. Sit down."

"I'm tired." He pointed over his shoulder. "I was going to go take a shower and rest."

"I called Jeanette from Lady Eyes Private Investigation. I told her about your case and how you're trying to track people down. She said if you're interested, she has an investigator or two she can put on the case. She's the same one who helped my cousin Byron back when he needed to track down Zoe."

Russell was both shocked and touched to find out she'd done that. "You called a private investigator for me?" Surprise made the words come out sharper than he'd intended.

She looked a little sheepish. "I hope I didn't overstep my boundaries. That meeting with Bryce didn't sit well with me. I know everyone who was at that party isn't in the area. Jeanette and her investigators are good a tracking people down."

He shook his head and softened his tone. "No, you didn't overstep. I appreciate you giving her a call. I'd hired a private investigator a few years back, but he didn't find out anything new. I felt like I'd wasted time and money."

Ashiya gave him a thumbs-up. "Jeanette is the woman. If there's something to find out, she'll be the one to find it. I'll send you her number. She's expecting your call."

She put down the wineglass and picked up her cell phone from the table. The strap of her tank top slid down her shoulder, revealing smooth, brown skin and a dark mark on her neck. A dark mark he'd left on her when he'd kissed, licked and sucked that delicious spot the night before. Instead of going to his room, Russell came around the couch and sat down next to her.

The sad look in her eye lessened the intensity of his frustration with her disappearing earlier that day. He'd get to the bottom of that, but first he wanted to know what was bothering her. "Why are you in here?"

"I'm watching television," she said blithely. Her eyes were still on her cell. The light cast a blue glow on her soft features that made him want to trace his fingers over her cheeks and lips.

Russell glanced at the nearly silent television and back to Ashiya. "You can't hear the television. Did everything go okay today?"

She put down the phone and gave him a tight smile. "It did. Levi was patient and accommodating, and he answered all my questions. He was even okay with me trailing along with him for lunch at his grandmother's house."

"Your Aunt Gertrude?"

"Yep," she said, her smile turning genuine and her features becoming even more enchanting.

"Good." Though he was happy for her getting to know her family, a hint of unease tightened his neck. "I guess if Levi is willing to help, you won't need me to continue to stick around much longer."

Her eyes widened, and her hand shot out to grip his arm. "Yes. I do need you. We still haven't found the blackmailer."

He suppressed the stupid grin that threatened to take over his face. She wanted him to stay. That eased some of the sting from the thought of her not wanting him around anymore. "How long do you think you'll want me to stay?"

"Are you asking because you have work to do for Elaina? I'll give her a call and explain. I'll even say there may be a way for Legacy and Robidoux Holdings to partner on something and she'll calm down."

"There's no need for that. I'll stay and help as long as you feel you need it."

Even though forming a future partnership between the Legacy Group and Robidoux Holdings was the reason Elaina asked him to come, Russell didn't want to stay just for that. He'd already gone over the deep end and slept with her. His brain might not agree with his emotions about how wise it was to be with Ashiya again, but the choice was made. He only wanted to stick around if she wanted him there.

The smile on her face sent ripples through his midsection. "Really? Thank you, Russell."

His cheeks heated. He was useless in the face of her admiration. "How did things go with your aunt at lunch?"

She nodded. "Really well. What Brianna said is true. My aunt wants to get the family back together after everyone drifted apart. Once I'm comfortable at the Legacy Group, I may work on that."

"Do you really want to put a lot of effort in reuniting the family that ignored you for years?"

"That's the thing, Aunt Gertrude said my mom blocked my grandmother's attempts to get to know me."

"Do you believe her?"

She shrugged. "I don't know. My mom always talked about how my grandmother was being stubborn and trying to keep me from my legacy. I couldn't imagine she would try to block her from knowing me."

"What happened between them?" He knew there was a history that involved her dad, but she'd never gone into detail.

Ashiya picked up her glass of wine. She studied the

contents for a second before taking a sip and speaking. "My mom married my dad right when the Legacy Group became a Fortune 500 company." She said slowly. She glanced at him from the corner of her eye. When he continued to wait patiently, she kept talking. "My dad fell in love with her and thought they were a love match. It wasn't until my grandmother cut him off from the company and any chance of inheriting anything that it came out my mom only married him because of the money."

Russell cringed. "Oh…damn."

Ashiya nodded and wrinkled her nose. "Yeah. It wasn't the most fun time. When he found out, I think my mom had fallen in love with my dad, but it was too little, too late. The damage was done. Ever since, they stayed together for appearances and to raise me. My dad said he didn't want me to grow up without a father, but with the way their marriage was, it wasn't much different."

"How so?"

"He traveled for work. A lot. He was often out of town, and when he was in town, they fought or ignored each other. I tried to play peacemaker. If they liked something I did or were both proud of an accomplishment, then I tried to keep it up. I wanted them to not have to worry about me. Grades, boyfriends, anything, as long as my parents were okay with it, then I was okay with it. They loved Stephen. He charmed my mom with his connections, and he was all buddy-buddy with my dad whenever he was in town. They both kept telling me to get married and settle down. I thought having Stephen and being in a steady relationship would mean they wouldn't worry about me growing up lonely or alone."

"What did they say when you two ultimately broke up?"

She chuckled darkly. "That's the funny thing. They

were indifferent. Daddy said as long as I'm happy he's happy, and Mom said she never liked him and only put up with him because she knows I like to live life on my own terms. That's when I really learned I had to stop living for my parents."

The bitterness in her voice surprised him. On the outside, Ashiya and her parents seemed like the stable members of the Robidoux family. Now that he thought about it, he didn't see her dad around except at occasional family events, and he didn't stick around long. George and Elizabeth Waters put on a good show of being happy, and Ashiya, always the perky, happy and slightly mischievous member of the family, never seemed to show any hints of being unhappy.

She glanced up at him. "Do you know why I don't like being alone in new places?"

He shook his head. He knew she didn't like sleeping in strange places, but assumed it was like most people who were uncomfortable with unfamiliar surroundings. Admittedly her need for sleeping pills just to sleep in the house she inherited was still a surprise to him.

She downed the rest of her wine and took a deep breath. She put the glass on the table and faced him. "Because I was locked in a basement for an entire weekend when I was eleven." She rushed on before he could ask a question. "My parents were fighting. We had to make an appearance at one of those home shows for a restored home. I arrived with my mom, but my dad was supposed to take me home. Mom wanted me to leave with her because Elaina had some recital or something the next day. They fought, and Mom thought Dad was taking me, and Dad thought he was doing right by letting Mom take me." Her voice shook, and she wrapped her arms around herself. "One of the kids at the party locked me in the basement when we were playing hide-and-seek. I kept waiting for someone to find me, but I fell asleep. The kid didn't tell anyone I was there, the house wasn't occupied, and my parents didn't realize neither had me until two days later."

Russell slid across the couch and tried to pull her into his arms. "Ashiya."

She shook her head. "It's okay," her voice trembled. She cleared her throat and spoke again in a steadier voice. "I mean, the situation was fucked up, but I'm okay. Okay enough that I can at least fall asleep in a strange place if I take sleeping pills. Still not so good with being alone in enclosed spaces, as you saw the other night in the kitchen."

"I'm sorry."

She rubbed her temples before running her fingers through her hair. "Yeah, me too. My mom blamed Dad. Dad blamed Mom. Neither admitted that they were too petty to check with the other one to make sure their child was safe. Which is why, as much as I don't want to believe it, I could see my mom keeping my grandmother away from me out of spite." More bitterness crept into her voice. Bitterness coated in sadness.

Russell rubbed his hand up and down her arm. The gesture was little comfort for knowing your parents' fight and pride resulted in being trapped and alone for two days, but he didn't know what else to do. He'd always assumed Ashiya being spoiled and doted on by her parents was one of the reasons she kept so much of herself locked away. Now he wondered if years of being rejected and sidelined by the very people who should have protected her made her wary of letting people close.

"Are you going to ask your mom about your grandmother reaching out to you?" he asked in a soft voice.

She threw up a hand. Her brows drew together. "Does it even matter anymore? I have the inheritance. I don't have to rely on either of my parents for anything ever again. Why should I care what my mother's reasons were?"

"The same reason you care that they let pettiness keep you trapped in the basement of a strange home for days. Even if they never apologize or acknowledge what they did, you have a right to let them know they hurt you. It's okay to let them know how you feel."

Ashiya met Russell's earnest gaze. Even if the hurt was unintentional or the blows weren't meant for her, Ashiya was injured in her parent's ongoing fight. She'd never once considered going to her parents with her grievances. That's the way things were in her family. Everyone ignored or covered up the things that were unpleasant or unpretty. She hadn't wanted to burden them further by letting them know how much their bickering, fighting and one-upmanship affected her.

"Telling them ruins everything," she admitted.

"Ruins what?"

"The image that I'm strong and independent. That I've found my own way without being influenced by the demands of being a perfect member of the Robidoux family or letting my dad know him not being around hurt me just as much as it hurt my mom. I don't want them to know that."

Russell shifted forward and squeezed her arm. "Why not?" His voice wasn't judgmental or accusatory, just curious and supportive.

"Because I don't want to add to their guilt. They know. I can see it in their eyes whenever I walk into a room when they're fighting. They both tried so hard to make things right after leaving me in that house for the weekend. I know that they know how upset I was, but talking about it forces us to admit our mistakes. Forces us to deal with the pain we've spent years avoiding."

Russell's hand slid down her arm. He laced their fingers together. "All I'm saying is that if you want an answer from your mom, go for it. Don't feel bad about asking for a reason she kept you from your grandmother. Ask your dad why he allowed your mom to keep the feud going if he knew about it. You don't have to feel guilty for doing either of those things. It's okay to show them how you feel."

Ashiya imagined having the difficult conversation with her family, and her stomach churned. Emotions, especially the messy ones, were not things she was comfortable with. Everything about her upbringing contradicted the idea that showing your true self helped any situation.

But when she looked into Russell's eyes and saw the compassion reflected there, she wondered if she could open herself up to him. "What about you?" she asked. "Is it also okay to show you how I feel?"

He glanced away, and her heart sank. Her suspicions were confirmed with that avoidance of her gaze. He didn't want to deal with all of her problems either.

Ashiya reached for her wineglass, then stood. "I need a refill. Do you want anything?" She walked to the door without waiting for an answer. She'd hoped the night before meant the start of a second chance. The doubts and concerns that drove her to leave the house early that morning rushed back. She'd almost forgotten her worry that he'd claim them being together again was a mistake.

Russell's footsteps followed her into the kitchen. She went to the wine fridge and opened it. "I bought this new wine Brianna told me about. The winery owners are Black women, and the wine is really good. I'll pour you a glass."

Russell's strong chest pressed into her back. The spicy scent of his cologne mixed with the delicious smell that only belonged to him wrapped around her. Heat spread deep in her midsection as his large body overshadowed her. His arms wrapped around her waist and hugged her close.

"Why did you leave me behind this morning?" His low, rumbling voice was like lighter fuel to the desire pulsing in her body.

"I had to get to work," she said in a soft voice.

He pulled her tighter against him. "You work with me. Instead, you left me behind. I woke up and reached for you, and you weren't there."

She sucked in a breath. "You reached for me?"

His lips hovered right over her ear. "I never stopped reaching for you. The only difference is this time you were supposed to be there beside me." His warm breath tickled her ear, sending goose bumps across her skin.

Ashiya bit her lower lip. "Why?" Hope squeezed and twisted her heart, extracting every ounce of anticipation from her in the one breathless word.

"Why what?"

"Why did you never stop reaching for me?"

He didn't answer. He kissed her ear before slowly running his tongue over the sensitive outer shell. "I wanted you beside me this morning." The whispered confession was followed by his teeth gently nipping against her ear.

Ashiya's nipples tightened, and need burned hot in her veins. "You didn't regret the night before or think that we made a mistake? I thought leaving was doing you a favor."

"You were avoiding me?"

She spun around and stared into his eyes. He hadn't answered her question, but if he was willing to admit that he wanted her beside him in bed, then she was going to press until he admitted why.

"Yes. Because I couldn't take you rejecting me again after what happened last night. I couldn't bear to see regret or, worse, disgust in your eyes. I messed up before, and I want you back. I want *us* back. I couldn't get my hopes up only to have you dash them into smoke while my body still trembled from every touch, squeeze, and kiss you gave me the night before."

His eyes burned into her. The fight in his gaze something she'd seen in the three years since she'd ruined their relationship. The fight that told him to pull away instead of accepting what was between them. He wanted her to surrender on his terms, but she couldn't let him have everything his way. Yes, she'd fucked up, but he wanted her too. If he was going to touch her, look at her that way, then he had to admit that he wanted them back together.

"Why do you still reach for me, Russell?" Her voice was low but demanding. "Why didn't you want to let me go?"

His gaze dropped to her mouth. "Last night reminded me of the way things were."

She pressed forward until her breasts were flat against his chest. This time her hand grabbed his waist and pulled him against her. "Was it a mistake? Do you regret what happened? Are you going to eventually say that we can't be together again?"

Russell's brows drew together. She pulled her lower lip between her teeth and slowly let it slip out. Desire burned hot in his eyes. The growing length of his erection pressed between them.

Ashiya didn't let up. "Why do you still reach for me?"

His eyes met hers, and his body shivered. "Because I

can't get you out of my mind. I fucking hate it. You broke my heart. You hurt me more than anyone ever has, but fuck, Ashiya, I can't forget you."

His head lowered, and his lips took hers in a hard kiss. His ragged confession tore her to pieces. She might not deserve the second chance, but she'd be damned if she let it go by. Ashiya's arms wrapped around his neck, and she lifted on her toes. Her lips parted and gave his tongue access to her mouth. The kiss was hot, raw, and driven by their need.

His large hands gripped her hips and held her firmly. His hold on her was tight and demanding, as if he were afraid she'd slip between his fingers. He didn't have to worry about that. If Russell was going to hold on to her now, she'd never let go. She wrapped one leg around his, opening her thighs so that the heat of her sex could get closer to the tempting press of his erection. She was close, but not close enough.

He lifted her hips. Ashiya jumped, and her legs wrapped around his waist. His hard dick pressed right in the slick junction of her thighs. That was so much better. She hadn't worn panties after showering and put on the light sundress to lounge around in. Yes, a part of her had hoped he would come home, want her, and notice her lack of underwear. Now, with the front of his pants brushing against the aching swell of her clit, none of her ulterior motives mattered.

Russell moved away from the counter. She thought he would take her to the bedroom, but instead he crossed the room to the wooden table in the kitchen and sat her on the edge of the cool, hard surface. Their mouths didn't part as he rewarded her again with a sexy kiss. His long fingers slid up her thigh in a light, teasing touch that stopped right at the edge of her dress. She squirmed on the table.

"Keep going up," she panted against his lips.

She felt his smile against her lips. "Why?" His fingers inched up a few delicious centimeters.

"You'll find out why if you listen to me." She grabbed his face and pulled him forward for another hard kiss.

His hands took their sweet time slowly getting closer, closer, and closer to the wetness between her legs. She was so damn wet. So damn needy, and if he didn't touch her she was going to explode. Finally, his fingers slid across the slick outer lips of her sex.

He groaned against her mouth. "No panties."

"You know I don't like wearing them at night."

"And you know what the thought of you in no panties does to me." He stepped back to shove up the edges of her dress.

Ashiya's legs opened wider for his view. She loved the way his body shook whenever he got a good look at her wet folds. "I think I may have forgotten?" she said in a teasing voice.

He cocked a brow. "Your ass didn't forget."

No, she hadn't forgotten. She couldn't get a single thing about him out of her mind. That's how she'd known that even if she'd moved on, met someone else, and eventually been happy with a new person, she still would have a soft spot for Russell. No matter what happened in her life, he was the one she'd always regret losing and secretly yearn for.

"Remind me." She didn't care that her voice trembled with a plea.

He grabbed her legs and pushed them wider. Ashiya grinned, then gasped at the raw hunger in his face. She leaned back on her elbows. Russell put one of the chairs between her spread legs, and then his lips and oh-so-skill-ful tongue were there. Licking perfectly, sucking just right, nibbling in every way she liked. Her head fell back, and her mouth fell open.

He gripped the outsides of her thighs, and pushed up and out so that he could get even deeper. His stiff tongue drove inside her, and Ashiya's cry of pleasure bounced off the stainless-steel appliances. His mouth took her to the edge and then backed out until she whimpered and begged him for more. Tightness drifted up from her toes, calves and thighs and culminated in her midsection. His lips slowed, and his tongue laved lazily right before his teeth gently slid across her aching clit. The tightness snapped free, and her orgasm exploded through her body. Her hand slapped the table and her throat hurt from her raw, uninhibited cry.

When she could finally catch her breath, she pushed herself up on the table. Russell watched her. Desire, satisfaction and a hint of adoration were written all over his face. He'd unbuttoned his pants and pushed them down around his ankles. One hand stroked up and down the hard length of his dick. Ashiya's body, and heart, trembled. There was nothing she wouldn't do to always have this man in her life, looking at her, and loving her like this.

She slid off the table, onto his lap, her legs straddling his thighs. She placed her hands on his cheeks and kissed him long and deep. The taste of her mingled with him. She would never get tired of that flavor. He stood and sat her back on the table. Her legs spread and she shifted forward. Then Russell pushed inside her.

Her nails dug into his shoulder. "Oh God," she moaned.

"Not God. Just Russell," he said in that sexy, confident way he had whenever they made love. His hips pulled back, then pushed in.

Ashiya met his thrust with one of her own. "Never just Russell."

He thrust in again, and her eyes rolled to the back of her head. His urgency from earlier was gone. He took on a steady rhythm that slowly built her desire all over again. Until she moaned and gripped at him as if he were her only lifeline to the world. When her desire was at his height again, his pace quickened. He always did that. Waited for her to catch up before taking them both over the edge. With one arm around his neck and his hands clutching her waist, they matched rhythm. Their eyes locked on each other. The connection, the feel of him deep, so deep inside her, and the happiness of knowing he was back with her, that they were back together, were almost too much for her to handle. Her orgasm started low and slow. Russell's eyes lit up, his thrusts turned fast and hard, and he stiffened, then released inside her just as she crashed over.

"Oh my God, Russell, I love you!"

His body froze. Ashiya's eyes clenched closed. She couldn't look at him. She'd seriously fucked up the mood.

CHAPTER TWENTY

SEVERAL DAYS LATER, Ashiya sat in the executive conference room at the Legacy Group, frowning at the latest profit report for the new shampoo the company released the previous quarter. Though the profits were above the projections, there was still something about the numbers that threw her.

"We lost a lot of money on the packaging," she said. She looked up from the report to Russell sitting across from her at the gleaming table. Whenever they came into the office, he opted for his suit, and Ashiya spent a good portion of the day imagining peeling every conservative layer off him the moment they got home.

"That's not the only placc," Russell said. "There was also a loss in a couple of areas during production, but because the overall production costs came in at budget, it's easy to overlook."

Brianna sighed and leaned forward in her chair next to Ashiya. "Which means whoever was skimming money is getting bolder."

Ashiya looked back at the numbers before her. "And getting sloppier. Before, the money that was taken wasn't easily seen. Now it's as if the person feels bold."

"Or desperate," Levi said from his chair next to Russell.

Ashiya met Russell's gaze. The grim look in his eyes reflected how she felt. The person responsible either knew they were on to them and was trying to go out with one last hurrah or felt the change in leadership was too inept to realize what was happening. Neither was a good situation.

Ashiya slapped the report down on the table in front of her. "I want to find out who's behind this, and I want to know in a week. I don't like being played for a fool. It's bad enough this happened before when my grandmother was in charge, but I won't let it keep happening under my watch."

Levi's hand tightened into a fist on the table. "I should have caught it sooner. I trusted your grandmother when she said the financial reports were good."

"The reports were good," Ashiya countered. "It's the backup reports that weren't. I know you don't want to hear it, but we can't ignore the fact that someone on your team is behind this."

Levi's dark eyes gleamed defensively. "I trust my team."

Russell turned to Levi. "Trusting your team is great, but you can't deny what's in front of you. Your group reconciles the reports. Someone either noticed what was happening and said nothing or didn't realize what was happening. Either way, we can't keep this up."

Levi jerked on his suit jacket. "Are you questioning my integrity?"

Russell shook his head. "No, but I am stating what you may not want to face. You're too close to the people on your team."

Levi's jaw tightened. Over the past few days, she'd witnessed how much pride Levi had in his employees and his dedication to the company. She didn't believe he was behind the embezzlement, but his trust in the people he worked with might have blinded him to the subtle stealing under his nose.

She spoke up before he could argue back at Russell.

"It's time to have one-on-one talks with the people over-seeing production and marketing. We need details on the losses and why they happened." Ashiya met Levi's frustrated stare. "Russell and I can do it under the guise of new ownership coming in. We don't know everyone and are more likely to notice if something is off."

"I want to be involved," Levi said. "I want to catch this person just as much as you do." The edge in his voice was hard and determined. Ashiya almost would have felt sorry for the person who'd deceived him, if they weren't skimming thousands of dollars from the company.

"We'll find the person, or persons, behind this. Don't worry," she said.

Brianna glanced at her watch, then at them. "It's lunchtime. We all should eat." Her eyes darted to Levi before coming back to Ashiya.

It was well past lunch, and Ashiya's stomach was about to protest. "Sure. How about I order something?"

Russell waved a hand. "No need. I'll go pick something up. Any preference?"

After a brief discussion of options, they settled on sub sandwiches. Russell wrote down what everyone wanted and left without giving her a backwards glance. Ashiya fought not to follow him out of the room. He hadn't officially agreed to getting back together, but he hadn't opposed it either. Even though she was living her fantasy and peeling off his clothes as soon as they got home every night, since their encounter in kitchen, she could tell he still held back a piece of himself.

It was the "I love you." Those three little words that had ruined perfectly fine relationships since humans created words of affection. Why had she said that? And right after sex, no less? It was too much too soon. She knew she wanted Russell now and forever, but he was just getting used to the idea of them being back together after she'd obliterated his heart before.

Levi stood after Russell left to pick up lunch. "I've got to make some phone calls before my next meeting."

Brianna sat forward, concern in her eyes and her voice when she spoke. "Aren't you going to eat?"

"I will when the food gets here," he replied.

Brianna pointed a finger at him. "I'll bring it to you. You will eat," she said in a stern voice.

Levi's lips lifted in a half smile. "You're just as mean as Melissa. Fine, bring the sandwich. I'll eat."

Brianna's lips pressed together as if she were suppressing a smile, and she nodded. After he walked out, Ashiya turned to her. "How do you do it?"

Brianna's brows drew together. "Do what?"

"Love him like that but not go after him? I don't understand."

Brianna blinked, and the sparkles in her eyes from her low-key flirting with Levi were hidden as her professional demeanor dropped down like a curtain. "I don't love Levi. We're just colleagues and friends."

"Oh no. You're crazy about him. How do you do it? I barely worked with Russell a week before spilling my feelings. You've worked with Levi longer."

Brianna snapped and pointed at her, her eyes bright with an aha gleam. "Even before that kiss I knew there was something between you two."

"There's too much between us. We dated three years ago, but things didn't work out. I wasn't sure if we'd ever get together again, but for whatever reason, he's softened a little."

If letting her in his bed without promises of tomorrow was softening, then she was taking it. Every day she yearned for the full warmth he'd had for her before, but was afraid that if she pushed too hard, he'd only retreat. Which was why blurting out that she loved him during sex was the wrong thing to do. She'd once again expected a talk about them moving too fast, or making a mistake, but no talk had come. He'd just acted as if she hadn't said anything. The words drifted away like lint in a breeze. Small, insignificant and easily forgotten.

"You two are dating?"

Ashiya lifted a shoulder and straightened the papers in front of her. "Kinda."

"Sleeping together, then," Brianna said knowingly.

Ashiya nodded. "That was never a problem between us."

Brianna shook her head. "That's why no matter how I may feel about Levi, I won't do that," she said with conviction. "I can't sleep with a man I know doesn't feel anything for me."

"He likes you," Ashiya argued. Brianna was one of the few people who made Levi sort of smile, and he listened to her opinion.

"Yeah, because he's known me for a long time, and I worked closely with your grandmother. Would he sleep with me? Probably, but that's all it would be. Sex, and I can't set my heart up to be broken like that."

"But sometimes just sex turns into more," Ashiya said confidently.

Brianna gave Ashiya a girl-have-you-lost-your-mind look. "That stuff only happens in books and movies. In real life, the guy who is emotionally unavailable and in love with someone else doesn't fall for the other women he lets in his bed in the meantime."

Ashiya's eyes widened. "He's in love with someone."

"Yep. Loved her for years and tried to be honorable and let the guy who was 'right for her' have her." Brianna made air quotes. "Now she's on the brink of divorce with that guy, and Levi pretends like he doesn't care, but he does. I know a lost cause when I see one. I'm not one of those women who believe the power of my coochie will change a man."

Ashiya flinched even though the words weren't aimed as a direct insult to her. Still, they hurt. She was hoping that rekindling their sex life would be enough to make Russell realize they belonged together. Was she just being foolish? Would he get his fill of her and then move on, leaving her heartbroken?

The door to the conference room slammed open. Ashiya and Brianna both jumped as a furious Melissa burst into the room. She pointed at Ashiya.

"How dare you try to connect me to something that I have nothing to do with!"

RUSSELL RETURNED FROM the sandwich shop next door and knew something was wrong the second he stepped out of the elevator. Not many people had offices on the executive level, but those who did stood in the hallway with pensive expressions and stared in the direction of the conference room. Immediately, his steps quickened. He'd prepared himself to, once again, remind Levi that Ashiya could fire him at any time she saw fit. Though her cousin was helping her and was cooperating with the investigation, Russell didn't miss the way Levi's jaw tightened or the thinly veiled frustration that took hold of his voice whenever Ashiya questioned one of his decisions. He hadn't stepped in or called him on it because Levi seemed to accept the fact that Ashiya wasn't going anywhere, but he'd also expected things to come to a head.

He was not prepared to walk in and find Ashiya and Melissa in the middle of a heated argument. Brianna stood between them with her arms up as if to keep them from lunging at each other. Russell dropped the bag of sandwiches on the table and rushed to Ashiya's side.

"What's going on?" he asked.

Melissa's eyes narrowed in on him. "You know exactly what's going on."

Russell's head jerked back. How in the world was he supposed to know the reason for this? Melissa hadn't been involved with their meetings this week, and he'd been happy to avoid seeing her.

Ashiya answered for him. "Melissa came here to accuse us of slander." She crossed her arms beneath her breasts and twisted her lips. She looked Melissa up and down as if she were a rat who dared to invade their space. "To me it sounds like she has something to hide."

Russell turned back to Melissa. They'd kept the investigation into the embezzlement to themselves because they didn't want to tip off whoever was behind it. Now that the person grew bolder, time was of the essence to clean out the bad people at the Legacy Group. This morning, Levi had taken the realization hard that someone underneath him was intentionally hiding the siphoning of funds. He hoped Levi hadn't mentioned their concerns to Melissa, and she took that as slander on her name.

"What type of slander?" he asked, keeping his voice calm. He needed to find out what she knew before revealing anything.

Melissa pointed a red painted nail at his chest. "I had nothing to do with whatever happened to your brother. Stop sending people to check into my past as if I did something. I told you already that I barely knew or remember him."

Her words slammed into him like an unexpected punch. Fast and clumsy but with enough power to knock the breath from him. Russell took a step back and tried to catch up with what was going on. "What does this have to do with my brother?"

Melissa's blue eyes were like glaciers. "You've got a private investigator knocking on my parents' door, asking questions about me and a spring break party from years ago. That's what I'm talking about."

Russell took a long breath as his brain caught up. He'd called Jeanette the day after Ashiya mentioned her willingness to help. She'd expected his call and immediately put one of her investigators on the case. She'd asked if he wanted her to keep the investigation private, and he'd refused. He didn't care whose feelings got hurt or feathers got ruffled as he searched for the truth. Fifteen years with no word on what happened to his brother was too long to care about the sentiments of anyone who might have been at that party and seen something but not said anything.

"No one is accusing you or your parents of anything," Russell said, barely managing to reign in his frustration. "I'm only trying to find answers."

Melissa looked at him as if he'd called her an idiot. "At my parents' house? They know even less about your brother or that party."

"But the party was hosted at their home," Russell said.

"They weren't there," Melissa shouted back.

Russell took a deep breath to calm his frustration and stop himself from lashing back at Melissa. "Not being there doesn't mean they might not have heard anything afterwards or noticed anything. No one is accusing you or your family. We're just trying to find answers."

Ashiya stepped forward, her arms still crossed, and glared at Melissa. "Exactly. So again, why are you so defensive if you don't have anything to hide?"

Melissa pressed a hand to her forehead and took several slow breaths. When she looked at them, anger still burned in her eyes, but her words were calm. "My parents didn't know about the party. They didn't know about half of the stuff I got into when I was in college. Your investigation means that now I have to deal with a guilt trip over a decade in the making. They say they can't trust me anymore and are refusing to speak to me. So, while you may not be accusing us of anything, you have caused a rift in my family that didn't have to be there."

Ashiya held up a hand. "Hold up. Wait a second. You're in here tearing my head off because your parents got mad at you for a party you held in secret years ago?"

"Yes, and while it might seem trivial to you, it's not to me. I rely on my parents a lot. I never gave them a reason not to trust me, and this revelation blew a huge hole in our relationship."

Ashiya scoffed and rolled her eyes. Russell put a hand on her shoulder. He appreciated her willingness to fight for him. Maybe more than he should, but like the three words she'd uttered a few days ago, he wasn't going to get into that or explore his feelings more. Right now, he had to deal with Melissa.

"Look," he said, trying to sound somewhat empathetic even though he didn't give a damn about Melissa's relationship with her parents. "I'm sorry about what's going on with you and your parents, but I'm not going to stop my investigation into finding out what happened to my brother. I'm going to keep digging and ask a hundred thousand times if I have to. You have a rift that can be fixed because your parents are still here for you to work things out. The rift in my family can never be repaired as we don't know what happened to my brother."

Melissa let out a huff. "Fine. I can't stop you from looking. I get that. Just remember that when you go digging up the past, you may also cause problems for others."

"I don't give a damn about those problems. I only care about finding out what happened to Rodrick," he said, his voice unflinching and his gaze unwavering from hers.

Her lips pressed into a tight line. Something flashed in her eyes. Maybe a challenge. He had a feeling all pretense of being nice and professional with him was gone after today.

"And also remember," Ashiya said smugly, "that while Levi is still the CEO, *I'm* majority shareholder of the company you work for. Levi may be able to shelter you some, but if you ever come at me like that again, I will not only fire your ass, but I'll make sure you never work for any major corporation in this state."

Ashiya's voice turned cold and calculating, her eyes hard with challenge. The quirk of her brow dared Melissa to argue back. If anyone on the Robidoux side of the family thought Ashiya hadn't picked up on their ruthlessness, then seeing her now would prove them all wrong. Seeing her so enmeshed in her role as the owner of the company poked the emotion he was ignoring in his chest and made him want to kick Melissa and Brianna out the room, put Ashiya on the conference table, and fuck her until they were both breathless.

Melissa's eyes widened, and her shoulders straightened. His declaration had made her mad, but Ashiya's words reminded her of her position. She nodded stiffly. "You're right. I apologize."

"I suggest you get back to work," Ashiya said haughtily.

Levi came to the door then, his brow furrowed and confusion in his eyes. "What going on? Did I miss something?"

Brianna shook her head and let out a humorless chuckle. "*Now* you show up."

CHAPTER TWENTY-ONE

AFTER DEALING WITH Melissa's meltdown, interrogating employees at the Legacy Group, and tap-dancing around the issue of where her relationship with Russell stood, Ashiya was more than happy to go home and be around the family she was familiar with. She didn't have to return for the fundraiser for one of the organizations her cousin Byron supported as the mayor of Jackson Falls, but Ashiya needed the break and the reassuring dose of being surrounded by people who cared for her.

The party was the usual thing. All the most important people in Jackson Falls along with clients and business partners from the state enjoying delicious food and expensive liquor at the sprawling Robidoux estate. Even though each one of her Uncle Grant's children had their own place, when it came time to raise money or show off their influence, the event would be held on the grounds of the estate the family had built to show how they'd turned a sharecropping legacy into a massive empire.

Ashiya mingled with the crowd and accepted the condolences that were quickly given before the person changed the subject to the real reason they suddenly decided to pay attention to her. Her inheritance. She'd expected some curiosity, but not the way almost everyone at the party wanted a piece of her. She'd intentionally tried to be the least influential Robidoux family member, and in one quick twist of fate, she was now the one most talked about. Even Elaina, who had warmed up to her a bit in the past few years but was by no means her bestie, made a point to slip her arms through Ashiya's and introduce her to several business associates.

An hour and a half into things and Ashiya was ready to go home.

She spotted India crossing the decorated backyard toward the back of the house and made her way to her cousin and best friend.

Ashiya slid up next to India and took her hand in hers. "Where are you going? Please tell me it's someplace quiet and away from all this."

India grinned and laughed. Her cousin looked radiant in a teal cocktail dress. The sleeveless floral lace bodice and flowing skirt that stopped above her knees looked flirty and comfortable.

"Tired already?" India asked with a teasing smile. "I thought you'd like to be the belle of the ball."

Ashiya shook her head. "Not at all. I miss my store, my own bed, and being known as Elizabeth Waters's daughter at these things. Now everyone wants to gawk at the newly interesting member of the Robidoux family."

"You're the owner of a Fortune 500 corporation now. Get used to the attention."

That was just it. Everything in her life had changed, and it all was happening way too fast for her. She wasn't so much worried about running the company anymore. The more she worked with Levi, the more she realized the two of them could make the Legacy Group even more successful. She was starting to like being tied to the company her dad was denied and reconnecting with the family she'd never known. What made her nervous now was seeing the way people suddenly found respect for her just because of what she had. She wasn't ready to deal with that.

"I don't think I'll ever get used to the attention." She glanced across the yard. Elaina, who stood next to a guy Ashiya didn't recognize, pointed in their direction. She was about to be introduced to someone else she didn't want to know. "Where are we going? I'd love a moment of quiet to catch up."

India glanced toward the back of the house, then at Ashiya. She bit the corner of her lip. "Well... I was going to the upstairs family room."

"Good. I'll go with you. There's so much I need to tell you." Ashiya pulled India in that direction.

India hesitated long enough to stop her. "Um... Travis is waiting for me up there. He promised to rub my feet. I may not be pregnant anymore, but my feet still swell up and hut whenever I wear heels."

Ashiya looked down at India's feet in cute but practical black pumps. Disappointment and, she hated to admit, a hint of jealousy twisted around her stomach. She and Russell and barely spoken at the party.

"Oh...well, I don't want to intrude," she said.

"Oh no, you won't be intruding. Come on. As long as you don't mind talking while he massages my feet. I know he won't mind." India headed toward the house and pulled Ashiya along.

Ashiya reluctantly followed. She did mind. She wanted to talk to India alone. She needed to talk to someone about everything going on with her. Especially about what to do with Russell. India didn't know about her relationship with Russell, or how terribly it ended. She wouldn't judge Ashiya, but she would tell her honestly if she was being stupid for sleeping with him again without defining what they were doing.

Russell had attended the party, and just like before, they'd pretended not to be together. Other than a quick hello when they were in the same group, there was nothing else. No secret glances. No stolen kisses in the shadows. No accidental touches as they walked by each other. Before, when she'd insisted they didn't do any of that when they were around her family, it was because she hadn't wanted to deal with the judgment of her family when she and Stephen ultimately reconciled. Now it made her stomach twist into a dozen knots. She'd treated Russell so badly when they were together.

Inside the house, Ashiya spotted her mom going toward the kitchen. She let go of India's hand and pointed in her mom's direction when India gave her a curious look.

"I'll come up in a minute. I need to ask Mom something," she said.

"Sure. See you in a bit," India said before hurrying toward the stairs to the private rooms of the family.

India didn't give her a backwards glance. Ashiya didn't have anything to ask her mom. She just didn't want to be the around a happy couple when she was in a dubious relationship.

Her mom spotted her and extricated herself from a group with Camille Ferguson and her mother to cross the room to Ashiya.

"Ashiya, come with me. There's something I need to show you," her mom said as if she'd been waiting weeks to talk with Ashiya.

"Sure." Ashiya glanced at Camille eyeing them with interest before quickly following her mom out of the sitting area to the quieter, empty study.

As soon as the door was closed, her mom sighed and rolled her eyes. "That Camille is just as aggravating as her mother. I thought I'd have to stab myself in the eye with a fork to finally get them to let me loose."

Ashiya chuckled and plopped down in the leather sofa. "I needed a break, too. If Elaina shows me off to one more business associate I just have to know, I'm going to be joining you in the fork eye assault."

Elizabeth shook a finger and crossed the room to Ashiya. The light in the room sparkled off the sequins on her mom's navy sheath dress, making Elizabeth look both elegant and dazzling at the same time. "What Elaina is doing is different. I told you years ago that you needed to cultivate your network. If you'd done that before instead of focusing on that little store, you wouldn't be bothered tonight."

The moment of camaraderie with her mom withered away. Ashiya pressed a hand to her forehead and took a fortifying breath. "My little store is the one thing that gave me sanity in the middle of all this Robidoux pomp and circumstance. Not only that, but I turned it into a very profitable business. Lindsey even mentioned the possibility of opening another location."

Ashiya checked in with Lindsey weekly to see how things were going. Not surprisingly, the store continued to run smoothly in Ashiya's absence. She'd known Lindsey was capable, but it was a huge relief to not have to worry about Piece Together while she learned the ropes at the Legacy Group.

"Why bother?" Elizabeth said as if expanding the store was one of the most outlandish things she'd heard all night. "You're the head of the Legacy Group now. I can understand you might care because you started there, but don't let what's-her-name distract you from the big picture."

"Her name is Lindsey, and she's worked there with me from the start. You've met her dozens of times, and she even came to one of these ridiculous functions with me." Irritation filled Ashiya's tone. Her teeth clenched, and her fist pressed into the cushion next to her.

"Don't get so upset, Ashiya. I know the girl's name. I like her, and I like her loyalty to you even more. That's something you can buy but not necessarily keep."

"Everything is about buying and selling and loyalty with you."

Elizabeth gave her a so-what brow raise. "You know that. Why are you getting upset about it now?"

"Because you talk about that and using every advantage given to you, but you don't play by the same rules."

Her mom crossed her arms and eyed Ashiya skeptically. "For example?" she said in a matter-of-fact tone.

Instead of defending herself, her mom always pushed Ashiya to come with evidence. And recent evidence at that. If she stuttered or didn't have a comeback, then her mom moved on and ignored the original complaint.

Ashiya stood and placed her hands on her hips. Her mom's dismissive expression and tone snapped something deep inside Ashiya. Something she'd held back for years because she didn't want to make things messy for others, even though keeping her thoughts inside made things messier for her.

"For example, if you really believed that, then you wouldn't have kept me from my grandmother when she wanted to get to know me. Why would you do that when you wanted the connection with the Legacy Group so bad you even married Dad when you didn't love him?"

Elizabeth watched her for ten long seconds before she finally answered. "Because she disrespected me and didn't deserve you."

Ashiya's arms dropped to her sides. Her lips parted with her surprised gasp. "Say what?"

Elizabeth continued in a defensive tone. "Your grandmother. She called me a gold digging whore who bewitched her son. I didn't like that."

Ashiya couldn't believe the words coming out of her mother's mouth. "You're the one who told me that if I wanted to get more, I sometimes had to deal with people I didn't like. Letting me get to know her would have gotten you the Legacy Group."

"Keeping you away from her prevented her from turning you against me, and you still got the Legacy Group. I don't see what the problem is," Elizabeth said as if this conversation wasn't even worth having.

Ashiya stared at her mom. As much trouble as her mom put her dad through, and all of the fighting and instilling into Ashiya that her dad's family had deprived her of what she deserved, her mom had only used those words to manipulate her and her father. Pride over being called out on her very real transgressions had kept Elizabeth from accepting any chance of a reconciliation when Gloria Waters was still alive.

"She was my family," Ashiya said in a raised voice. "I would have liked to know my dad's family."

Elizabeth waved a hand and shrugged. "You're getting to know them now. Again, what is the problem?"

Ashiya scoffed and shook her head, disbelief growing into anger with each what's-wrong-with-you look from her mom. "No, you never do. You and Dad fight and ignore each other, and if I'm caught in the crossfire, then oh well. It doesn't matter."

"Crossfire? Ashiya, please."

Ashiya pointed at her mom. "It's the truth and you know it. As long as you both continue to keep your pride, you don't care if I'm hurt in the process. Or left behind."

Elizabeth's lips pressed together. Her nostrils flared with a deep breath as frustration glazed over her eyes. "Is that what this is about? The time we forgot you at that house." Her mom sounded incredulous.

Ashiya's hands balled into fists. "Don't say it as if you left me for a few hours. You left me for three days, Mom! I was locked in a basement in a strange house, alone, for two days. All because you and Dad were too busy ignoring each other to ask about your kid."

Elizabeth glanced over her shoulder quickly at the closed door. When she turned back to Ashiya, there was a hint of guilt in her eyes. "It wasn't like that," her mom snapped back.

Ashiya's anger only grew. Her mom was still more concerned about who might overhear them than Ashiya's feelings. "Then what was it like? Because I remember being down there, in the dark, and scared for those *two* days."

"Your dad insisted on taking you—"

"And you insisted that he just come home and stay with us for the night. But instead of getting on the same page, you both ignored me."

Elizabeth's jaw trembled. She shook her head in a jerky motion. "No! I wanted to give him what he wanted. I tried to make things work with your dad. I hoped he would see that, but…"

"But you both were too prideful to actually talk things out and make sure one of you actually knew what your daughter was doing." Ashiya scoffed and rolled her eyes. "I took every single emotional hit from you two. I tried to be independent and successful and happy so you wouldn't have to worry about me. I hid all the pain and took any scrap of love or affection as the standard because all I got from you and Dad was posturing and being used to hurt each other."

"Ashiya, that's not fair."

"It doesn't have to be fair to be the truth," she said in a hard voice.

Her mom's mouth snapped shut. Elizabeth's chin lifted, and even though regret hovered in her gaze, all the excuses she'd thrown out formed a layer of defensiveness and justification Ashiya wouldn't be able to break through. Not tonight. Maybe not ever.

The weight of her anger and the pain of holding it back made her shoulders slump. She didn't want to deal with her mom anymore. Didn't want to smile and network with the people outside who were suddenly interested in her because she'd inherited a fortune. Didn't want to go upstairs with India and watch as her cousin was showered with affection from her loving husband. She was so tired of it all.

Why had she thought coming back to this would make her happy? She almost longed for the judgmental looks of The Dragons, the challenge to meet Levi's expectations, and Brianna's you've-got-this attitude. At least their reactions and emotions were real and not hidden behind fake smiles and niceties. Everything here came at a price to her sanity.

"Give my best to Uncle Grant, Byron and Elaina," she said dryly. "I'm going home."

CHAPTER TWENTY-TWO

RUSSELL LOOKED AROUND at the mingling people at the Robidoux estate and sighed. He was tired, had a lot of work to catch up on from being away for so long, and would likely cut the next person who asked him if Ashiya's inheritance was really as big as everyone said.

He turned to his cousin standing next to him at the bar. "I'm going to head out."

Isaac shook his head. "Nah, man, you can't leave. We've barely been here an hour."

An hour was long enough for him. "I'm beat and I've got some things to do. Me leaving doesn't mean you have to leave. Stay. Enjoy the alcohol and the networking."

Isaac placed a hand on his arm. "You can't leave. You know these people. I don't. I need you to introduce me."

Any other day, Isaac's pleading gaze would have squeezed at least another forty-five minutes out of Russell. Today was not the day. He couldn't do this. Being around Ashiya and not letting on that they were together was a heavier burden than listening to everyone speculate about her newfound wealth. Tonight just reminded him of how superficial their relationship had been before, which only made him question his good sense for being with her again.

Russell gently pushed Isaac's hand off his arm. "I've already introduced you to all the important people. The rest is up to you. I'm going home to catch some rest."

"You sure? I saw Ashiya just go into the house. Are you chasing after her?" Isaac asked suspiciously.

Russell scowled and jerked back. "What? Man, whatever." He turned and headed toward the house before Isaac could see how close he'd come to the truth.

Isaac hurried and followed him. "Nah, what's up with that look?"

"What look?"

"The look that said you are chasing after her. What happened? I knew something was going to happen as soon as you said you were staying in the house with her."

"Nothing happened," Russell said between clenched teeth. "I told you I stayed in the house because it was easier, and I'm in a completely different wing than she's in. Believe me, there's nothing there."

The words scratched his throat like rusty barbed wire. The truth of them hurt almost more than the idea of getting clowned by Isaac for sleeping with Ashiya again. If he'd thought anything about their relationship was different, tonight proved that nothing had changed. When he'd arrived she'd given him a polite nod and hello before getting lost in the crowd. Not once after had she acknowledged him. She'd gone back into the pattern of before. Giving no indication of what was between them. He was done playing games.

Years ago, he'd fooled himself into thinking their hidden relationship was scandalous and sexy. He'd thought he'd known a secret part of Ashiya that no one else had seen. He'd relished the idea that the cute and quirky member of the Robidoux Family who everyone underestimated was really the smart, brilliant and sexy woman sharing his bed. He'd listened to other men talk about their frustration with not being able to get close to her and silently gloated that she was his and that's why their efforts were in vain.

Except he hadn't been the reason. He'd just been a distraction and prop while she got the man she really wanted to come back to her side.

He didn't know what he expected to be different this time. That she'd tell her family they were sleeping together? Out of the question. He could imagine the automatic assumptions that he was suddenly with her because of her fortune. Still, he hated being shoved back to the pretend-we-don't-know-each-other zone.

Isaac kept rambling about all the reasons he knew Russell and Ashiya would get back together along with all the reasons Russell needed to keep away from her. Every single reason was true, but that didn't stop his eyes from scanning the crowd for her on his way out. It didn't stop him from wanting to ask her how it felt going from the ignored member of an influential family to the most sought-after. It didn't stop him from wondering if she was okay.

He was a damned fool.

"Look, Isaac, I get it." Russell said once they were in the house. "You don't have to tell me over and over. I'm staying away from her. There is nothing going on between Ashiya and me except work. Now, will you please leave me alone about her?"

"Fine. Just know that I'm looking out for you. I don't want to hate on her, but she fucked you up last time. I don't want you to get caught up again."

Russell stopped and placed a hand on Isaac's shoulder. "I'm not going to get caught up with her again. I'm good. Seriously."

Isaac studied him for a few tense seconds, then nodded. As much as his cousin got on his nerves with the anti-

Ashiya talk, Russell knew he came from a place of love. He had been messed up after Ashiya broke his heart. Isaac just didn't want him hurt a second time.

The sound of heels clicking on the floor in a quick clip caught both of their attention. Ashiya hurried down the hall with long, determined strides. Her face was blank, but he noticed the way her lower lip was pulled between her teeth. A sign that she was holding back her emotions. Only Isaac next to him kept him from going to her immediately to ask her if everything was okay.

Ashiya spotted him, and her chin trembled. Russell took a step forward. Isaac held him back with one hand. Ashiya hurried across the hall and threw her arms around him. Her lips lifted, and like a magnet to metal, his were drawn to hers. The kiss lasted only a few seconds, but in those moments, he knew he would never get her out of his system.

She pulled back, her eyes shiny with tears. "Take me home."

He vaguely recognized the surprised gasp of Ashiya's mother behind them. Isaac mumbled something about Russell being stupid. There were even interested murmurs from the guests. He didn't care about any of that. The comments from others faded away. The only thing that mattered were the tears in Ashiya's beautiful hazel eyes, the plea in her voice to escape. A fierce protectiveness along with happiness that she'd come to him made him tighten his hold on her.

Russell's brushed away the tear at the corner of her eye. "Let's go."

"YOU READY TO tell me what happened?" Russell asked Ashiya later.

They'd arrived at his place, and she'd barely given him a chance to close the front door before she was pulling on his shirt and kissing him. Clothes were discarded throughout the house on the way to his bedroom. A small voice in the back of his head said he should ask more questions. That he shouldn't just fall into bed with her after she'd spent the night ignoring him. That he was once again playing the fool for a woman who said she loved him, then acted completely different. He'd almost pulled away and stopped. Almost.

When the softness of her hand wrapped around his hard dick like the warmest of gloves just as her tongue slid across his lips, he no longer cared about the reasons. He had the woman he'd wanted and craved more than he cared to admit. Ashiya was there, in his arms, in his home, and ready to fall right back into his bed.

They'd made love hard and fast. Both gripping and pulling at each other as if they'd been lost without the other. It had happened so fast, all he remembered was the softness of her skin, the oh-so-tight heat of her surrounding him, and an orgasm that drew a whimper out of him he'd be embarrassed to remember the next morning.

He lay on his back. Ashiya's head rested on his chest. One of her legs sprawled across his thighs. The top sheet and comforter were somewhere on the floor on one side of the bed. The air circulated by his ceiling fan was cool against his sweat-soaked skin, but Ashiya's body, hot and soft in his arms, made him ignore the chill.

"What happened?" she said referring to his question. "You mean other than the obvious awfulness of suddenly being sought after by the same people who ignored you before?" she said dryly. The warm caress of her breath on his chest as she spoke stirred something in his midsection. God, he'd missed having her here.

Russell rested one arm behind his head while the other

played lazily across the smooth skin of her back. "You knew that was going to happen."

"I did. People who would say hello right before their eyes drifted away to search for a more influential member of the family suddenly had plenty of time to talk with me. Now they want to know about Piece Together and when I plan to sell it now that I've inherited so much."

"Are you going to give it up?" He couldn't imagine her giving up the store. She'd worked so hard to make it profitable and was proud of it. The store was just as much a reflection of Ashiya as the Legacy Group, because she'd started it.

"No," she said as if the idea were preposterous. "I know I might not be able to give it as much attention as I used to now that I've got the Legacy Group, but I don't want to let it go. I can let Lindsey run it. I don't plan to move to Hilton Head permanently. Once things are settled, I can travel between the two."

"But it wasn't the people questioning your ability to run a small business and a large corporation, was it?"

She sighed and ran her fingers through the hair on his chest to the cross charm he wore around his neck. He loved it when she did that. "No. It was Mom. I listened to you and did what you said."

Russell shifted his head and looked down at her. "What's that?"

"I told her that leaving me alone in a strange house for three days over the weekend because she and Dad were too proud to talk to each other was wrong, and it hurt me."

"Let me guess. That didn't go over well."

"Nope. She told me I was being overdramatic. Like, seriously? Overdramatic?"

Her body and shoulders tensed. Russell ran his hand up

and down her back until her body relaxed and she let out a breath. "What brought that conversation on?"

"She was doing her usual spiel. Telling me I should be irritated about the people suddenly wanting a piece of me and that I should take advantage of every opportunity. If that's the case, then why keep me from my grandmother? Things blew up from there."

"Did she have a good reason to keep you from your grandmother?"

Ashiya's hand curled into a fist on his chest. "Pride. That's it. Just because my grandmother accused her of being a lying gold digger who got pregnant to get a chance at my dad's fortune. That's the only reason." She let out another sigh. "The thing is, Mom does love Dad. By the time she realized she loved him, he'd found out the real reason she married him."

Russell wondered if Ashiya realized she and her mom reacted the same way in relationships. Elizabeth started a relationship on false pretenses only to realize too late that she'd fallen in love. The same with Ashiya and him. Were they no better than her parents?

"Did she ever tell your dad how she felt?" Had George stayed with Elizabeth because she loved him, only to regret his decision later?

Ashiya shook her head. "Not that I know of. Mom would never admit that. My mom and Uncle Grant kind of believe love is a weakness. Even if she did, I don't know if he would believe her." Her body froze, and she sat up quickly.

Russell was so startled by the loss of her body heat and the movement that he jumped up too. "What's wrong?"

Her eyes were wide, and they stared into his, horror on her face. "That's why you didn't say anything."

"Say anything about what?"

"When I said I loved you. I messed up so much before with Stephen that you don't believe me now. That's it. Isn't it?"

Her words were dead-on. She slapped him with a truth he'd struggled with from the moment he'd kissed her again. The truth that, deep down, a part of him was still ashamed to know he'd gone back to her after she'd used him to get back the man she really loved. The man she'd loved for almost ten years. How could one year of a clandestine relationship with him really undo all of that? That's why he hadn't believed her words of love. Words she'd blurted out during an orgasm. Millions of people swore they were in love when they had sex. That didn't mean they really were.

He shifted away and looked on the floor for the covers. "I didn't say anything because I'm taking things slow."

She reached out and placed a hand on his shoulder. "Slow, because you don't trust me. It's okay. You can tell me the truth. I know what I did was wrong."

The sadness in her eyes. Borderline pity and self-doubt made something inside him snap. He jerked his shoulder, and her hand dropped.

"Stop that. Stop with the sad eyes and the *I'm so guilty* routine. I don't need it on top of everything else."

"I'm not doing a routine."

He shifted away from her in the bed. "You've done a routine from the moment we broke up. You were sorry. You know you messed up. You were wrong. I deserve better. You say all those words, but you still try to play me, Ashiya. You think I don't see it? I know you well enough to know when you're pressing my buttons. And like a dumbass, I keep falling for it. Stop that shit."

He jumped up from the bed. She scrambled off the mattress and rushed to block him from walking out of the bed-room. "Russell, wait."

He stepped back to avoid her touch. "What?" Anger, with him, with her, with his insecurities, all came out in that one word. If she gave him another hollow *I'm so sorry, I love you, please forgive me* speech, he was done. He would not become the sequel to her parents' relationship.

"I'm—" Her words cut off when he glared at her. She dropped her hands and then crossed her arms over her breasts. She looked at the floor, the wall, his stomach, then finally met his eyes. "You're right. I played with your emo-tions and wanted you to feel sorry for me."

Her honesty was the only thing that kept him from rush-ing out of the room. Still, it wasn't enough. He needed her to understand, truly understand, what he meant. "Why? Why do that to me if you claim to love me?"

"Because I don't know any other way to love. I don't know any other way to be with the people I care about. My parents were too busy fighting with each other to show me anything but how to use the other person. I know they love each other, but what kept them together was appearances and manipulation. Even when they both should have just let things go. Maybe that's why I held on to the first rela-tionship I had that felt genuine for so long. Stephen was the first person who seemed to really love me, but we did the same thing. Whenever he said he needed a break, I went along with it because I thought that would keep us together. So I dated other people, too. He'd get jealous and come running back. Just like my parents. When I met you, I didn't think I'd care. I thought we would just be another relationship I had until Stephen was ready for the break to be over. Except I let my guard down. You were so gen-uine, loving, and open with your feelings that I just responded in kind. I was myself. Before I knew it, you were in my heart, but when you believed Stephen's lies about me cheating with him and cut me off, I went back to what I knew instead of fighting for something new and scary."

She took a long, shuddering breath. "I don't know how to just be happy. How to trust the person I love will stay without a reason. Am I really enough? Just me? I wasn't even enough for my parents to remember me when I was locked in a basement."

His anger vanished, but frustration remained. He wanted to shake her parents for making her think she wasn't enough. Wanted to shake Stephen for taking advantage of that. Mostly, he wanted to shake himself for contributing as well. He couldn't do this with half of his heart. Not if he was going to ask her to do the same.

He stepped forward and placed his hands on her shoulders. "Ashiya, you're more than enough. If you haven't noticed, I'm crazy about you. But we can't be together like before. No more games. No more manipulation. No more hiding. Unless you're willing to do that for me, you need to leave now."

EVERYTHING RUSSELL ASKED for was reasonable. An emotionally stable, grown-up, and responsible relationship should be free of manipulation and games. The panic and fear swelling in her chest shouldn't be there. The fear of trusting love to be enough made her want to put on her best running shoes and get out before her heart was broken.

The growing disappointment in Russell's eyes as the silence stretched between them let her know walking away now meant she'd never get another chance. He was ready and willing, and all she had to do was be ready and willing as well. She had to believe they could get it right this time and toss out everything she ever believed or thought about how to make a relationship work.

Russell's eyes dropped from hers. He took a step back. Ashiya's heart jumped into her throat. She'd been too quiet for too long. He turned away, and she wrapped her arms around his waist. His body was stiff. Tight with tension and probably disappointment.

"Do you really want all of me?" she asked in a trembling voice.

His hand rested on her forearm. "Ashiya, that's all I've ever wanted from you."

She loosened her hold on him and shifted around to his front. "Then I'm yours. No games. No manipulation. Just me."

Her heart beat hard and fast, but she pushed aside all the worries. All the beliefs that no one would want to stick with her without incentive or coercion. She shoved out the fear that the reason he hadn't said he loved her too was that he still wasn't sure. That he was waiting to see if he could love her as she was.

Instead she focused on the happiness in the sexy brown-and-green swirl of his eyes. The way his hands gripped her hips tight. The way the tension seeped out of his body with each quick breath he took. She'd brought that joy to him, and that was more than enough for now.

Russell's head lowered, and she lifted on her toes. Their kiss was slow and deep. His lips and tongue gliding over hers in such a thoroughly decadent fashion, there was no more room for any thoughts. Only the taste of him. Filling her and drugging her with need.

Though they'd just made love, she felt more naked, more exposed now. This wasn't sex to distract, sex to deflect, or sex just for quick pleasure. He looked at her as if seeing her for the first time. Each kiss felt as if it were the start of something new.

His hands swept over and across her breasts as he led her back to the bed. His fingers gently stroking, then lightly tugging the hard tip of her nipple sent a shot of desire straight to her toes. His eyes kept coming back to hers. Checking in. Making sure she was still there with him. Witnessing the raw and open pleasure his body invoked in hers.

His fingers and sweet lips caressed, touched, and kissed every inch of her body as if he were rebranding her as his. Pleasure grew and expanded through every nerve and vein until her body trembled and she begged him for more.

By the time he settled between her legs, her sex ached for him. Russell's fingers slid across her wet, swollen folds before pressing against her clit. Ashiya's back arched, and her legs spread further.

"Please, Russell," she begged.

He didn't make her wait longer. He slid into her strong and sure. His hand pushed the hair back from her face. He rested his forehead on hers and locked eyes with her. His hips circled, and he took her body with bone-melting steady strokes. The entire time, he watched her. His demanding gaze dared her to look away.

She was open and exposed. A part of her wanted to look away. Tighten her legs around him. Pinch his nipple and take him over the edge first. Do anything to break the hold of his gaze, but she didn't. She let him see. Let him watch her own pleasure. Let him watch as he broke her down and brought her back again. He wanted her all, and Ashiya knew there was no other person she'd rather give her all to.

CHAPTER TWENTY-THREE

RUSSELL EXPECTED THE phone calls the next day which was why he cut off his cell phone after he'd woken up in the middle of the night with Ashiya in his arms. He didn't want a ringing phone with someone's unsolicited opinion or weak attempt to get the latest gossip about them on the other end to wake them early and break the magic of the night.

He drove her home right before noon. They both needed to pack and prepare to go back to Hilton Head later that day. After the week of interviews, they were beginning to get an idea of how the money was being embezzled which would bring them closer to finding the person stealing, and the plan was to push hard on Monday morning to flush out the thief.

He didn't turn his phone back on until after he'd dropped her off, showered, eaten, and finished packing the clothes he would need for the week. Immediately, the chimes and dings of text messages and voice mails assaulted his ears. The phone rang again as he pressed the button to check the messages. His cousin Isaac's number.

Russell sighed and pressed a hand to his temple. He might as well get this over with sooner rather than later. Isaac was the last person he wanted to know about him and Ashiya, but he was also his closest friend and the one person who might give him shit for his decision but eventually would accept it.

Russell took the call and brought the phone to his ear with a weary sigh. "What, man?"

"What, man? What, man?" Isaac repeated in a mocking tone. "Don't 'what, man 'me. What was that about last night? I knew you were still fucking with her. Why, man, why? Why did you go back to her? You know she's not right for you. Remember how she did you last time. What the hell is wrong with you—"

"Isaac, chill!" Russell snapped, his voice hard and laced with irritation.

"Chill? You want me to chill? Remember when I had to drag your ass upstairs and leave a bucket by your bed because you got so drunk after she went back to that guy? Remember how I had to take your phone away from you so you wouldn't call her ass and curse her out for playing you? Remember how you swore you would never talk to her again, and just the sound of her name made you punch a damn hole in your wall? Because I remember all of that, man. All of it."

"I remember," Russell shot back. He remembered every single thing. Every single second of pain after realizing the woman he'd fallen in love with hadn't loved him back.

"Oh really?" Isaac's dubious voice came through the receiver. "Because from the way her ass kissed you last night and then you damn near carried her out of there like a knight in shining armor all because her lower lip wobbled said you don't remember. All of that shit said you were back with her and were ready to make the same mistakes again."

"It's different this time." He tried to make his voice strong, confident, but Isaac's prodding of his old wounds tried to stir up some of the doubt he'd let go of the night before, when Ashiya looked him in the eyes and asked him to have all of her.

Isaac sucked his teeth. Russell could imagine his cousin shaking his head and looking at him as if he were a damn fool. He couldn't blame him. If the roles were reversed, he'd be on Isaac's case just as hard.

"Different? What makes this time different? She's no good for you, man. You need to let it go. I'm telling you—"

"Isaac, for real. Stop." Russell's voice was firm. "Look, I get it. You don't want to see me in the same situation as before. Nothing I say is going to make you believe that this time is different."

"Hell no. Not a damn thing," Isaac grumbled.

"But what you won't do is talk about her while we're together. If I'm making a mistake, time will tell, and you can call me all kinds of a fool."

"Oh, I will call you a fool," Isaac said.

Whether his decision to trust Ashiya again was right or wrong didn't matter. The decision was his to make. This time they'd entered the relationship without any pretense. If he let Isaac bash Ashiya and throw doubts on their relationship every time they talked, then he might as well say he wasn't willing to truly move on.

"Isaac, I'm serious. We're back together. We talked it out. I know I'm taking a chance, but it's my life and my choice. Unless you've got something nice to say, keep my woman's name out of your mouth."

"Oh, so now you're going to let her come between us?"

"I'll never do that. You're my family and even more, you're like a brother to me. I can't make you understand, but I hope that because you are like a brother, you'll at least respect my decision. I'll always have your back, but

I won't stand for you talking shit about Ashiya. The past is the past. Deal with the Ashiya I'm with from this day forward."

A tense, uncomfortable silence stretched. Russell could imagine his cousin's disbelieving expression. Isaac had talked so much trash about Ashiya after she'd broken Russell's heart. Russell, angry and heartbroken, had let him. He'd felt just as angry and bitter. But if he and Ashiya were going to really try to make this work, no games and no manipulation, then they needed a clean slate on both ends.

Finally, Isaac sighed. "Fine. You want to give her another try, then more power to you. You're better than me. I won't disrespect her, but I'm also not going to sit around and watch her disrespect you. I'm here for you. Not her."

"I'll take that." It was more than he would have expected from Isaac.

His cell phone beeped. He checked the screen and cringed. "Damn, man, I've got to take this call."

"Is it her?" Isaac asked as if he couldn't believe Russell would get off the phone with him for Ashiya.

Russell almost laughed. Isaac was not going to have an easy time getting used to Ashiya being back in his life. "No, this is Elaina. Let me see what she wants."

"Probably to find out why the guy who tried to date her sister is now going home with her cousin," Isaac said smugly.

"You know what, fuck you," he said with no bite. "I'll talk to you later."

He switched over the call to Elaina with the sound of Isaac's told-you-so laughter in his ear.

"Hello, Elaina," Russell said, switching to his professional voice.

"Russell," she said in the cool, clipped voice she used

whenever she was irritated with someone. "I'm going to get straight to the point. You left with Ashiya last night. Are you using my cousin to further your own goals?"

Russell blinked and held up a hand even though Elaina wasn't there. He paced the room. "Hold up, what? No, I'm not using her."

"Because if you do plan to use Ashiya, then I can't trust you as my CEO."

Russell froze, pulled the phone away to stare at the screen, then put it back to his ear. "Wait a second. You're the person who told me that helping her would convince you I'm on your side."

"Helping her make the Legacy Group strong. Even if Robidoux Holdings doesn't acquire them, it's still a strong connection to have. But last night, I saw the way she looked at you. Ashiya is in love with you. I didn't consider that when I first asked you to work with her. That was wrong of me. I won't let you use her. If all of this is just to get the CEO position, then stay in Jackson Falls, and we'll assign a consultant to help her. I'm not like my father. I don't want to use the emotions of my family members to get ahead."

The regret in Elaina's voice lowered his defenses. Maybe she really had changed and softened a bit. When she'd asked him to help Ashiya, he'd assumed Elaina was only soft where her husband Alex was concerned and was still willing to be ruthless and use any means necessary to get what she wanted in business. Now, although her voice was strong and haughty like a true Robidoux, he heard the underlying plea. She didn't want him to hurt her cousin.

"I'm not using her," Russell said, letting conviction enter his voice. "I care about her."

"I know what she did to you," Elaina said. "I know she secretly dated you to make her ex jealous. I also know she went back to that jerk for a while. You hid things at work pretty well, but I could tell you didn't realize you were on the receiving end of one of our family's machinations. I'm not excusing what she did. It was wrong, but I do believe that afterwards, she regretted it. I also saw the way she looked at you once she realized Stephen wasn't the right person for her. I'm not as close to Ashiya as India, so she won't confide in me, but that doesn't mean I won't protect her."

"You don't have to protect her from me."

"Don't lie to me. If you use this to get revenge on her, I will destroy you." The cut in Elaina's voice was as cold and precise as a surgeon's scalpel.

"I'm not afraid of anything you would do to me."

He wasn't afraid. Elaina had reach, and she could destroy his career and possibly make his life a living hell, but he'd lost so much already in his life that her threats didn't frighten him. There were things that could hurt him worse. Losing his parents, Isaac, Ashiya. If he used this opportunity to get revenge on Ashiya, he would destroy both of them in the process.

"I love her too much to hurt her like that," he confessed.

His heart pumped. The words scared him. The truth of those words had chased him like rabid bloodhounds from the moment they'd broken up. He wanted to run from them. Escape from the emotional chains that kept him bound to her. But he'd tried that. For three years he'd ducked, dodged, and dived around how he felt. He was going to trust the look in her eye, the sincerity in her voice, and the promise in her heart.

"Do you really love her?" Elaina's voice was skeptical.

He'd said it once but wouldn't repeat it. Ashiya needed to hear the words out of his mouth. Not secondhand from

Elaina. "Just know that I meant everything I said today. Ashiya cares about the Legacy Group. She's going to do great running the company, but if you want to keep the ties with her, then stop trying to push her to connect with people who've ignored her for her entire life. Let her build her own reputation. She never wanted to ride the coattails of the Robidoux Family. She might step away from you all for a while as she starts this new venture, but believe me, she'll be back. Trust her."

Elaina was quiet for several seconds. "What about you? Are you planning to continue to work for her? Are you no longer interested in the CEO position?"

Russell hadn't thought about the position in weeks. He'd hoped access to power, money and influence would give him the answers he wanted. But hiring a better private investigator hadn't resulted in new leads, and being connected to one of the most influential families in the area where his brother disappeared hadn't made anyone remember anything new. As much as the thought of never finding out what happened to Rodrick make his insides twist, he was starting to think no matter how much power he gained, he might never get the answers he wanted.

"I don't know," he answered honestly. "If it's offered, I'll consider."

"It's offered," Elaina said. "Ashiya mentioned you were helping her execute her new ideas, but that her cousin is stepping in to help. I'll give you a few more weeks, but after that I need you back here. If you want the job, then be back in Jackson Falls by the end of the month."

CHAPTER TWENTY-FOUR

ASHIYA SCANNED THE finance report in front of her and compared the numbers to the invoices for the last marketing campaign. It was the fourth time she'd gone over it in the past half hour. She was about to fire someone for embezzlement and press charges. The accusation was huge, and even though all the evidence pointed to this person, she knew she couldn't start this process unless she was entirely sure.

A hand clasped her shoulder and squeezed lightly. She put down the report and looked up into Russell's concerned eyes. "Are you ready?"

Ashiya took a slow breath. She tried to smile as she placed her hand over his but could barely muster the enthusiasm to lift her lips. Even though it had to be done, getting rid of an employee who'd been with the company for a decade wasn't something she was excited about doing.

"As ready as I'll ever be," she said.

"You've looked over the evidence a dozen times this morning, not to mention meticulously following the money trail hundreds of times during week."

"I know." She looked back at the stack of materials they'd gathered.

All of it proved the mismatched reporting of expenses and the overpayment of refunds for products and services that were claimed to not be delivered. All of it went back to one man in the finance department. A guy who'd been with the company for years. An unassuming member of the finance team who reconciled the spending for certain marketing projects and submitted the reports to Levi for final review and approval before they were given to the board of directors. He'd been steadfast, loyal, and good at his job. No one suspected he'd been the person slowly stealing money from the Legacy Group.

"What's wrong?" Russell asked.

"I know he did it. The evidence is clear."

"But?"

Ashiya shrugged. "I want to know why. He'd worked here for ten years. He was recognized, promoted, and according to his performance evaluations, he was a good worker and respected. Why did he start stealing from the company two years ago?"

"Who knows why people do the things they do?" Russell continued to gently massage her shoulders. "Greed comes in all forms. If there was a quick way to tell which person was most likely to be a crook, then life would be a lot easier."

She sighed. "I guess you're right. It just bothers me."

"I understand. This person appeared to be loyal to the company. The reason why he chose to steal doesn't matter. He did. The only things that matter now are making sure he no longer gets the opportunity and letting the rest of the staff know this type of behavior won't be tolerated."

"It won't be tolerated," she said in a determined voice. "Whatever the reason, my grandmother trusted this person. So did Levi. If we want to keep the Legacy Group as successful as it is, then we can't be tolerant. Regardless of the situation."

She closed the folder. Russell dropped his hands from

her shoulders and stepped back. Ashiya immediately missed his touch. The solving of this mystery also meant the end of needing him to stick around and help her. On their drive back, he'd mentioned that Elaina wanted him back for the CEO position. Ashiya knew how much he wanted that position. It was the only reason he'd agreed to help her in the first place. She wanted him to continue to help her at the Legacy Group, but she couldn't keep him as a consultant forever. Levi was the company CEO, and Ashiya didn't have a reason to or want to fire him.

For now, she didn't want to think about what she would do when Russell left. How that would affect their relationship. Though she didn't plan to give up Piece Together, she wanted to stay in Hilton Head longer. She had a lot more to learn about the Legacy Group and her family, and selling the house her grandmother left her was out of the question. For the foreseeable future, she'd be in South Carolina. Would she and Russell survive long-distance after just agreeing to reconcile?

That was a thought she was willing to continue to put off.

"Let's do this," she said instead of letting heavy, what-if feelings about her future with Russell take over.

"I told Levi we'll meet him in the conference room."

She nodded and picked up the paperwork. Levi had given her a vacant office in the executive suite to use. The same one her grandmother used to occupy but stopped a few years before. Ashiya liked being close to the action. She got to learn more and stay up-to-date on everything happening with the company without getting in anyone's way.

They made their way to the conference room. Levi and Melissa joined them soon after. Melissa smiled tightly and nodded at her and Russell. Ever since the confrontation about questioning her parents, Melissa had given both her and Russell a wide berth. From what Ashiya understood, Levi had also given her hell for coming at Ashiya the way she had. Ashiya still felt the woman knew more about Russell's brother's disappearance than she let on, but until the private investigators produced more concrete proof, they were at a standstill.

The four of them settled around the conference room table. Before they could start the small talk, the head of human resources entered with the culprit from finance close behind him. Danny Norris was an unassuming man. Average height, balding, with glasses and the beginnings of beer belly, Danny didn't give off the appearance of someone who would steal from the company.

His eyes scanned the room. They widened when they landed on Ashiya and Levi before darting back to Melissa. When the human resources director indicated for him to sit, he hesitated before gingerly pulling out a chair across from Ashiya.

"Mr. Norris, do you know why we're here?" Ashiya asked, getting straight to the point. She wasn't excited about firing him, but she also didn't want to drag this out unnecessarily.

"Not particularly," Danny said nervously. His gaze continued to bounce between the people in the room.

"For the past few years, there have been discrepancies related to the expenses coming out of the marketing department. The discrepancies don't match the financial report you put out quarterly. Money is missing, and we're trying to figure out why."

"You think I took it?" His voice rose to a high pitch.

"Didn't you?" Ashiya replied with a cocked brow. "Everything points to you." She spread out the information in her folder. "The funds were transferred to personnel accounts, and from there, funding in the same amount showed up in your checks as bonuses and overpayments. You also signed off on these transfers and payments. Do you deny that?"

He shoved his glasses up his nose and shook his head. "It's not what it looks like."

Levi crossed his arms and leaned back in his chair. "Then tell us what's going on, because it looks like you've embezzled funds from us for the past two years."

"It's not embezzlement," Danny said.

"Then what is it?" Ashiya asked.

"I… I just…" Danny glanced around the room. He looked first to the human resources director, then to Melissa, as if searching for a friendly face to bail him out.

"Just what?" Ashiya asked. "If you tell us what's going on, then we'll try to settle this with as little fuss as possible."

Danny's brows drew together. "What does that mean?"

"I don't want to drag this out in the media. I also don't want to paint you as a bad guy. It's obvious from your years of service that you have been a good employee for the Legacy Group up until a few years ago. I also can't allow this to slide by without letting the rest of the company know that this type of fraud won't be tolerated."

"You want to settle?" he asked hopefully. "Out of court?"

Ashiya did not want to settle out of court. She was going to press charges, and he would face all the consequences, but she didn't want what happened to turn into a media frenzy that might hurt the company's image. For now, she just wanted the answers.

She clasped her hands together, placed them on the

table, and gave Danny a small smile. "I want to get this resolved quietly."

He twisted his hands and stared at the surface of the table. "Fine. I did it."

Relief should have rushed through her, but her shoulders remained tense. This was too easy. "Why did you do it?"

Danny looked up, glanced around, then lowered his eyes again. "I had my reasons."

Levi shifted forward and glared. "What reasons?" Irritation was thick in his hard voice. "Were we not good to you? Did the company do you wrong, and you decided you wanted to get back at us?"

Danny shook his head. "No. it's not like that. I just... I..." He glanced at Russell, then Melissa, before looking back at Ashiya. "One day I saw a mix-up in the numbers. If I reported it, things would be fine, but if I didn't, then I could divert a few thousand dollars my way. I tried it and it worked. No one caught me, so I did it again. After that... I was in over my head." He lowered his voice and his head as if ashamed.

"Are you working with anyone else?" Ashiya asked.

There were several moments of tense silence before Danny shook his head. "It was just me. I kept it from my coworkers."

Ashiya let out a breath. "Then you'll be the one to pay the price for deceiving us."

LEVI AGREED TO come back to Ashiya's place with her, Russell and Brianna for a celebratory drink. to say she'd been surprised he'd agreed was an understatement. Ashiya knew the discovery of someone embezzling funds under his watch was a tremendous blow to Levi. She was glad that he'd agreed to help her find the person and that he'd softened somewhat when it came to her being involved in the decisions at the Legacy Group. He could have made her transition, and this whole process, a lot worse.

They sat outside on the patio. The late evening breeze helped with the lingering humidity in the air. Ashiya had lit the tiki torches to drive away the mosquitoes, and old-school music played quietly in the background as they talked.

Ashiya lifted the glass of wine in her hand toward Levi. "I want to thank you for all your help these past few weeks. I know you didn't want me here."

Levi raised his own glass and shrugged. "It wasn't that I didn't want you here."

Brianna laughed. "Excuse me? I'm pretty sure I remember you telling her to go back to where she came from."

Levi waved a hand. "I did, but that was only because I thought she was just here to get her hands on the company. I'll admit I misjudged you."

Ashiya's grin didn't leave despite his begrudging tone. She leaned forward and winked. "Does that mean you're okay working for me?"

Levi sighed and shook his head, but the corner of his mouth raised in an almost-smile. "I'm okay working *with* you," he countered. "You've still got a lot to learn about the company."

"But you're willing to stick with me while I learn," Ashiya said in an aha tone of voice. "That's a vast improvement from when I first got here."

Russell grunted. "Most definitely." He took a sip of his drink.

Levi chuckled and looked at Russell. "I thought you were going to tear my head off that first day."

"I was if you would have kept talking to Ashiya like that," Russell said without a hint of a joke in his voice.

Ashiya smiled and took a sip of her wine. She was giddy with happiness, and she didn't care. Back when Russell stood up for her, she could only hope he did so because he felt something for her. Now that she knew he did, and they were giving each other another chance, she wasn't about to hide her joy.

Levi didn't seem bothered by the lingering warning in Russell's voice. "My bad. I've never been good at being subtle with my feelings," Levi said. "I was wrong when you first came. I didn't trust either of you. I thought for sure I'd be gone if you didn't think I could find the person behind the embezzlement."

Ashiya sighed. "I just wanted to find out who was behind it and get things cleaned up."

"Really?" Levi asked incredulously. "I thought I'd be the first person you'd suspect."

"I suspected you, but I didn't want it to be you. I grew up close to the cousins on the other side of my family. I'm excited to get to know more of my family. I really didn't want our first interaction to be me firing you."

Levi lifted a brow, then nodded. Ashiya was glad things worked out. If she had fired Levi, she might not have found the thief as quickly, and even if she had, she wouldn't have been able to entice him to come work for her again easily. The company would have lost a valuable employee either way.

Brianna raised her glass. "I'm glad things worked out for both of you. You did such a good job finding and getting rid of Danny that I think you work well together. With you two running things, the Legacy Group will be even better."

Russell reached over and took Ashiya's hand in his. "I think so, too."

Levi leaned forward in his seat. "Does this mean you're going to stick around and continue to work here, or will you go back to Jackson Falls and only come down for board meetings?"

Ashiya shrugged. "I'm not sure. Right now, I think I need to stay longer and see how things settle after getting rid of Danny. After that, and I learn more about the company, then maybe I will move back."

Except she wasn't excited about the idea of going back home. Her store was there, and she loved Piece Together, but her mom, the increased scrutiny of being the newly famous member of the Robidoux family, and the expectations to continue to climb and use her new connections to make Robidoux Holdings stronger were also in Jackson Falls. While she loved her family, getting away and building a life apart from them had an appeal. She'd have to apologize to India later for giving her such a hard time for staying away for so long.

Russell squeezed her hand. She looked up and met his reassuring smile. "Take your time to figure things out."

She nodded. "I will."

She knew what she wanted. She wanted to stay in Hilton Head, but she also wanted things to work out with Russell. Elaina was waiting for him to return and take over the CEO position. The position he'd wanted so much it drove him to come down here and help her. If she moved away from Jackson Falls and he stayed, could they really make this tenuous relationship work?

"Despite the shake-up, I think things will settle down pretty quickly at Legacy," Levi said.

"Why is that?" Brianna asked.

"Even though Danny's embezzlement was a shock and surprise, Ashiya's quick action will let everyone know she's serious about the company. One bad employee hasn't spoiled everyone else. Those who are leaning toward being shady will jump ship, and we can replace them. The ones who stay behind will work harder."

"I hope so," Ashiya said, slightly surprised by the confidence in her abilities that rang out in Levi's voice. "I still find it hard to believe no one else new about what he was doing."

"That bothers me, too," Brianna admitted.

Russell tapped the back of her hand with his thumb to get her attention. "Do you want to question the people in his department again?"

"Not right now, but I do feel like I'm missing something," she said. "It was a lot of money, but he doesn't have much to show for it."

Levi lifted a shoulder. "He was the last person to see all the reports before they came to me. He could easily change numbers and move things around without those under him realizing what happened."

"Still, it just rubs me the wrong way." Ashiya sighed and shook her head. "But enough about that for tonight. Tonight, we're going to be happy we got rid of the person trying to cheat the Legacy Group."

"I'm good with that." Levi tilted his glass in a toast. "And here's to making the company even stronger than it was before."

Ashiya grinned. "I'll drink to that."

Later, as Ashiya and Russell lay in bed wrapped in each other's arms, her mind drifted back to the earlier conversation. She should be happy and content. She should be looking forward to implementing some of the new ideas she had. Why couldn't she shake this thing with Danny?

"What's on your mind?" Russell asked. He pulled her closer into his embrace and kissed the top of her head.

Ashiya sighed. "Work. Danny. The Legacy Group."

"What about it?"

"I'm being silly and overthinking."

"No, you want to make sure you didn't miss anything. I understand. It's the first big shake-up to happen under your watch. You want to be successful, but you don't want to be further duped."

"That's it exactly. What if there's more and I'm missing it? The company would be in jeopardy."

"Then take a few days and think it out. It's okay to be cautious, but don't beat yourself up if the numbers continue to add up to the same thing. You're just starting out. It's one thing to be thorough and another to be overly paranoid."

She nodded and fingered the gold chain around his neck. "You're right. It's going to take a while for me to get used to this owning a multimillion-dollar company thing."

"You'll figure it out. I believe you can." His lips brushed her forehead.

"And…will you wait for me while I figure this out?" she asked tentatively.

"Why wouldn't I?"

She lifted on her elbow to look down at him. "I know Elaina offered you the CEO position. If I stay, will we continue to work out?"

He slid an arm behind his head and gave her a questioning look. "Why wouldn't we work out?"

She poked his chest. "Because I'm here and you'll be there. It'll be long-distance. Can we really make that work?"

Russell wrapped his fingers around her wrist and pressed her hand to his chest. "If we want it to, we can. I want to make it work. Do you?"

He sounded so confident. So sure. Maybe that's what love without games gave you. Peace of mind. "I want us to work."

He nodded and squeezed her hand. "Don't borrow trouble, Ashiya."

"I'm not. I'm just being honest with you about how I feel. It's hard to admit that I'm afraid of long-distance. That I'm afraid you'll go back, remember all the reasons why you shouldn't be with me, and change your mind."

"I've already gone over all the reasons why I shouldn't be here, and you know what?"

"What?"

"They don't matter anymore. You make me happy. I'm happy talking to you and having you in my life. That's all that matters now."

When he said things like that, it only made her love him more. She wanted to blurt out the words again. She wanted to tell him every day that she loved him, but she held the words back. She'd hold on to them until she was sure he'd repeat them back, because even though he'd taken her back, it might take longer for him to trust her enough to love her.

She slid over until she straddled him. Desire flashed in his eyes as he placed his hands on her hips. His dick flexed against her in the most delicious way.

"Talking to me and having me in your life. Is that all that matters?" she asked innocently and rotated her hips.

Russell hissed. His fingers pressed into her flesh. "Well…there's a few other things I like about you."

Ashiya chuckled as she shifted forward and then back against the growing length of his erection. "Just a few?"

Russell flipped her over so quickly that she gasped, then giggled. "Quit playing with me, woman. I'm about to show you everything I like about you," he said in a raspy voice before kissing every inch of her body.

CHAPTER TWENTY-FIVE

RUSSELL LOOKED UP as the door of the coffee shop in the specialty shopping center near the beach opened. He lifted his hand and waved as Jeanette came through the door. The private investigator had called him the night before to say she would be in town with an update on his brother's case. Her last update hadn't given him much hope of learning anything new. Too many people didn't remember the party, who was there, or his brother.

After years of believing the police department hadn't cared or tried hard enough to find Rodrick, he was begrudgingly wondering if maybe he could cut them a sliver of slack. He still believed if they'd searched harder for Rodrick right after he disappeared, then they might have gotten a lead on his brother before the trail went cold, a decade passed, and everyone forgot a night drinking at a party.

Jeanette gave him a tight smile that brought out the dimples in her cheeks as she pulled out the chair across from him in the coffee shop. The sunlight filtering through the windows brought out the gold highlights in her reddish hair. Jeanette was average height with a heart-shaped face and a cute smile. Her sweet and harmless appearance probably served her well as a private investigator. No one would suspect her of digging up their deepest secrets.

"Sorry I'm late," she said. "I was held up by a phone call before I got on the road."

Russell shook his head. "It's fine. I took the time to catch up on emails while I waited." He closed his laptop and slid it into the leather messenger bag in the chair to his right. "Do you want to grab a coffee or something to drink before we talk?" he asked out of politeness. He wanted to immediately jump into why she'd called and asked to see him. He was desperate for any word on his brother, but he would try to be patient enough to wait for her to at least order something to drink.

Jeanette shook her head. "No need. I might get something later."

He nodded and leaned forward in his char. "You said you've found out something new about my brother?"

Jeanette pulled out her cell phone and tapped the screen. "I did. I had one of my agents track down several of the people we knew were at the party along with anyone they might remember who attended. We found out about a man named Lemuel Wells who was also there."

"That name doesn't sound familiar." He'd reviewed numerous reports from the night of the party and the subsequent investigation. He'd damn near memorized every name.

"He was at the party that night almost in the same way your brother ended up there. A friend of a friend invited their group to this huge bonfire at Melissa's house for the end of the week. He pretty much corroborated everyone else's story. There was a ton of drinking, sex, and other shenanigans at the party."

"Does he remember seeing Rodrick?" Russell asked, barely able to keep his thoughts together. He'd always believed there were more people at the party than originally reported. More people who might have answers to his questions.

Jeanette nodded, and her voice filled with excitement. "He does. He says he saw your brother and remembers him because Rodrick was one of the few other Black guys at the party. He said there were probably about a handful of them there. He even talked to Rodrick briefly. Mostly about where they went to school and how they ended up at the party."

"Is that all he remembers?" Russell couldn't hide the deflated feeling in his chest. He'd waited so long for information, and if all he would find out is that Rodrick had talked briefly to another guy at the party, that didn't give him any new answers.

"That's not it. He went on to party, but says later he noticed your brother, drunk and being led away by a white guy and girl. He went up and asked them if Rodrick was okay, and they both said yes. They put him in the guy's truck and left. Lemuel didn't think more of it and finished his night after the party."

"Who were the guy and girl?" Russell asked.

"He didn't remember their names, but when I showed him their picture, he recognized Melissa and her ex."

Russell's hand balled into a fist. He'd known it. He'd known from the moment Melissa gave him a sorry-not-sorry smile that she knew more. That she remembered his brother. "Melissa and Bryce never mentioned taking my brother away from that party. They've always said he left on his own without them knowing. Why didn't this guy come forward before?"

If he'd given a statement from the start, they might have gotten answers years ago.

Jeanette shook her head and slid her cell phone out of the pocket of her jeans. "He didn't know your brother went missing. He left and went back to school in Georgia two days later. Your brother's disappearance only made the local news back in your hometown. A lot of people who were at that party and might have remembered something wouldn't know he'd gone missing. That and the fact neither were directly invited. No one would know Lemuel was there or how to get in contact with him to make a statement."

"Is he willing to testify to what he saw?" Russell asked. As far as he was concerned, he was ready to request that Melissa be brought in for questioning immediately. She'd lied not only to him but to investigators for years.

As if sensing his urgency, Jeanette held up a hand in a not-so-fast gesture. "It's not that easy. He does seem willing testify, but that still doesn't mean we'll find out what happened to Rodrick. Melissa can claim she brought him back to his hotel room or dropped him off somewhere. Unless we actually find a b..."

Jeanette cut herself off and leaned back. Russell pressed his fist into the table. He knew what she was going to say. It was the same truth he'd tried to accept when his parents legally declared Rodrick dead. A truth he didn't want to, and probably never would be ready to accept. A part of him continued to hope his brother would come home safely one day.

"Until we find Rodrick's location, it's just this guy Lemuel's word against hers," he finished for her.

"It is. We're still looking. Lemuel agreed to go to the police and tell them what he knows. That will at least give them a good reason to question Melissa and her ex again. Hopefully, learning someone saw her leave the party with your brother than she'd believed will put a little pressure on her to remember."

Jeanette was right. Rodrick leaving with Melissa didn't automatically mean he'd get all the answers he wanted, but Melissa might reveal more information that could lead him to his brother. He'd take what little bit he could right now.

"Even if it doesn't tell me where Rodrick is, this is the

first lead we've had in years. Thank you, Jeanette," he said sincerely. She'd gotten more information for him in a few weeks than anyone else had in years. Proving, once again, why she and her team were some of the best investigators in the state of North Carolina.

"It's what I do," Jeanette said with pride.

"Maybe so, but the last private investigator I hired gave me nothing new. I didn't have the means to pay someone a lot of money, nor did my parents."

"It's hard for me to turn down a missing persons case regardless of what a client may have. Especially when it comes to one of our kids. They already don't get the same media coverage. If you had come to me before, I still would have tried to help. And I'm going to keep trying to help. Believe me."

Her dark brown eyes reflected a determination that gave Russell the first bit of confidence he'd get answers about Rodrick he'd had in years. Fifteen years had passed. The news about what happened to Rodrick might not be what he wanted, but he believed Jeanette would do everything she could to help him learn the truth.

Russell pushed away the feeling of unease and focused on the positive. They had a lead. "I do. Thank you."

Ashiya tried not to spend her first Saturday with no plans obsessing about whether she'd missed something when it came to Danny. When The Dragons invited her over to talk about their plans for a family reunion the following summer, she'd agreed and hoped spending the day getting to know her family would be just the distraction she needed.

Between talks about venues and potential dates, the three of them gave Ashiya an earful about each family member they hoped would show up and what it would take to get everyone together. There wasn't any real animosity between everyone. Their kids and grandkids had grown up and grown apart. Her grandmother's passing had brought home to each of the women how much they wanted to spend more time with their families and bring back the family closeness they'd experienced as kids.

The women had a variety of reasons they wouldn't be able to get the family together for the reunion. Everything from busy schedules, to feuding cousins, to general apathy toward the family. All things that were probably true, but seeing the growing disappointment in their eyes, Ashiya knew she couldn't just accept defeat.

Ashiya slapped one fist into the palm of her hand. "We'll get everyone here. It might not be easy, but we can make it work."

Her Aunt Gertrude pulled a butterscotch out of her purse and opened it slowly. "Do you really think so?"

Ashiya didn't know half of the cousins they mentioned, but she wasn't going to let that stop her. If she could win over Levi and find an embezzler at the Legacy Group, then she could at least throw a family reunion. "Even if we have to blackmail and bribe, we'll get the family together."

Maggie paused in the middle of her crocheting to point at Ashiya. "I like the way this girl thinks. Maybe my sister wasn't so wrong for putting you in charge of Legacy."

Helena snuffed out her cigarette and nodded. "Maybe Gloria did know what she was doing."

Ashiya left them with smiles and a heavy weight on her shoulders. Away from their hopeful stares, she wondered how in the world she'd be able to get all of her family together like she'd promised. She chuckled to herself at the thought of trying to hold a reunion with people she'd hadn't wanted to hang out with for most of her life.

She called Russell to tell him about her new project, but

he didn't answer his phone. He'd mentioned meeting with the private investigator on his brother's case today. She hoped he'd found out something new. As much as he tried to remain hopeful, she saw the disappointment and grief in his eyes every time he received another update with no news.

She glanced at her watch. It was almost two in the afternoon. He might still be in the meeting.

Instead of going home, she decided to drop by the Legacy Group office. The Dragons had done a great job of distracting her for a little while, but now that she didn't have anything else to focus on, the paranoia that she'd missed something with the Danny situation came back. She'd left the information she'd gathered on the case in her desk. She could spend just a little bit of time going over the evidence one more time before driving home and getting caught up with Russell.

The parking lot was empty except for a few cars. Not surprising since there were security and cleaning crews who came in over the weekend. Ashiya didn't expect anyone to be working at the corporate offices today. The security desk was empty when she entered the lobby. A cup of coffee and a book opened facedown on the desk sat next to the security screen. Ashiya glanced around, but the security guard wasn't in sight. She assumed the guard had stepped away.

She'd talk to them on her way out. She used her ID badge to buzz past the lobby doors toward the elevators to the upper floors. When she got out on the top floor, she made her way to her office. The sound of a voice coming from Levi's office stopped her halfway down the hall.

Frowning, she slowed her steps and eased up to the door leading to her cousin's suite. The door wasn't closed completely. She peeked through the crack toward the office. Melissa stood behind the desk, her back to the door, and a cell phone lodged between her head and shoulder. She held a stack of papers and steadily fed them into the paper shredder.

"I'm not worried about Danny. If he knows what's good for him, he'll keep his mouth shut." Melissa paused and continued feeding papers. "Of course I trust him. He's stupid and thinks I love him. I told him that if he were ever caught, I'd cover for him."

Ashiya pressed her hand to her mouth. Her heart stuttered and shock made her stomach clench. She knew there was more to the story, but Melissa? She'd never seen Melissa and Danny interact with each other. How could she do that to Levi? Why would she do that?

"Don't worry about him," Melissa continued. "He thinks Levi and Ashiya will go easy on him. By the time he realizes they're going to throw everything at him, it'll be too late." Melissa stopped loading papers, straightened, and pressed the phone to her ear with her free hand. "Will you quit being paranoid? I'm getting rid of everything now. You just have the boat ready. Even if he changes his mind, we'll be gone. I'm sending Levi my letter of resignation on Monday. He's another one who trusts everything I say. By the time he puts me together with this, we'll be gone."

Ashiya frowned. So not only was Melissa a thief, but she planned to bail and leave Danny to take the blame for everything. Not if Ashiya had anything to do with it. She'd never liked Melissa. She was going to make sure this woman went down along with whoever was on the phone with her. She pushed the door open slowly.

"This would be so much easier if that damn Russell hadn't come with Ashiya. If I wasn't worried about him finding out the truth, I'd just get Danny to shut up and keep my position here."

Ashiya froze at the door. Learn the truth? What truth? Dread sent cold chills across her skin.

"Levi was just about to promote me." Melissa's voice was petulant. "I'd have more control and the chance to get even more from this damn company, but Russell won't stop pressing. If he keeps digging, he'll find out the truth about his brother, and I can't be around for that."

Rage snapped Ashiya out of her shock. "What did you do to Rodrick?"

Melissa yelped and spun around. The papers in her hand flew to the ground along with her cell phone. Wide blue eyes stared back at Ashiya.

"How did you get in here?" Melissa asked.

"I own this company and this building. I can come whenever I damn well please." She placed her hands on her hips and glared at Melissa. "I knew there was someone else working with Danny, but I didn't think it was you. Why would you do this?"

The frightened surprise in Melissa's eyes warped into a smug smirk as she glared back. "Why wouldn't I? I deserve just as much as anyone else from this company."

"How? Levi trusts you. Why deceive him like this?"

Melissa flipped her hair over her shoulder. "It's his fault for being so trusting. My family was once the most prominent family in the area. Then suddenly your grandmother's little soap company turns big. Now people are sucking up to them. I'm just taking back a little bit of what we had before."

Ashiya stared, dumfounded. "That has to be the dumbest thing I've ever heard," she shot back. "Just admit you're a lying, greedy thief, and you saw an opportunity to take advantage of someone, and you did."

Melissa shrugged, but her eyes narrowed. "Call it what you want."

"And Russell's brother." Ashiya took a step further into the room. "You know what happened to him. What did you do to him?"

Melissa's eyes darted away. "I don't know what you're talking about."

"I heard you on the phone." Ashiya pointed to Melissa's dropped cell on the floor. "You said everything was fine until Russell started digging. You don't want the truth to come out." Ashiya stalked closer. "What happened to Rodrick?"

Melissa raised her chin. "I didn't do anything to him." Her voice wobbled, and a frightened look glazed over her eyes.

"Where is he? What happened?"

"I don't have time to deal with this," Melissa said, sounding frustrated at being interrupted but not at all worried about Ashiya catching her.

"You're going to have a lot more time for this. There is no way I'm letting you get away with it." Ashiya slid her hand into her purse for her cell phone.

Melissa raised a brow. "I've gotten away with this and so much more for so long. You're not going to stop me now."

The cold detachment in Melissa's voice was the first warning sign. Her eyes narrowed just as her hand clenched around her cell. Melissa's quick glance over Ashiya's shoulder and nod was the second warning before pain erupted across the back of her head and everything went black.

CHAPTER TWENTY-SIX

ASHIYA WOKE UP to blinding pain in the back of her head. She groaned and tried to sit up. Her head spun and her stomach flipped. The only light she saw was from the stars behind her eyes. She groaned and brought a shaking hand to the back of her head. Her hair was wet and sticky. Shivers ran through her body as the memories from before came flooding back.

Melissa was involved in the embezzlement. She also knew what happened to Russell's brother. Someone, not Melissa, had hit her in the back of the head. Hard.

She was going to kill that woman!

She took another deep breath and opened her eyes. The darkness remained. Panic was like a vise around her throat. Choking off her breath and silencing her voice. She blinked several times, but there was still nothing but darkness. Her hands patted around her. She was on the floor. There was carpet beneath her. Pushing herself up, she leaned into a wall behind her. She spread her hands out. They didn't go far. The vise around her neck tightened.

Wherever she was, the space was small. Memories of being left alone for days in the basement as kid came back. She opened her mouth and yelled.

"Help! Hello! Someone please!" She banged on the wall.

She was frantic for what felt like an eternity. Screaming and pounding on anything around her. She pushed up and spun to the wall at her back. Not a wall but a door. The barest hint of light came from beneath the slit at the bottom. If there was a door, then there was a way out.

She shoved up to her knees. Her head spun with the sudden movement, and her stomach rolled. She pressed her forehead against the door and took another deep breath to steady herself. She slapped at the door, slid her hand across the surface until she got to the knob.

Relief lived for the briefest flicker and died as swiftly as she turned. Nothing. The door was locked. She banged on it.

"Please! Someone help!" she yelled. Her hands slapped and punched against the door.

She'd be in there forever. Just like last time. She was trapped. No one cared. No one would come for her. She'd be alone in the dark. This time injured. Her body shook.

"No!" she yelled. She closed her eyes and controlled her breathing. "No. you're not going to die in here, Ashiya. You're not a kid anymore. You can get out of here. Think. Just…think."

It took several more breaths and repetitions that she wasn't going to die before her heart calmed and her breathing evened out. She was obviously in a closet. Probably still in the Legacy Group offices. That's where she'd been last. Someone had been there with Melissa and hit her in the head.

Ashiya touched the knot and winced. They'd hit her hard. No one knew she was here, but Russell would look for her. He might have already tried to reach her.

Cell phone! She needed her cell phone. She could call him and get out. She felt around the floor of the closet. She found her purse, but when she reached inside, the contents were empty. She felt around the small space again, hope diminishing with each passing second. They'd taken everything out of her purse.

Before panic could rise again, she took another breath. Okay, no cell. She was still alive and in an office that would be filled with people on Monday. Even if Russell couldn't find her, she wouldn't be here forever.

"I just have to make it until Monday." The depressing thought brought tears to her eyes.

She was tired, hungry, her head hurt like hell. She was going to beat the shit out of Melissa when she got out of there.

"Think, Ashiya, think," she mumbled to herself. "Don't panic. Think."

Her eyes popped open. She jerked forward, froze to let the nausea and dizziness subside, then felt around the floor again. Her hands brushed over something small and cool, a paper clip. She grinned and quickly straightened out the wire. She'd taught herself how to pick locks after being trapped as a kid. A trick she'd hoped and prayed she'd never have to use.

"Thank goodness my fear of being here again has worked out," she said dryly into the darkness. A hysterical laugh bubbled up. She let it free. If she didn't laugh, she'd break down and cry again.

She put the paper clip into the knob and twisted. The dizziness came back full force. The barely-there light under the door darkened. Breathing became harder. She blinked and tried to focus, but her hands shook. Tears spilled from her eyes.

"It's okay," she said. "It's okay. You're just tired. You can pick it later." Still she worked on the lock.

She banged on the door. "I'm going to kill you, Melissa!" she half yelled, but her sentence ended on a sob.

For all she knew, she'd been there for a day already and Melissa was long gone.

"Get the boat ready." She hadn't forgotten those words. Melissa already had an escape plan.

The light under the door flashed brighter. "Ashiya!"

She froze. Her heart beat wildly in her chest, and tears came faster. She banged on the door. "Russell! In here! I'm in here!"

The knob twisted and the door opened. The light from the other side sent shards of pain through her brain. She flinched and raised her hand.

"Thank God!" Russell said in a trembling voice and dropped to his knees.

Ashiya fell forward into the embrace of his arms. The blurred vision of Levi behind him and Legacy Group security filled the room before she passed out again.

RUSSELL SAT NEXT to Ashiya's hospital bed and cradled her hand in his. She was going to be alright, but that didn't stop his heart from squeezing from all the what-if possibilities. Things could have gone so much worse.

She shifted in the bed. Russell sat forward in his seat and gripped her hand more firmly. Ashiya's eyes blinked open. She stared toward the ceiling; her brows furrowed before she turned her head his way.

"Russell?"

"How are you feeling?"

She blinked again and tried to sit up. She winced and leaned back. "My head hurts."

He almost smiled at her cute pout and the affront in her voice. Even injured, she was spirited. "You've got a concussion. The doctors said you can be released later today."

"Concussion?" Her frown deepened. Then her eyes wid-

ened. "Melissa…she hit me. I mean, she was there when
someone hit me."

Russell nodded. "I know."

"How did you know? Did you find her? She also was
behind the embezzlement."

Russell patted the back of her hand. "They're looking
for her now. She got on Bryce's boat. From what we could
find out, they are on the way to the Bahamas."

"No, she can't get away with this. She knows more
about your brother." Ashiya tried to sit up and scowled.

Russell pressed a hand on her shoulder and gently
pushed her back down. "I know that, too."

"What?"

Russell thought about where to start and decided his
meeting with Jeanette was as good a place as any. "I met
with Jeanette, and she found another witness from the
party. He saw my brother leave the party. No, he saw Melissa and her ex dragging my brother away from the party."

Ashiya gasped. He hand twisted around until she
cupped his in hers. "Oh no, Russell."

"We went straight to the police after our meeting. She
gave them the number to the witness. Thankfully, the detective wants to solve this case. He called the guy and corroborated the story. He was on his way to Melissa's house
to question her, and I went home to tell you."

"How long was I in that closet?" she asked, her voice
wavering.

"Overnight." His voice hardened at the memory. He'd
almost lost his mind not knowing where she was or what
happened. "Your phone was off. We didn't know where
you'd gone other than to visit your aunts."

"How did you eventually find me?"

"A hunch that you would have gone to the office. Your

car was there, but there wasn't any record of you checking into the building."

"I signed the book. The security guard wasn't at the desk. I wanted to leave the record and follow the procedures."

Russell frowned. "There wasn't anything there. The security guard who was supposed to be on duty wasn't there either. We called in the rest of the security team to search for both of you in the building. We found you, but not the guard."

"Do you think he was the one who hit me?"

"I hate to think that the problems of the Legacy Group go that deep, but it looks that way."

"Melissa is a psychopath," Ashiya said.

"She's something. I just hope the police find her." She could give him answers about his brother. They had her on assaulting Ashiya, and abetting the embezzlement if what Ashiya said was true, but that didn't mean they could prove she knew the whereabouts of his brother.

Russell brought her hand to his lips. "I was so worried when I couldn't find you. Are you okay? I mean, the closet…"

Ashiya squeezed his hand. Her fingers trembled. "I was afraid when I woke up. More than afraid. I was petrified. I did panic, but then remembered I had to be in the office. Someone would find me eventually. I wouldn't be stuck forever."

"Did that work?" He could only imagine her fear. The way she'd reacted when she'd been locked in the pantry haunted him. He could kill Melissa for locking Ashiya in the darkness like that.

Ashiya tried to smile bravely, but her voice shook. "A

little. I tried to pick the lock. I was about to black out again when you found me."

He leaned forward and kissed her forehead. "I'm so sorry. I wish I could have gotten there sooner."

"If you'd gotten there sooner then you might not have found me. It wasn't long after I woke up that you got there. If you had come earlier, I would have been passed out on the floor."

Her trembles increased. Russell pressed the back of his hand to her cheek. "Shhh…you're okay now. When I get my hands on her…"

"You don't have to worry about it," Ashiya said in a hard voice. "If I ever see her face again, she's going to wish she'd never laid a damn hand on me."

He smiled, relieved to have the fight chase the fear from her eyes. "Right now is when I should remind you to let the police handle Melissa."

She grunted. "The police may need to handle me." She threaded her fingers through his. "Thank you for looking for me."

"Why wouldn't I?" When she shrugged and glanced at their entwined hands, he tugged so she'd look back up at him. "I wouldn't leave you there. If you ever disappear out of my life without a word, I will come find you. I'm not your parents. I'll never leave you behind."

Her eyes glistened with tears. She pulled on his hand, and he leaned forward and kissed her forehead. Ashiya pressed a shaky hand to his cheek when he pulled back.

"I love you so much, Russell."

The ache in his chest when she'd gone missing had become heavier when she'd passed out in his arms and almost unbearable when the doctors said she'd been hit with a blunt object and had a concussion. Now the ache eased to bearable proportions. He doubted it would go away until she was out of the hospital, healed, and back to herself again.

He loved her, too. Had fought loving her for too long. The thought of losing her, of something terrible happening to her and never getting the chance to tell her he loved her, had chased away any lingering regrets about being back with her.

"Ashiya, I—"

A knock on the door interrupted them. They both glanced up at the slender white man in his early thirties dressed in a brown suit standing at the door.

"Detective Mitchell." Russell straightened.

"Sorry for the interruption," the detective said. "I wanted to give you an update on the case, and the woman at your place said you were still at the hospital."

"I haven't left since she was admitted," he said.

Ashiya's hand in his tightened. He glanced at her, and she smiled shyly. She seemed surprised by his admission. He didn't understand why. There was no way he'd leave her here alone.

"We found Melissa and her ex-husband," Detective Trent said.

Ashiya moved to sit up and hissed. "You did?" she asked in a voice laced with pain.

Russell pressed the button on the side of the bed to lift the head so she wouldn't have to struggle to sit up again.

"She's in custody?" Russell asked after Ashiya was settled.

Detective Trent nodded. "She is, but not here. She was picked up in Florida. They pulled in for fuel and were recognized. We put out an APB for her and Bryce up and down the East Coast. They're both being extradited back to South Carolina."

Russell let out a long, relieved breath. "Good."

"What happens when she gets back?" Ashiya asked.

"We'll question her about the attack on you and the embezzlement, along with the missing persons case."

"I heard her on the phone," Ashiya said. "She helped Danny steal the money."

Detective Trent didn't seem surprised by Ashiya's words. Instead, a grim look came over his face. "Once Danny found out Melissa left town and was heading out of the country, he spilled everything. Apparently, the two of them started having an affair a few years ago. That's when the embezzlement started. It's also the reason she ended things with Bryce. Except they didn't really break up. She had both men on the hook to do whatever she needed. Them and the security guard who hit you."

Russell blinked several times. He hadn't trusted Melissa, but he'd only guessed her for a liar. Not a triple-timing thief and assailant. "Did you find the security guard?"

Detective Trent nodded. "We did. He was found upstate. When he was questioned, he said the whole thing was Melissa's idea. He was another guy who thought she was in love with him and would do anything to protect him."

"How many more?" Ashiya asked.

Detective Mitchell shrugged. "I don't have a reason to believe there are additional people at the Legacy Group, but we'll know more when we question her. Now that we've got Danny willing to testify to her involvement with the stolen funds along with Levi implicating her in your brother's case, she may be more likely to cave."

"I won't get my hopes up," Russell said. After the way Melissa feigned concern and almost cried when he pushed her for information on his brother, he wouldn't be surprised to find out she'd manipulated dozens of other people.

"I'll get back to you when we have her in custody," Detective Trent said.

"Thank you," Russell said.

Detective Trent looked at Ashiya. "If you're feeling better, then I'd like to ask you a few questions. We need to get your official statement."

"Do you have to do it now?" Russell asked. "She woke up right before you came in."

Ashiya rubbed his forearm. "It's okay. I'm ready to tell him everything I heard and what happened to me."

Russell didn't want her to exert herself. He wanted her to rest more, but the determined look in her eyes told him that he wasn't going to win this argument. There would be time later to make sure she rested and felt better.

"You sure?"

"I'm sure," she said with a careful nod. "Whatever I can do to get this bitch behind bars, I'm ready to do."

CHAPTER TWENTY-SEVEN

TWO WEEKS LATER, Russell stood in the gravel driveway leading up to Melissa's parents' property at the outskirts of the county. Ashiya stood by his side. Dozens of cops and forensic experts covered the grounds. A bulldozer had knocked down the shed in the middle of the property, and a crew had just finished breaking up the concrete floor and removing the slabs.

Melissa had been extradited to South Carolina. When faced with the fact that not only Danny but also the security guard had snitched, she'd admitted everything. She'd been the first person to notice the glitch in the numbers. Once she realized how easy it was to move money without being noticed, she'd convinced Danny to go along with it. She also seduced and paid off the security guard to let her and Danny in on weekends to handle the paperwork and clean up the trail without signing in or providing a record that they'd been there. It's how she'd gotten away with things for so long.

She'd still tried to insist she didn't know anything about Russell's brother or what happened to him. It was Bryce who'd cracked under that pressure. Rodrick had gone to the party with them. He'd drunk too much during a drinking game. Melissa and Bryce dragged him into the house and left him on his back in a bed. He'd gotten sick, chocked and later died without anyone realizing until it was too late. Instead of calling the police, Melissa and Bryce buried him out of fear. Melissa's parents helped their daughter cover things up instead of risking their baby girl getting in trouble. Her father built a shed over the makeshift grave that same summer.

Someone at the worksite yelled. "We've got something."

Russell's heart lurched. He staggered back. Ashiya's arm slid through his, and she hugged it to her chest. The feel of her, steady and sure beside him, kept him from running away like he wanted.

"Are you going to be okay?" she asked. Her voice was filled with empathy. The look in her eye said she'd drive him far away from here if he said the word.

He didn't have to be here for this. But after going for over a decade with no word of his brother, he couldn't stay away. He had to know for sure.

He nodded and used his free arm to rub her shoulder. "Yes. I'll be okay."

Activity around the site increased. The buzz of conversation rose. More people rushed over. Officers took notes, pictures, and pointed toward the ground. Several agonizing minutes later, Detective Trent walked over to Russell and Ashiya.

He looked at Ashiya and then at Russell. His grim expression told Russell everything he didn't want to know.

"We found a body," Detective Trent said. "We won't know until we get the remains back to the lab and conduct DNA samples if it's your brother."

The rest of the world faded away. Russell tried to breathe as his throat closed up. He didn't need DNA samples. The agony of waiting and wondering was over. The question of whether one day they'd get what they wanted and find his brother was answered. Except it was answered in the worst way.

His shoulders shook. He pressed his mouth closed and turned away from Detective Trent. He wanted to scream, run, beat something. Anything to channel the hurt and the pain swelling inside him.

Ashiya stood in front of him. She rose up on her toes and wrapped her arms around his neck. The pain drowned him. He buried his head in the crook of her shoulder and sobbed.

ASHIYA WALKED THROUGH Russell's parents' house and made sure the dozens of guests cramming the place were okay. She picked up discarded cups of half-filled drinks and took them into the kitchen. Cleaned away the stray tissues and plates of uneaten food. Made sure the food put out for guests was replenished but the carrot cake she knew was Russell's and his mom's favorite remained hidden in the pantry for them later.

Though his family had legally declared Rodrick dead years before and held a small funeral, she knew Russel and his parents had held out hope for a miracle. Once his remains were found and verified, they'd held a funeral for friends and family to say their final goodbyes. Ashiya was overcome by the outpouring of support Russell and his parents had received.

Things had gone from bad to worse in the weeks since they'd discovered what Melissa had done. Ashiya spent more time at the Legacy Group working with Levi to keep the company stable. Levi had been rocked by Melissa's betrayal and the extent of the problems she'd caused. They were going back through all the employees and cross-checking anyone who had ties to Melissa. Those people were put on watch, and after the threat of retaliation from Melissa was gone, many had come forward with examples of the ways she'd coerced or bullied people in order to get what she wanted. It was going to take a lot of hard work to undo the damage she'd done.

While they'd dealt with the issues at work, Russell dealt with telling his parents about Rodrick, continuing with the charges pressed against Melissa, her parents and Bryce for hiding his brother's death, and helping his family plan a funeral.

Ashiya didn't know where she stood with him, but she knew her promise to be there for him, no games and no manipulation, was still there. That's why she'd respected the space he needed while his family grieved and tried to be supportive without demanding his time.

She missed him. She wanted to make sure he was okay. She wanted him to know that whatever he needed to get through this, she'd try to help him get it. But she also didn't want to be another thing he had to worry about.

Ashiya entered the kitchen with a handful of plates and cups she'd taken from around the house. Russell and his cousin Isaac were in there. They both had glasses with brown liquor in their hands, and Russell had a rare smile on his face. When he looked at Ashiya, his smile slowly faded. He didn't seem upset to see her, but she couldn't make out the emotion behind his expression.

"Everything okay?" she asked. She took the dishes to the trash can to scrape out the food.

"It is," he said. "Isaac and I were just laughing about the way Rodrick used to prank me when we were younger."

"Oh really?" Ashiya smiled when she heard the humor in his voice. It was the best he'd sounded since things went down.

"Yeah, he was always doing something silly. There was this one time I'd worked so hard to rack up all these points in this video game. I spent all summer getting to one of the top levels, and I had a collection of weapons and prizes."

"What happened?" Ashiya took the empty plates over to the sink.

"He did something to make it look like the game had been reset. I thought I lost everything. I was so pissed."

Isaac laughed and shook his head. "You were more than pissed. You cried."

"I didn't cry," Russell said playfully hitting his cousin's arm.

"Yes the hell you did. I remember. There were tears."

"Oh no!" Ashiya said giggling. There were a ton of dishes piled up. She placed the stopper in the sink, turned on the water and added a squirt of dish detergent. Russell's parents didn't have a dishwasher, and she didn't want to leave them with more things to worry about.

"Oh yes," Isaac said, still grinning. "He cried like a baby."

Ashiya put some of the dishes in the soapy water. "What happened?"

Russell lifted a shoulder. "Rodrick realized I was really upset and told me what he did. All my stuff was still there. I didn't have to start over. Then he helped me get to the top level."

"That was cool," she said.

"It was," he said, fondness in his voice. "That's the kind of brother he was. He might play pranks on me, but he always did what he could to make things right if I ever got upset. He was my best friend." Russell's voice trailed off. He stared down into the glass in his hand and took a long breath.

Ashiya stopped the water and went over to him. She placed one hand on his arm and the other on his back. "I wish I had been able to meet him."

"Yeah…me too," he said.

She wanted to pull him into her arms and hold him the way she had when he'd cried the day the body was found. She wanted him to know he didn't have to be strong or hold himself together when she was around. She loved him. She didn't want him to suffer alone.

Russell sniffed and hastily brushed his eyes. He shifted, and her hands fell away. "I need to check on Mom and Dad. I left them with some of their friends from the church, and I think Mom is getting tired."

Ashiya nodded and stepped back. She wouldn't push. She'd give him his space. "Sure. Go take care of them."

He glanced at her, gave her a tight smile, and then hurried out of the kitchen. Ashiya watched him go with a heavy heart. She didn't want him to think she was in the way. A burden he shouldn't have to deal with. He hadn't said he loved her back. She'd told him those words in the hospital, but he hadn't reciprocated. What if he just wanted her out of his life while he dealt with this?

She didn't want to focus on that right now. Instead she went back to the sink to wash the dishes.

"You know, you don't have to do that," Isaac said.

Ashiya glanced at him over her shoulder. "I know, but I want to."

"Why?" he asked, sounding suspicious.

"Because they've got enough to deal with. A sink full of dishes shouldn't be another thing." She grabbed the sponge and started cleaning.

"They've got a whole house of family here do to that." Isaac said in a dismissive voice.

"I just want to help."

"Why? So you can show Russell what a good girlfriend you are, and he'll forget about the way you treated him?" Isaac's voice was filled with ridicule.

Ashiya spun around. "What?"

Isaac glared back as if she were an intruder in their sacred space. "You heard me. I was there after you broke his heart. You're not good for him. So this good girl act you're trying to put on now isn't working. Russell has enough going on in his life right now without having to worry about dealing with your flighty ass. If you really care about him, then you'll go ahead and get out of his life."

Isaac gave her one last dismissive glare before stalking out of the kitchen. Ashiya stood there dumbfounded. Her hands trembled as she turned back to the sink and her vision blurred. She finished washing the dishes and left.

CHAPTER TWENTY-EIGHT

ASHIYA WAS IN the middle of packing her items to go back to Hilton Head when her doorbell rang. Groaning, she swiped the tears from her eyes before throwing a shirt into the suitcase. She was ready to get the hell out of Jackson Falls and back to the relative safety, comfort and privacy of her home in Hilton Head.

Funny how the first few nights she hadn't been able to sleep in that house, and now it was the one place she wanted to retreat to.

With a sigh, she made her way to the front door. One look through the curtains and a glimpse of her parents sent alarm through her. They didn't visit her at her place, and they damn sure wouldn't come together.

Ashiya rushed to open the door. "What happened? Is everyone okay? Please don't tell me someone is hurt."

Her parents stared at her, stunned, before her mom stepped forward and placed her hands on either side of her face. "We came to check on you. You were the only person hurt recently."

The answer was so surprising that Ashiya pushed her mom's hands away and scoffed. "Really? You didn't have to come over here for that."

Ashiya turned and went into the house. Behind her, the glass screen door creaked as her parents scrambled through to follow her inside. She stopped in the living area and turned to face them. She almost laughed at the incredulous looks on their faces. Her mom's mouth was pinched into a tight line, and her dad's nostrils flared as if she'd cursed them.

Her dad spoke first. "How could you say we didn't need to come over here for that? You were attacked and left in a closet."

She lifted a shoulder. "Maybe because you didn't seem that concerned when I was left in a basement as a kid. I figured it would be like last time and you two would just act as if it never happened."

Her mom stepped forward. "Ashiya, don't say that. Of course we care. This is different."

"Why? Because I was hit over the head before going in? It was no scarier then the last time I woke up alone in the dark with no idea if or when someone would come find me."

Her throat thickened, and she took a deep breath. She crossed her arms and swallowed hard. She was not going to cry in front of them. Not over this and not over what happened with Melissa. Just like last time, she'd gotten over what happened, and she'd do the same now. She didn't need coddling from her parents, Russell, or anyone else.

"I'm sorry," her mom said. "We're sorry." She pointed at her dad, then back at her. "You're right. We shouldn't have left you there."

Her dad stepped up next to Elizabeth. "And we shouldn't have pretended everything was okay afterwards."

How long had she waited for them to admit they were wrong? How long had she wanted to see the looks of regret and sorrow on their faces? She'd expected to feel validated, relieved, cared for. Instead, their afterthoughts of pity only made her angry. Apologizing now didn't take away the years of hurt.

"No. You shouldn't have. I was a kid. All I wanted was for you two to be happy. I didn't want to be the one hurt in your never-ending fight to get back at each other. Sometimes I think it would have been better if you'd just gotten a divorce instead of acting as if everything was fine."

George looked at Elizabeth. Her mom gave a jerky nod. When her dad looked back at her his eyes were sad. "That's why we are getting a divorce now," he said solemnly.

Ashiya dropped her arms and frowned. "You are?"

Her mom nodded. "After our confrontation at the party, I told your dad what you said. We both had to come to the realization that our attempts to hurt each other also hurt you. You're right, it wasn't okay, and we were wrong."

George stepped forward and held out his hands as if he were begging for forgiveness. "We don't want to continue to hurt you or each other. You've got a new start with the Legacy Group. It's time for us to start over as well."

"But…" She glanced first at her mom and then at her dad. "You two still love each other. I know you do."

Her parents shared a glance. Her mom's sigh was sad and full of regret. "We did love each other. I'll always care about your father because marrying him gave me you. But there's no way we can come back from the years of what we've done to each other."

"Or what we've done to you," George said.

Ashiya tried to figure out all of the emotions swirling through her after her parents' revelation. Yes, they needed to get a divorce. Should have left each other years ago when they realized their egos wouldn't let them get past the hurt and heal. She was mad it had taken this long. That it took her getting hit over the head and locked in a closet to make them finally realize that their fight had scarred her.

What did they want from her? For her to say "good job" and give them a hug? She wasn't in the space to give that right now. She had her own stuff to deal with. Getting things settled with the Legacy Group. Nurturing her relationship with Russell. Getting rid of the nightmares that blended her time alone as a kid with the time as an adult that had popped up after in the aftermath of what happened.

"If you're happy, then I'm happy," was all she could say in a tired voice. "I'm okay. No lingering side effects from the concussion. Melissa is behind bars waiting to be sentenced for a ton of charges. I'm packing my clothes so that I can get back to Hilton Head tomorrow."

"So soon?" her mom said.

"Already?" her dad said at the same time.

She would have laughed at the disappointment in their voices if she weren't so tired. Now they wanted her around. She wasn't writing her parents off, but she needed space to heal. Her parents' feelings were no longer her top priority. Still, she cared about them, and no matter how much they infuriated her, she wouldn't intentionally be cruel.

"I need to get back to work. There are a lot of things to settle there."

"What about your store here?" her mom asked.

"I'm going to turn over full management to Lyndsey. She's handled things well while I've been gone. I think she'll continue to make the place profitable."

She'd had that talk with Lyndsey the day before the funeral. She wasn't going to let go of Piece Together. It was the first thing she'd built, and she was proud of it. Instead, she was going to let Lindsey purchase a portion of the business and continue to run things while Ashiya focused on working with Levi to keep the Legacy Group going.

"But you put everything you had into that store," her dad said. "Now you want to give it up to work at my mom's company?"

"I put everything into that store because I didn't want to be a part of the Robidoux family fight for power. When I went to Hilton Head, I expected to be involved in another fight and try to get out of it just as quickly. Instead, it turns out I work pretty well with my cousin, I like my aunts, and I want to see the Legacy Group rebound from what happened. Just like you need a fresh start, so do I. This is mine."

She could see the fight start in her mom's eyes. Her dad placed a hand on her arm and shook his head. When he looked back at Ashiya, he said, "If you're sure, make certain you're doing this on your own terms."

Ashiya nodded. "I am. I finally feel as if I've found a place for me."

"What about Russell?" her mom threw out. Knowing her mom, she was still trying to find a way to keep Ashiya close. "I hear he's going to be working with Elaina. Does this mean your relationship with him is a way to tie the two corporations together?"

"My relationship with Russell is something we both want and has nothing to do with the companies. If anything, I plan to keep them both separate for as long as possible. He feels the same. We both agree we won't accept interference from anyone on this."

She met her mom's gaze and kept her voice direct. She meant it. Whatever happened between her and Russell would be between them. If she had to craft a contract that said the two companies would always remain separate, she would. She didn't know if the things his cousin said had come from Russell or were just Isaac's own thoughts, but if there was even a small crumb of a chance Russell disagreed with Isaac, she wanted him to know she was not her mom, Elaina or anyone else in her family. She was coming to him as just herself, with her heart, and her honest intentions.

Her dad smiled at her and nodded. "Good. I want you to be happy, Ashiya. Don't make the mistakes we made."

"I don't plan to," she said honestly.

Her mom sighed, and her shoulders relaxed. She came over and wrapped Ashiya in a hug. When she pulled back, her eyes were bright. "Fine. Your mom will learn to stay out of your business. For once I'll agree with your dad in front of him. Be happy, Ashiya. Don't ever settle for less. Don't end up heartbroken like us."

RUSSELL SAT ON the swing on his parents' back porch. Their backyard hadn't changed much in the years since he'd left. His dad's shed full of tools and lawn equipment was still in the left corner. His mom's small vegetable garden occupied the right corner. In the middle was the birch tree his mom planted when his brother disappeared. The tree symbolized hope. The day she planted it, she'd said it was a physical representation of her belief her son was alive and coming home.

Russell's vision blurred. He wiped away the tears and sniffed. He was surprised he even had tears left. The rational part of his brain had told him years ago that Rodrick was dead. When they'd declared him dead, he'd thought he'd dealt with all the emotions of losing his brother. The funeral they'd had this week brought up all the shit he'd thought he'd dealt with. His brother really and truly wasn't ever coming home. That hurt more than anything.

The back door opened. He glanced over and gave his dad a weak smile. "Is the house still full?"

His dad chuckled and came over. He'd gotten rid of the black jacket of his suit and the tie and was dressed in a white button-up shirt untucked from his slacks. "Yep, though some people have left. Your mom's sisters aren't going anywhere anytime soon. They know she needs them."

Russell slid over and give his dad more room on the porch swing. "What about you? What do you need?"

His dad let out a long, heavy breath. "Nothing."

"Really? Cause I feel like I need to hit something, have another hard drink, or just run and hide." He tried to lighten his tone, but the pain still bled through.

His dad squeezed his shoulder. "Doing that won't bring Rodrick back. We all knew this day would come."

"Still… I didn't want it to be like this. He shouldn't have gone like that."

"He shouldn't have. I think about all the lectures I gave him before he went to college. Don't party with strangers who won't care about you. Don't drink too much when you're out and about. Be careful of the company you keep. I think about that, and a part of me wants to get mad because he didn't listen, but getting mad won't bring him back either."

"I feel like getting mad is all I have left," Russell said.

"It's not, son. We've got a lot left. I've got your mother, who I love with my whole heart. I know she's hurting just as much as I am, but we'll get through this together. I've got you." His dad squeezed his shoulder again. "My baby boy who grew up into a responsible man. You gave us the closure we needed. You didn't have to pursue this the way you did, but I'm glad you did. We wouldn't have known what happened. We wouldn't have been able to lay him to rest."

"I wish I'd found better news," Russell said.

"You could have found nothing. I'll take bad news rather than the no news we had before. Did we want Rodrick home alive? Yes. Did we all know deep down he wasn't coming back?" He let out a heavy sigh. "Yes." He paused for a second before continuing. His voice solemn but sure. "We've got answers. The people who hid what happened will pay. That's more than a lot of other people get."

Russell nodded. He looked back at the tree. "Are you going to cut it down?"

"Nah. Your mom already said she's keeping it. Now she's hoping for grandchildren to climb it."

Russell coughed. "Grandkids! What? Where did that come from?"

His dad laughed and pounded him on the back. "From you bringing Ashiya around. We noticed how much she helped out around here. Your mom is ready to open the door to the next chapter. I think I even heard her and your Aunt Delphina talk about a wedding next year."

"Hold up, Mom is already planning a wedding?" Russell asked, surprised.

His dad gave him a sharp look. "Shouldn't she? Or are you not serious about her? Because the way she stood by your side and helped out the family says she's a long-term kind of person."

He met his dad's stare for a few seconds before looking away. "I've thought about it, but…"

"But what?"

Russell didn't want to tell his parents about what hadn't

gone well with Ashiya. He liked that they liked her. He wasn't ready to plan a wedding, but the idea of her being his wife one day didn't fill him with panic as it once would have.

"We tried before. It didn't go well."

"I won't ask what happened. I will say that relationships have good times and bad. You have to decide if the good times outweigh the bad. Do they with her?"

He thought about the way she'd fought for him since he'd come to Hilton Head. How she'd planned the celebratory barbecue after the meeting with Bryce to get his mind off things. Her smile after surviving the first board meeting. The way her eyes filled with love and the softness of her voice when she uttered those words.

The corners of his mouth tilted up. "Right now they do."

"Then you've got that, too. I'll tell your mom to hold off on wedding plans, but know that we like her."

"Is she still inside?"

He hadn't seen Ashiya since they were in the kitchen earlier. Foolish as it was, he hadn't wanted her to see him cry again. She'd held him when he'd sobbed the day they'd found Rodrick. She had enough on her plate without worrying about his emotional support. He hadn't wanted her to worry about him, but he also hadn't been able to send her away. Her being around was the one thing that made this easier.

"I don't know."

"I'll go check." Russell stood. He took a step toward the door, then turned around. "Love you, Dad."

His dad smiled. "Love you, too."

Russell smiled and went in. Most of the people had left. He found his mom and her two sisters sitting at the kitchen table. He glanced around.

"Where's Ashiya?" he asked.

"She left a few hours ago," his mom said.

"Why?"

Why would she leave without saying goodbye?

"I don't know," his mom said. "She just told me she'd washed the dishes in the kitchen and straightened up, but that she had to get home to pack before going Hilton Head. You didn't know?"

Russell shook his head. "No, I didn't know." He crossed the room and snatched his keys off the hook next to the door. "I'll be back."

"Hold up," his mom said. She stood and went to the fridge. She pulled out a plate covered in aluminum foil. "I fixed her a plate. She saved all the stuff we liked from the rest of the family. I don't think I ever saw her eat anything when she was here. Make sure she eats all of this."

Russell thought about what his dad said as he took the plate. In all his life, his mom had never sent him to one of his girlfriends' houses with a plate. She'd liked the women he'd dated okay, but she'd also given him a look that told him she wasn't exactly impressed.

"You like her, huh," he said.

She lifted a shoulder. "She might be a Robidoux, but she's okay. Tell her thank you and that I'll cook for her the next time she comes." His mom raised a brow. "There will be a next time?"

He nodded. "Yes, Mom. There'll be a next time."

CHAPTER TWENTY-NINE

THE SUN WAS setting when Russell arrived at Ashiya's place. Her car was parked in the drive, but the house was dark. The blinds were open and no lights shone behind them. He hoped she hadn't gone somewhere with her cousin India or someone else. The funeral was done. His brother was laid to rest. His parents were going to be okay.

On the drive over, he'd thought about what his dad said. He still had a lot to be thankful for. He hopefully had a long life ahead of him. He didn't want to spend the rest of his life being afraid to move forward because of the problems in his past. He loved Ashiya, and he wanted to step out on faith that their love was a strong enough foundation for them to build a lasting relationship.

He rang the doorbell and waited. After a few seconds, he rang the bell again and knocked on the door. He glanced at her car in the drive. If she had left, no problem. He'd go to her.

He pulled out his cell to call her when a light became visible behind the glass panel of her door. The door opened, and Ashiya squinted up at him.

"Russell? What's wrong?" Her voice held the huskiness he was used to when she just woke up. Her hair, which had been curled cutely earlier, was now disheveled.

He stepped over the threshold. "You were asleep?" It

was so early, he hadn't expected her to be down for the night.

She shook her head and reached for his hands. "It's okay. Did something happen? Are your parents okay?"

"They're fine." Russell smiled at her concern and took her hands. They were clammy and shaky. He looked at her closely. Her breathing was ragged, her pupils were dilated, and a sheen of sweat covered her forehead. "What's wrong? What happened?"

He pulled her into his arms, and she squeezed him tight. Her body trembled as she pressed her cheek against his chest.

"Nothing. I just fell asleep on the couch. It was a… I had a nightmare. It's silly. When the doorbell rang, it jerked me out of it."

"A nightmare? About what?" He pulled back so he could look into her eyes.

She continued to stare at his chest and lifted a shoulder. "Nothing, it's nothing." She briskly wiped at her eyes.

"It's not nothing. What was it about?"

She lifted a shoulder. "I was in the closet and I couldn't get out." She waved a hand. "No big deal. I'm okay now that I'm awake."

Russell felt like the world's biggest ass. Of course she was having nightmares. She'd gone through something traumatic. Something so similar to what she'd gone through when she was younger, it would have triggered those bad memories. He should have realized she would have nightmares afterwards. He'd gotten so wrapped up with finding his brother that he'd taken her everything-is-alright facade as the truth.

He bent, put his arm behind her knees and swept her up into his arms. Ashiya took in a quick breath before her arms wrapped around his neck. She was light against him, lighter than she'd been when he'd carried her to the bedroom what felt like forever ago, back in Hilton Head.

"What are you doing?" she asked, some brightness coming back into her voice as she smiled at him.

"I'm taking care of you for once," he said. He strode down the hall to her living room. The inside of her place was dark. He sat on the couch with her in his arms.

"I'm fine," she said even though she leaned her head against his shoulder.

He reached for the lamp next to the chair. Ashiya's palm pressed against his bicep, and she pushed downward. "No. Leave the light off."

"I didn't think you'd want to be in the dark."

"The dark doesn't bother me. Not when I'm in your arms like this." She sighed and snuggled closer to him.

Russell wrapped his arms around her and settled back on the chair. "How long have the nightmares been back?"

"They never went away," she said in a soft voice. Her fingers pulled the chain with the gold cross out of his shirt, and she ran her fingertips around the edges. "I've had them off and on since I was a kid. They get better and I think they're going away, and then bam, they're right back."

"But with what happened with Melissa, that made them worse."

Her head shifted on his chest as she nodded. "It did. Now they're blended together. I'm a kid when I'm locked in, and then I'm an adult with a bloody bump on my head. The ending doesn't change. No one finds me. I'm stuck and alone."

His arms tightened around her. He brushed his lips across her forehead. "I'm sorry I didn't notice. I should have been there for you."

"You had your own stuff to deal with."

"I know, but I still shouldn't have taken advantage of you after what happened."

Ashiya's head tipped back, and she frowned up into his face. "Take advantage of me? How did you do that? You've been so busy with the funeral and taking care of your brother's remains that you barely bothered me."

Even though she hadn't said it in an accusatory tone, he still felt worse after hearing the words. "I know that I pulled back after Rodrick's rem…" He cleared his throat. He still had a hard time thinking of that day. "After they found my brother. I didn't know what else to do. I was in so much pain. It hurt so much, I didn't want to drag you down into the dark place I was in, but I also couldn't push you away when you came around. I accepted every bit of help you offered. Accepted and appreciated every meal you dropped off, every note you left telling me to eat and drink something, every phone call you made to the funeral home to help my mom make the arrangements, every dish you picked up at the house today to put things in order and keep my parents from having to deal with a mess."

"You did?" The surprise in her voice sliced him. He hadn't realized just how much his pulling back must have affected her.

"I did. You were the only light in my life these past few weeks. You're the reason I made it through the day when the hurt and the rage made me want to go find Melissa and Bryce and bury them under a shed for fifteen years."

"But you seemed so… I don't know. As if I was in the way."

"You weren't. I tried to protect you from my feelings but also relied on you being there. Instead of doing that, I should have checked in on you, too. I should have made sure you were okay. I should have noticed you were losing weight, the dark circles under your eyes, the troubles you were going through. I'm sorry."

"I'm so used to getting through things myself, I didn't even expect more from you. I got through the incident when I was a kid alone, and I just planned to get through things this time alone as well."

He sat up and turned on the light before she could stop him. She squinted and blinked several times to adjust to the light. He waited for her gaze to clear up and meet his. He wanted her to see him and know exactly what he meant.

"You don't have to get through anything alone anymore. Not while we're together. I guess we both have a lot to learn about sharing and relationships. After Rodrick died, I was afraid to get attached to anyone again. I didn't want to hurt like that, and watching my parents' pain made me not want to burden them with my own feelings. I pulled back after asking you to be open and trusting with me. I'm sorry."

Her eyes lowered, and she laced her fingers with his. "My parents came by today. They're getting a divorce. It's a long time coming, and I'm happy for them, but it also made me wonder."

"About what?"

"About life, love and relationships. Holding on to things you should have let go of. Russell, I don't want you to feel guilty about mourning the loss of your brother because I was also reliving something awful in my past. Your grief and my trauma don't outweigh each other. We both were dealing with something hard the best way we knew how. You don't have to use it as an excuse…" Her voice trailed off.

"An excuse to do what?"

"An excuse to keep this going if it's not what you want," she said in a rush.

Her words were such a surprise, he nearly dropped her off his lap. "What? Why wouldn't I want to keep this going?"

"Your cousin Isaac said I was a burden. That I didn't need to try so hard. I didn't do all of that to make you stay with me. I did it because I wanted to help. If you don't want to keep—"

"I'm going to fucking kill Isaac." He took her chin between his thumb and forefinger so she could look him in the eye. "Ashiya, I love you. I loved you before everything happened with Melissa and my brother, but I was too afraid to say it because I thought you'd leave again. I was going to say it when you were in the hospital, and I realized being afraid of you possibly leaving me didn't compare to the terror I felt when I literally almost did lose you, but the detective came in. I came here tonight, not knowing about any of the bullshit Isaac said you to, because I wanted to tell you how much I love and appreciate you. I want to spend the rest of my life making sure you understand you're not alone. If you have a nightmare, I'll be there to hold you. If you're lost, I'll find you. I don't care about what happened between us in the past. All I care about is our future."

Her lips parted, and tears glistened in her eyes. "I love you, too."

He pulled her against his chest in a tight hug. Ashiya's trembling laugh lifted him to new heights, and she squeezed him back.

"I love you so much," he said, then kissed her. Her stomach growled, and he jerked back. "Oh crap."

She frowned. "What? Did you change your mind?"

He shook his head. "Never that. I left your plate in the car. My mom sent you a plate."

Ashiya's bright smile made his stomach flip. "She did? For real? I think your mom likes me," she said with the cutest of smug smiles.

"She does. She's already talking weddings and grand-kids."

Ashiya's eyes widened. "Grandkids?"

He laughed. "We've got plenty of time to worry about that, but I kind of like the way she's thinking. I like the idea of you and me together forever."

Ashiya gently tugged on the front of his shirt and pulled him closer for a kiss. "I like that idea, too."

* * * * *

Want to spend more time with the Robidoux family and see how the Jackson Falls series began?

Turn the page for a peek at Forbidden Promises

When her brother needs her help with his high-profile political campaign, India Robidoux has no choice but to stay and face the one man she's been running from for years—Travis, her sister's ex-husband. One hot summer night when Travis was still free, they celebrated her birthday with whiskey and an unforgettable kiss. The memory is as strong as ever—and so are the feelings she's tried so hard to forget.

Travis Strickland has one regret. Impulsive and passionate, India always understood him better than anyone else. And the longer they work together on the campaign, the more torn he is. Coming between her and her sister is out of the question. But how can he let love pass him by a second time?

CHAPTER ONE

A LARGE CALLA LILY bouquet came entirely too close to slapping India Robidoux in the face the moment she entered her family's home for the first time in four years. Only a quick slide to the right saved her from that indignity.

The woman carrying the flowers rushed by with a barely audible "excuse me."

India jumped back to avoid being hit by another bouquet as a different woman with an equally large arrangement hurried by. The ornate oak-and-glass front door swung open behind her. India stutter-stepped to the right to avoid being hit. Maybe she should have taken up dancing instead of the violin. She clearly had the footwork down.

The front door opened again, and a man carrying a large box rushed through. "Where do you want these?" he asked her. He shifted and the sound of glasses clinking together came from the box.

India's mouth opened, then closed. She glanced around in the hope he was talking to someone who had some clue what was going on.

The man loudly cleared his throat. "Ma'am?"

Blinking rapidly, India pointed down the hall where more noise came from the back of the house. "Um…the kitchen?" That had to be where glasses needed to go.

The man nodded and hurried on his way. Yet another

woman carrying a huge bouquet, roses instead of calla lilies, rushed by.

India moved out of the entryway and the line of people going back and forth. She pulled her cell phone out of the back pocket of her jean shorts and checked the date. No one's birthday, no anniversary and no major holiday. Why were there dozens of people zipping around making the already impressive interior of her family home even more extravagant?

People were everywhere, placing flower arrangements, hanging decorations, carrying crates and cleaning every nook and cranny. The effort put into whatever was going on wasn't surprising. Her family didn't do anything half-assed. It was as if four years hadn't passed and she was back home in time for another *Robidoux Family* production.

"I told the caterer there were to be no oysters, at all. If my brother dies from an allergic reaction to oysters at his own party because the caterer is too dumb to remember my instructions, there will be hell to pay." Her sister's cool Southern accent was laced with frustration.

India rolled her eyes and sighed. Apparently, Elaina's tendency for overdramatic threats hadn't diminished recently.

The quick apologetic reply of the unfortunate assistant her sister spoke to accompanied the sound of heels clicking along the marble in India's direction. For a second, she considered hiding, but dismissed the urge. There was no reason to hide from her sister. Their relationship wasn't the closest, but neither were they enemies. Elaina always viewed India as the annoying baby sister in need of her guidance. Adulthood hadn't changed that perception.

Elaina and a woman India didn't recognize came into

view. Elaina's deep sepia skin, dark almond-shaped eyes and perfectly flat-ironed hair hadn't changed at all. Even though Elaina was thirty-two, India swore her sister had stopped aging at twenty-five.

Elaina's furious pace didn't slow down even though the other woman struggled to keep up with her. Seeing they would continue right by her—probably assuming India was just another person helping with the party, which apparently was for her brother—India sighed and stepped away from the wall. "Byron isn't going to die from eating an oyster, Elaina, and you know it."

Elaina froze midstride. Surprise registered for a millisecond before her gaze traveled over India's body.

India automatically stood straighter. She was considered the artist of the family, and her brother… Well, he was the son, which made him their father's pride and joy. Everyone agreed Elaina was the beauty, but that didn't stop her big sister from quickly sizing up India every time they were together. That didn't make her sister's scrutiny any less annoying. So, India wasn't dressed to impress. She'd come straight from the airport, leaving her luggage in the car in her rush to get inside and figure out why there were so many vehicles in the long drive. She wore jean shorts with a white tank top that sported the words Plays Well With Others beneath musical notes. Elaina's peach silk blouse and tan pencil skirt easily outshone India's wardrobe, but India had traveled all day and opted for comfort. That had to count for something, right?

Elaina's full lips finally spread into what India assumed was supposed to be a welcoming smile. "Well, you're back. I wondered if you would actually come. I guess Daddy hasn't completely lost his hold on you."

India took a deep breath and smiled just as sincerely as

her sister. "I'm not here for—" she looked around at the decorations "—whatever is going on. I have a break in touring and now I'm home."

Elaina's dark eyes widened. "Oh. Well, you're home just in time." She turned to the woman next to her. "Gwendolyn, I've got to get my baby sister up to speed. You go check to make sure the crystal glasses were delivered. Please let Sandra know India's back."

Sandra was the head housekeeper for the estate. India didn't know her—she had started after India had already left. According to Byron, the woman was a saint.

Gwendolyn gave India a curious look before she nodded at Elaina. "I will, and I'll make sure there are no oysters anywhere on the menu."

"Please see that you do," Elaina said in an exaggerated tone.

When Gwendolyn walked away, Elaina strolled over to India. "Gwendolyn is a straight-up pit bull when it comes to party planning. If there is an oyster in the house, she'll make sure it's destroyed."

India's lips twisted. "She sounds delightful."

Elaina smiled ruefully. "Actually, she's a little scary."

"Scarier than you?" India said with disbelief. Elaina was nearly a carbon copy of their late mother. Witty, smart and unwilling to take shit from anyone.

Elaina lifted one slim shoulder and placed the tips of her manicured fingers on the other. "No one's scarier than me."

India smiled and some of the tension eased from her spine. She'd forgotten that Elaina made her laugh occasionally. "So, this thing is for Byron?"

"You really don't know?" When India shook her head, Elaina motioned for her to follow. "Come on, let's go upstairs. It's a madhouse down here. Byron is running for

Senate and he's formally announcing his candidacy to-night."

India froze at the bottom of the curving staircase. Shit. Damn. Motherfucker! She'd hoped to come home, spend a few easy days, maybe a week, catching up with her family and then get the hell out of there. Not arrive in the middle of what was sure to be a full-fledged Robidoux family drama complete with television cameras, adoring friends and political posturing. There was no way her daddy would stand for her popping in and out during her brother's po-litical campaign. If she'd known, she would have gone straight to Los Angeles instead of opting for a family visit.

Elaina either hadn't noticed India wasn't climbing up the stairs or hadn't cared, and continued her assent. India resumed her stride and followed her sister to the second-floor family room. Though the downstairs rooms were ornate and grandiose with their antique furnishings, ex-pensive wall hangings and polished surfaces, the upstairs was relaxed and welcoming. This was where the family got together to talk, watch television and spend time to-gether. Dark carpet covered the family room floor and large leather sofas and recliners filled the space before a large television screen on the left. A pool table and mini-bar occupied the right side of the room.

Elaina went to the bar and pulled a bottle out of the small fridge and two goblets from the cabinet. "Wine?"

"Please," India answered.

Elaina raised one arched brow. "And here I thought you weren't a day drinker."

"A lot's changed in the years I've been away." Truth-fully, nothing had changed. Any other day, she'd say one in the afternoon was too early for wine. But any other day she wouldn't be home facing her demons.

Elaina poured them wine, then walked over and handed a glass to India. She held up her glass. "Welcome home, sister." Elaina's voice didn't carry any warmth or fondness. That was Elaina. Cold beauty and pragmatism. Warm and fuzzy was not her style.

India clinked her glass to Elaina's and took a sip. As the crisp flavor of the wine played across her tongue, she glanced around the room. Pictures of her and her siblings along with the various awards Robidoux Tobacco, the vast empire that supported their lavish lifestyle, had won over the years filled the bookshelf. The faint scent of cigar smoke hung in the room that was the heart of the family.

India took a deep breath. The smell of home. Tobacco had made her family rich and turned Robidoux Tobacco into one of the most profitable tobacco producers in the country. Despite arriving in the middle of a publicity storm, India had missed home.

She walked over to get a closer look at the pictures. "I can't believe Daddy still has these up."

"As if he'd take them down," Elaina said with a trace of humor. "He loves to brag about his children's accomplishments. From fourth grade spelling bees to traveling the world with a renowned orchestra."

India smiled at some of the pictures from the events Elaina mentioned. There was even a framed newspaper clipping of a review of the Transatlantic Orchestra from the *New York Times*. Her dad hadn't wanted her to go, but he'd still been proud enough to brag.

Her gaze slid across Elaina's wedding photo, then jerked back. Her chest tightened as if her heart was in a straitjacket. The photo of Elaina in the arms of her ex-husband, Travis Strickland, during their wedding dance instantly made India wish she'd gone on to LA. They were smiling and staring into each other's eyes. Elaina and Travis had been happy that day, and India had wanted to cry. She hadn't expected to still feel so disappointed.

"I hate that picture," Elaina said. India jumped and whirled around to face her sister. "Daddy loves it," Elaina continued. "He still thinks it's fate the boy he saved fell in love with his daughter." She took a long sip from the glass. "I've considered throwing it out the window, but he'd just print another."

India swirled the wine in her glass. "It is a good story."

Elaina laughed softly and drank the rest of her wine. "The story sounds nice. The ending isn't so happy." She stared at the picture a few more seconds. No emotion on her face, but her hand tight on the wineglass before she turned and sat primly on the edge of the couch. "How long are you here for?" she said in a cool, let's-change-the-subject tone of voice.

Usually, when Elaina intentionally tried to change the subject, India would use the opportunity to keep pushing. That was part of the little sister code of conduct—tease older sister relentlessly. But, when it came to Elaina's marriage, India was more than happy to stray from the habit.

Besides, Elaina and Travis were divorced now. Elaina had called her two years ago to tell her she and Travis were ending things, but because Travis was their brother's best friend and partner in a successful law office, she'd have to keep him in her life. Elaina hadn't said what caused their split, and India hadn't asked, even though she'd wanted to know. In the end, the why didn't matter. She couldn't go after the man she'd always wanted when he was her sister's ex-husband.

"I'm only going to be home a few days." India sat on the other end of the couch. "The orchestra's tour for the year is over. I'm taking some time to recharge. I submitted my request to audition for the Los Angeles Philharmonic."

Elaina tilted her head to the side. "Los Angeles. Impressive."

"Only if I get the job."

"You will. You're persistent and that violin was always attached to your damn hand. You'll be fine." She said the last with a wave of her hand and more than a hint of pride. Elaina may be cold and distant, but India would never call her unsupportive. As if realizing she'd let her pride show, Elaina frowned at India. "How did you get here?"

"My plane landed about an hour ago. I rented a car at the airport."

Elaina looked confused. "Why? Daddy would have had a car waiting for you."

"I didn't want that. I hoped to sneak in. I wasn't ready to see everyone just yet." She looked away from Elaina and turned the glass in her hand. Her dad would be hurt she'd sneaked home, but he'd also be happy to see her. They'd Skyped and video chatted while she'd toured, but she hadn't been home in years. Somehow seeing Travis when he was free of Elaina had seemed harder than seeing them together.

"He'll be happy to know you're here for Byron's announcement," Elaina said. "He's worried your prolonged absence reflects badly on Byron."

India froze with the glass of wine halfway to her mouth. "How?"

"You being away makes it look like our family's torn apart."

"What? Where on earth did that come from?"

Elaina's lips twisted into a small smile and she shook her head. "I wish I could blame it on his overactive imagination, but I do think this is from Byron's campaign manager. You running off and not coming home for years does make it look as if you don't want to be around."

"I didn't run off. I've been touring." That's what she told herself anyway.

"Doesn't matter. You know Daddy only thinks three things are important. God, family and Robidoux Tobacco." Elaina raised a manicured finger with each word. "To him, you've turned your back on two of the three. I'd admire you for doing what you love instead of sticking around here and doing what he wanted, if it hadn't made my life so damn difficult."

"Sure, Elaina, I left just to make your life difficult," India said sarcastically.

The corner of Elaina's mouth lifted for half a second before she sighed. "I'm the one who argues with Daddy. Byron hangs on to his every word and you're the sweet one who can do no wrong. Did you really think you could go traipsing off across the world and Daddy wouldn't shift your share of the pressure to live up to the family's legacy onto me and Byron?" Elaina brought her glass to her lips, frowned when she realized the glass was empty and stood. She quickly crossed the room to the bar.

"I didn't think he'd take things out on you two." Honestly, she hadn't thought about how her leaving would affect Elaina and Byron. She'd only known she couldn't stay and pretend as if her heart wasn't breaking every time she saw Elaina and Travis together.

Elaina poured another glass of wine. "You should have known Daddy wouldn't be easy to deal with after his favorite daughter defied him."

India rolled her eyes and fell back onto the chair. "Don't be dramatic. I didn't *defy* him. Daddy knew about the offer to play with the Transatlantic Orchestra. I told him I wanted to go."

Elaina strolled back to the couch. "Yes, and he said you couldn't go, remember? That meant the case was closed. Even I thought you were staying. You never went against what Daddy wanted. What happened?"

The need to go against her dad's wishes had never been a problem before, because until then their dad hadn't denied her anything she'd wanted. He'd disciplined her when she'd messed up and pushed her to be not just good but great in everything she did. She hadn't fought him on things the way Elaina used to, so he never had a reason to say no to India's requests.

The urge to tell the truth about why she left was on the tip of her tongue. To shed light on things in the open and unravel why events had played out the way they had. India sat forward and swirled the contents of her glass instead. Confessing her sins and fighting with Elaina would make a difficult homecoming worse.

"I wanted to go, that's what happened. I was tired of being Daddy's baby girl. It was time to live my life." That part was true, as well. She'd had no identity before leaving. The youngest Robidoux. The sweet baby sister. Leaving her family behind had allowed her to grow and depend on herself. For that, she'd never regret her decision.

Elaina scoffed and sipped her wine. "You're Grant Robidoux's daughter. You don't get to live the life you want."

India swore there was bitterness in Elaina's voice, but her face held no sarcastic or angry smirk. Instead she stared off into space. Grant Robidoux making demands of his family was no secret. Everyone was expected to do their part to uphold the traditions their paternal grandparents started when they opened Robidoux Tobacco. Their mother had helped market the company before she'd passed away nearly ten years ago when India was twenty. Elaina worked at the company and oversaw some of their other holdings and was primed to take over the helm. Byron had been one of the many legal counsels for them before opening a law firm with Travis. Not to mention all of their aunts, uncles and cousins who also worked somewhere in the company.

India was the only one who hadn't wanted to grow the empire. As his baby girl, her dad had let her indulge in her "little violin hobby" until she got serious about making music her career. He couldn't accept that what he considered a hobby was a passion for her.

"Where is Daddy anyway?" Except for the noise of preparations downstairs, the house was quiet.

Elaina smiled widely. The expression was so unlike Elaina that chills of foreboding skittered down India's spine. "He's off with his new project. You're going to love this." The glee in her voice only increased India's unease.

"Forget the dramatics and let me know where he's gone." Her words were confident, but her stomach quivered.

"He's off with Russell Gilchrist. The newest young executive at Robidoux Tobacco. Marketing division. Daddy's bringing in all this new blood to revitalize the brand. Russell's one of them."

"Okay, so why are you smiling like Cruella de Vil?"

"Because, I heard Daddy say he can't wait for Russell to meet his baby girl."

India started shaking her head before Elaina finished talking. "Don't tell me he's playing matchmaker and he doesn't even know I'm home."

"Daddy's always planning for the future. Apparently

since I can't make babies, and Byron won't get married and make any, he needs you to carry on the family line."

India cringed. During her first Skype calls with her dad a few months after she'd left with the Transatlantic Orchestra, he'd told her about Elaina's miscarriage. India hadn't even known her sister was pregnant. When she'd tried to call Elaina afterward, her sister discussed the medical details as if she were going over a business proposal before rushing her off the phone. "Don't talk like that."

Elaina's lips tightened. "Don't patronize me. Look, forget my broken womb and prepare for yours to be claimed faster than the last yeast roll at Sunday dinner. Daddy's ready for you to get married and make little Robidoux children. Our cousins are being fruitful and multiplying. If we don't catch up, the company will end up completely in their hands. So, beware of Russell."

India shook her head. "No, no, no. I'm not going to let him coerce me into anything. I'm only here for a few days."

Elaina sipped from her glass and raised one slim shoulder. "I wouldn't complain. Russell isn't bad. He's young, smart, good-looking. I don't think you'd find it hard to cozy up to him."

India scowled. "Then you cozy up to him."

"I'm not the cozying type." Elaina waved a hand. "Enough about that. I'll wait and see who wins that battle after we get through the party tonight."

"Where's Byron? If this party is for him, I'd expect him to be here."

"As if the favored son would dare take the time to plan his own party," Elaina said without any animosity. Byron had always been spoiled and doted on by their father and late mother. Even India, his baby sister.

"He's off with Travis. They'll be in later," Elaina said.

India's stomach twisted as if she'd had six glasses of wine instead of half of one. "Will Travis be at the party?" she managed to ask in a steady voice.

"Of course, he will. He and Byron are joined at the hip." There was one emotion Elaina wasn't afraid to show and that was irritation, something which was thick in her voice as discussed her ex-husband and brother.

After what happened between her and Travis, every time India saw him with Elaina it felt like jagged claws sinking into her chest. The pain had dulled somewhat over the years, but Travis had never belonged to her. Elaina had been married to him. They'd shared so much. India could only imagine how hard it must be for Elaina to see him so often. "That doesn't bother you?"

Elaina ran a finger over the rim of her wineglass. "Travis and I don't love each other. He worked for the company and is my darling brother's best friend." The words sounded like a carefully crafted public relations statement.

"That doesn't answer the question."

Elaina pointedly looked India in the eye. Her push-me-on-this-and-I'll-eviscerate-you feelings were very clear in her direct gaze. "No. It doesn't bother me," she said carefully. "I don't love Travis and shouldn't have married him. Our divorce was the best thing that could have happened to either of us." She capped off the very mature-sounding words with a serene smile.

The words were little comfort to India. She was happy her sister wasn't heartbroken, but had they really not loved each other? She'd consoled her own bruised feelings and reasoned that Travis had married Elaina because in the end he realized he had loved her. That maybe he'd felt guilty after what happened the night of India's birthday and had tried to make things right. For Elaina to say they never loved each other made the bitter disappointment she'd felt back then come back even more.

That doesn't mean he would have married you. It doesn't mean anything would have been different. She'd been too young, too idealistic and too romantic back then. Maybe the truth was Travis had just been looking for a Robidoux sister to marry so he could further his own goals. Just because he kissed her once on the edge of the tobacco field, whispered words that she'd longed to hear, didn't mean a thing.

She managed a small smile. "I'm glad you two are still friends."

Elaina's shoulders relaxed along with the tightness around her smile. She clearly had not wanted to continue to explore any of her feelings for Travis. "I'd thought Daddy lost his mind, plucking him from that trailer park and training him up, but he's proved himself to be loyal. That's all the family needs."

India opened her mouth to ask what Elaina needed, but footsteps sounded in the hall right before a man walked into the room. India's breath rushed from her lungs.

Time had only enhanced his good looks. Dark brown skin smoother than the finest mahogany. Midnight-black bedroom eyes that used to pierce through her shyness to the bold girl she'd tried to hide from her daddy. He had a swimmer's body. Tall, sleek, well-defined. He wore a maroon polo shirt and dark brown slacks that complemented his dark skin. His full lips were parted in a big smile. He hadn't noticed them, as he looked back and smiled at her brother behind him. Yet flashes went through her mind of his lips brushing her neck and his eyes staring at her beneath lowered lashes in the moonlight.

Byron saw them and his grin brightened the room. "India. You're home."

Travis swung around. His dark gaze collided with hers.

"India?" His deep voice washed over her. She'd forgotten the sound of her name on his lips: low, smooth, intoxicating. As if he savored the syllables as they rolled off his tongue.

Her stomach tightened and she chugged the remaining wine in her glass. Heat prickled across her skin like a thousand needles. She should have gone to LA. She should have realized running from a problem didn't make the problem go away. Her brain screamed *run* and her feet twitched with the urgency to obey as the one answer she'd come home to find out robbed her of the ability speak. She was still in love with her sister's husband.

Don't miss Forbidden Promises, *available now from HQN Books!*